Stealing
Ho Chi Minh's
GOLD

Stealing Ho Chi Minh's GOLD

Jim Miller

We are all slaves to someone or something. Worldwide there are more people in slavery today than any time in history

STEALING HO CHI MINH'S GOLD

iUniverse books may be ordered through booksellers or by contacting:

iUniverse
1663 Liberty Drive
Bloomington, IN 47403
www.iuniverse.com
1-800-Authors (1-800-288-4677)

Because of the dynamic nature of the Internet, any web addresses or links contained in this book may have changed since publication and may no longer be valid. The views expressed in this work are solely those of the author and do not necessarily reflect the views of the publisher, and the publisher hereby disclaims any responsibility for them.

Any people depicted in stock imagery provided by Thinkstock are models, and such images are being used for illustrative purposes only.
Certain stock imagery © Thinkstock.

ISBN: 978-1-4917-5070-4 (sc)
ISBN: 978-1-4917-5071-1 (e)

Printed in the United States of America.

iUniverse rev. date: 11/05/2014

TUESDAY, CURRENT TIME

His phone vibrated on the night stand, once, twice and again. Kelley lifted his head, let it fall back and exhaled deeply. His hand groped and finally found the offending instrument, slid his thumb across the screen and tried to answer. His voice cracked from dry sleep.

"Hullo."

"Mister Price, Mister Kelly Price?"

"Yeah, what do you want?" Kelly hunched, bringing his knees up towards his chest in an awkward sitting position.

"You missed the reading of the will, Mr. Price."

Now, Kelley was collecting himself and getting irritated. "What will, what reading and why the hell are you calling me at two in the morning?" He was beginning to focus and the digital numbers on his clock were clear.

"Oh dear, I'm so sorry. I messed up the Mainland time zones again. You're later, not earlier than we are."

Kelley ran fingers through his hair. He was awake though groggy. Curiosity kept him talking. "So who are you and where are you?"

"Yes, yes, I'm Clayton Sheppard of Kennedy, Tanaka and Schiller, Honolulu, Hawaii. We are the custodians and executors of your Uncle Tooney's will."

"What are you talking about? Uncle Pat is dead?"

"Oh dear, I thought you knew. We sent a letter to your Edison, New Jersey address."

"That's nice but I haven't lived there since I attended Rutgers nearly twenty years ago. What did Uncle Pat die of?"

"I'm...I'm so sorry. I don't know... natural causes I believe. I didn't realize I would be the one to notify you of his passing. Please accept our sincere..."

"It's okay, we weren't close. In fact, we hadn't spoken for years. I can't even remember the last time. Old Pat was a colorful character, a little nutty. My mother and he exchanged Christmas cards but that was about it."

"And his sister, your mother, how would we contact her?"

Kelley leaned back on his pillows. He wasn't sure how to react. "The only way to contact my mother would be through a medium. My parents died in a traffic accident three years ago."

"Oh... I guess that makes you the sole surviving beneficiary. Your two brothers were specifically excluded. Several people claiming to be nieces and nephews showed up at the reading but they had no documented connection. That happens when we post information online." The lawyer sighed. "I guess you get everything."

Kelley chuckled under his breath. "Well, just send it to me. I can't imagine Uncle Pat had much of an estate. As far as I know, he hadn't held a job for years."

The line was silent for a long time before the lawyer spoke. "Actually, his bank account balances totaled $138,740. There are other assets. He owns three houses outright, a condo in Waikiki, another property on the Kona Coast and a waterfront home on Kauai. The real estate total value is well over three million. I'm afraid you'll have to come here to handle the transfers."

Kelley was wide awake now. "Three million? I can't believe it. How could..."

He breathed deeply. *God, could I use that kind of money. The divorce, losing my job, the bad economy... bless you Uncle Pat, however you amassed your fortune.* After a moment, he grinned and spoke into the phone. "Mr. Sheppard, I'll be there tomorrow and I'll get the time right."

WEDNESDAY

The offices of Kennedy, Tanaka and Schiller were less impressive than the name implied. A sign led to a second story walk-up over "Mister Chang's Very Good Chinese Restaurant" on Kukui Street in Honolulu's Chinatown. Kelley Price, red-eyed and weary, paused to take in the smells and sounds. He was a tall man but with none of the confidence tall men usually display. He had a little too much dark hair and it tended to fall in his eyes. His shoulders stooped slightly and he carried his head down.

Traffic was thick with occasional horns and surging engines. The Chinese restaurant fronted colorful gold dragon carvings on red columns. Other stores were festooned with paper lanterns and garlands of plastic flowers. There were shouts in English and other languages. Tourists and locals crowded and pushed along the sidewalk. Soy, ginger and incense aromas mixed with a faint hint of rotting cabbage.

Kelley was too tired to appreciate the postcard scene. Multiple plane connections left little time to catch sleep. He took a deep breath and started up the stairs. Three million dollars waited at the top. He could stay awake all week for that kind of money.

Clayton Sheppard sat behind an antique teakwood desk. He wore a bright flowered shirt with, of all things, a matching bow tie. He squinted through round glasses under a blonde buzz cut and extended a wimpy handshake. "Mr. Price, happy to meet you."

He pointed to a small conference table piled thick with paper. "Everything is ready. I'll be brief. I'm sure you're exhausted."

Kelley plopped in a chair, wiped his hands over his unshaven face and forced a smile.

"Okay then, first things first. Here are your uncle's remains and a receipt for you to sign." The lawyer pushed a square cardboard box forward. Kelley put his hand on the box—all that remained from his uncle, his benefactor.

"Was there a funeral?"

Lawyer Clayton made an uncomfortable face. "We followed Mr. Tooney's directive and had a discreet cremation. There was no service." He paused for a moment. "Ah, let's get on with the details."

Kelley was still staring at the cardboard box.

"Okay, most of this is just legal boilerplate already covered in the formal reading. I'll just skip to page six..." Clayton flipped through a document and put his finger in the middle of a page. "All my assets, real and otherwise, to my sister and her youngest son, Kelley Price, in turn, should she predecease him. In addition, Kelley Price should receive my dragon box and use it wisely."

Clayton pushed another box forward. It was wrapped in brown paper and heavy enough to make the lawyer strain.

"There, now for the details of your inheritance." He produced a manila folder. "This is the title, list of condo covenant restrictions and information for the transfer of utilities to your name. I'll file the actual title transfer with the city." He placed a key ring on top of the folder. "It's a great location, twelfth floor with an ocean view and large balcony."

Clayton gathered two more folders, both thicker than the first. "The other properties are more of a challenge. The beach house is managed by a resort broker who wants to renegotiate the contract. It's not a big deal but it will take five or six workdays. I'm confident I can get a guarantee of $2,500 a month with additional revenue based on occupancy. So far, it has almost a 90% rental rate, which boosts your monthly income to over $3,000. The broker takes care of maintenance, furnishings and housekeeping."

Kelley nodded. He was feeling the jetlag.

"The Kona property is more difficult and I don't know how you're going to feel about this proposal. The place is under a one-year lease to Haida Corporation, a Japanese company that wants more control. By law, a foreign entity cannot own the property. They are offering a ten-year contract...prepaid. That would be one point two million dollars in cash. If you agree, they will take care of everything including security. You probably won't even be able to get into the compound." Clayton looked at Kelley cautiously.

"Have you asked about the price? Is it competitive?"

Clayton shrugged. "Yes, in today's market, it's more than fair, generous actually. The question is, what will values be in ten years? For the last decade, prices have risen only slightly. The decade before, they doubled. It's anybody's guess what the future holds. The one thing that recommends this deal is that they will pay the taxes and there is no doubt taxes are going up."

Kelley took all the folders. "Tell you what, I'm going to look these over after I've had some sleep. Is that okay?"

"Yes, sure. But before you go, here is a cashier's check for $129, 752. That's the balance of Mr. Tooney's local accounts, less our fees."

Kelley started to protest the fees. In Clayton's phone call he quoted an amount nine thousand dollars higher for Uncle Pat Tooney's accounts.

"Oh, and the car. Here are the keys and transfer papers for his Audi TT. It's a two-seat convertible, great car for Hawaii. It's somewhere in your condo's parking garage. If you gather your papers, I'll drive you there. Ready?"

JUNE 6, 1969

Patrick Tooney screamed. He was tumbling, confused, out of control and disoriented as he plummeted into black night sky. Then his parachute jerked opened and an electric pain shot from his groin. He hadn't tightened his leg straps and the opening shock of the canopy dug them deep, crushing into his testicles. In desperation, he spread his legs to reduce the pressure. It worked a little bit but he had bigger problems than the pain. His canopy was gyrating, whipping him around like a carnival ride.

In the dim moonlight, everything was spinning in wild, eerie confusion. He was breathing too fast, puffing like a steam engine. *Control your breathing, damn it. Control yourself. Remember your parachute training.* Ha, that was a joke, being towed fifty feet in the air to parasail behind a truck. Ten seconds of floating in the air before smacking the ground, *some training*.

Now he was out of control, spinning in a dark sky, terrified and falling into enemy territory. Nobody trained him for this. *Never mind. Remember what they told you. Pull your risers.* What the hell were risers? He looked up. Four sets of heavy straps were all that attached him to the parachute canopy lines. *Okay, those straps had to be the risers. Pull one. Stabilize yourself.*

He reached up and pulled with all his might as though trying to lift himself. All he was really doing was pulling a corner of the parachute down. Still, it seemed to work. The parachute, which had been oscillating in a wide spiral, settled down, stabilized. *Good, now think about the landing.* He knew it wouldn't be long before the earth rose up to strike him.

For just that moment, he almost forgot the pain in his crotch. There was no sound, no sound at all, except the breeze ruffling his chute. He was still pulling on the riser and that made the parachute rotate slowly. In other circumstances, it could have actually been kind of fun. Then the panic returned full force. In the distance he saw a billowing ball of fire that a minute ago had been his airplane. *What happened? Why did he bail out?*

He should've been horrified at the humanity—as many as sixteen crewmembers on an AC-130 airplane—falling to their deaths. But strangely, there was no sound. The distant slow-motion falling star was silent. There was only the sound of wind. It was surreal.

Could he possibly be the only survivor? He watched in morbid fascination, even as the fireball impacted the ground and continued to boil and burn like an erupting volcano. His mind was blank, drained of all emotion. It just couldn't be real, couldn't be happening.

The toenail sliver of moon shone just enough to make him aware of the fast-rising earth. He couldn't discriminate shapes. He couldn't tell if he was headed into trees or rocks or whatever, but he knew it was coming fast and it was going to be hard. *Remember your training. Elbows in, legs bent, tuck and roll,* he repeated over and over. It didn't matter.

He slapped the ground like a sack of concrete. It knocked the wind out of him, may have even knocked him unconscious. When his senses began to return, he was being dragged along by the parachute. He bounced slowly, feeling every rock, every bump and every dip.

Remember your training. Release the riser clips. Where the hell were the riser clips? He clawed at his chest. The clips had to be there. He was sure they were there. He felt a large metal square, flipped open the cover, and yanked on the clip. One strap flew away. The parachute deflated and collapsed.

And now the silence was complete. There wasn't even wind, just his own labored breathing. He untangled himself, unbuckled the parachute harness and stood on shaking legs. He was alive, banged up, hurting, but nothing seemed broken.

But where was he? He didn't have a clue. It was too dark to tell anything except that he was standing in waist-high grass. He turned in a full circle, almost losing his balance in the darkness. He could barely discern a horizon, no lights, no buildings, and no people. He might have been on the dark side of the moon.

As his eyes adapted somewhat, he could tell that beyond the grassland were hills on both sides of him but he couldn't tell much more than that. He tried to remember his survival training. He tried to remember what little he had been taught about escape and evasion. He couldn't remember a damn thing.

This was only his second flight, his second flight as a gunner on the AC-130 Gunship and his training had been pretty sketchy. It sure as hell didn't prepare him to get shot down behind enemy lines. He had been so excited about this flight, about actually going into combat, he didn't pay much attention to the pre-flight briefing. He didn't even pay attention to where they were supposed to be flying. *What did it matter?* It all looked the same to gunners inside the darkened plane. He wasn't even sure what country he was in. All he remembered was that this area was called "Barrel Roll."

Which way was home? He didn't have a clue. *Maybe he could tell directions from the stars.* He scanned the heavens. They looked different than back in Iowa. He couldn't find the Big Dipper. He couldn't find Orion. He couldn't find north. He didn't know where he was and he didn't know where he should go. He couldn't concentrate with the screaming pain in his groin.

He was on the verge of tears when he heard something. Now, he was alert and really shaking. He heard someone moving here in enemy territory. He really didn't know much about the enemy. He knew that the North Vietnamese were the real scary ones. There were others, Viet Cong and Pathet Lao. He had heard these names but they meant nothing to him. Whoever was out there, he was sure they were the bad guys. He had to hide.

"Hey, Petunia, is that you?"

Patrick Tooney recognized the voice. It was Dewey, Dewey Block, his chief gunner. At least somebody else made it out of the plane, but why did it have to be Dewey? Big mouth, big belly and big smelly cigar, Dewey was a bully.

Patrick half whispered, "Over here, I'm over here."

Dewey crunched through the tall grass. Even in the dark, Patrick could smell the bigger man, his soggy unlit cigar and the lingering hint of whiskey and sweat seeping out of his pores.

"Ah, there you are, Petunia."

"My name is Patrick."

Dewey stopped short. "Pat Tooney, Petunia, what's the difference? You're still a mousey little shit that don't amount to much. I'm a Master Sergeant and I'll call you whatever I want. You got that, Airman Petunia?"

There was a hard moment of silence between them before Dewey ordered, "Now, let's police up your parachute so we don't leave a great big flag that says, 'Hey, come catch the American running dogs.' That be all right with you, Airman?"

Patrick said nothing but he did set to work gathering the silk billows of his chute and stuffing them back into the harness pack. It didn't fit, of course—the old "ten pounds of shit in a five pound sack."

Both men stiffened at a sound. Someone else was coming. Someone was climbing a hill, huffing and grunting with exertion. Someone was very close. Dewey and Patrick both sank to their knees and listened. Dewey fumbled with his survival vest and managed to draw his Air Force issue revolver. Patrick did the same. The stranger paused, gasping, trying to catch his breath. In clear American English he wheezed, "Damn, I've got to quit drinking and get in shape."

Dewey sounded unsteady, "Who goes there?"

"Oh shit, is that you, Dewey? I saw two other chutes beneath me and I hustled over to where you landed. Have you hooked up with the guy in the other chute yet?"

"Well damn, if it isn't Lieutenant Eli Lee. I got Airman Petunia right here and now I'm going to have to babysit you, too."

The lieutenant's breathing was becoming more even. "You watch your mouth, Sergeant. I'm your only hope of getting back alive. You two losers don't have a clue where you are, do you? Well, I do. I'm a navigator and I know where we have to go so you're going to do exactly what I tell you and keep your ignorant opinions to yourself. Got it?"

Dewey answered, "Yes Sir," in a voice of pure sarcasm.

"All right then. Airman Tooney, take out your survival radio and attach the earpiece. Then turn it to 'monitor' and listen on the headset. You'll hear a constant, very irritating, whoop, whoop, whoop. What you are waiting for is a voice, any voice. If you hear one, hand me the radio."

Patrick was heartened by the Lieutenant's authority. Even in the darkness, his six foot three frame loomed large and his voice was just as big, just as intimidating. Moreover, the man seemed to know what he was doing despite his reputation as a barroom fighter and alcoholic. Patrick gathered his courage and asked, "Sir, do you think they will come and get us with helicopters or something?"

Lieutenant Lee had pretty much recovered from his climb. "Not likely. Most of the airplanes involved in Mister Nixon's Secret War against Laos are down in the long T-bone part of the country we call 'Steel Tiger.' There are probably two hundred planes a night down there bombing trucks on the Ho Chi Minh trail. There's not much going on up here in the part of the country we call 'Barrel Roll.' It's not likely that anyone will even know we got shot down until we're overdue back at our base in Thailand."

Dewey perked up. "What about our escorts? They'll call in and start a rescue effort."

The lieutenant's voice seemed flat. "We didn't have any escort fighters. This was supposed to be a low threat mission. There wasn't supposed to be much anti-aircraft artillery to suppress. To make things worse, our targets were classified. Moonbeam, our Command and Control, didn't even know we were flying. It could be days before they get it sorted out." He paused. "I think we're pretty much on our own."

Dewey sounded angry. "So we're hung out here with nobody knowing about us? Just how are we supposed to get back?"

"Well," the lieutenant said, "luckily, we were at the southern edge of our search area, only thirty miles from Thailand. There's a dirt road just over that hill. If we follow it we can walk out in four hard days."

Dewey sounded skeptical. "Oh sure, we just walk along the road. What about the bad guys? They control this area, don't they? What do we do about them?"

Patrick felt a twinge of panic return. They were lost in enemy territory. This was no time for junior high school bickering. They needed to work together.

The lieutenant's voice sounded steady, almost casual. "Dewey, my boy, you're just worried that you can't go four days without a shot of bourbon. We're used to flying at night. We'll walk at night and hide during the day. With luck, our rescuers will eventually send a Jolly Green Giant helicopter to pluck us from this shithole. Otherwise, we'll just walk to Thailand and call from a payphone. Now, let's get moving."

"The road was a ribbon of moonlight." As he stumbled in darkness, Patrick Tooney recited from a poem he had been forced to read in high school. It took his mind off his throbbing genitals. "And the highwayman came riding, riding." *Why did he remember that silly poem?* He wished the road they were wandering was a ribbon of moonlight. But his moon had set leaving the countryside a dark, shapeless void. Only ruts of tire tracks bordered by stands of shoulder-high Elephant Grass kept the three men oriented, going forward to…wherever the hell they were going.

Dewey whined, "How long have we been walking? It seems like hours." He was not cut out for physical activity and his breathing sounded like the beginnings of emphysema.

Lieutenant Lee answered. "It's two thirty. We've been on the road for an hour and a half. How are you holding up, Tooney?"

Patrick shrugged but realized no one could see him. "I'm good Lieutenant, but how can you see your watch? I can't see anything. You got X-ray eyes?"

"Radium dial. I got the watch from Army surplus. The numbers glow. Sometimes, when I was bored on the airplane, I would look at it through the night vision scope. Light amplification made the numbers look like the Las Vegas strip. It was really groovy."

Patrick chuckled and tripped on a dirt clod. "I wish we had that night vision scope right now. It's dark."

The lieutenant's voice came out of the nothingness. "I had to jettison the scope to bail out. When I first saw that fire, I didn't have time to think. I just grabbed my chute and dove out the door head-first. I fell for a good ten seconds before I was able to get my chest-pack parachute clipped on and pull my rip cord. I've got to tell you, it was a relief to feel that canopy pop." He paused for a second. "I was standing in an open door spotting targets. That made bailout easy for me. But how did you two get out?"

Patrick thought before answering. "I'm not sure. I don't remember the fire or the bailout. I just remember my parachute opening and being scared shitless—no idea how I got out of the plane."

Dewey grunted, "I pushed you, Petunia. You were going nuts. The plane was burning like a giant blowtorch and you were just standing there frozen. Worse, you were blocking my way. We couldn't get to the open ramp because the fire completely filled the ass end of the plane, so I pushed you out one of the emergency exits. I even pulled your rip cord for you—saved your life, I reckon."

Patrick said a tentative, "Thank you." He wasn't sure he believed Dewey but maybe it was true. Then he was distracted by a crackling noise in his earpiece. The lieutenant told him to listen for voices on the emergency radio but the constant background noise bugged him and he had been slowly turning down the volume as they walked, turning it down until it became subliminal.

He fumbled to turn up the volume. There were indeed voices, scratchy and weak. "Lieutenant, I hear something on the radio."

Lieutenant Lee tromped back, grabbed Patrick in the darkness and fumbled for the radio. He shouted into it, "Mayday, mayday, mayday, this is Specter three zero, three survivors on the ground. Does anyone copy?"

He waited. They all waited…no response. The radio crackled and bits of distant words could be heard. The lieutenant tried several more times but there was no answer. With a sigh, he grabbed Patrick's hand and slapped the radio back into his palm. His voice seemed less energized than before. "Keep listening. Maybe someone's still flying around in radio range."

Patrick stiffened. His hearing was excellent. They told him that on the auditory part of his induction physical. Without the distraction of the radio bud in his ear, he could again hear small sounds, night insects, a slight breeze, even the breathing of his companions. He heard something else, something far off.

"Lieutenant, I hear vehicles coming."

The lieutenant put on his command voice. "Everyone off the road. Find the deepest grass you can and get down. Let's go." They clomped into tall grass and brambles, tripping and floundering before settling in. Three trucks lumbered by. The lead truck had little eyebrows over each headlight that deflected their beams right in front of the wheels. Patrick was surprised to see a thick morning mist had formed reducing the headlights to a soft fuzzy glow. The two following trucks were invisible in the fog, blindly driving off the leader to prevent detection from marauding American aircraft like their AC-130.

Dewey moaned and announced, "Oh damn, I gotta take a shit."

Patrick was horrified. "What? Not now. Just wait. You can wait a few minutes." There were more trucks coming, heavy trucks. Patrick heard them, but they were coming very slowly. In just moments three more trucks rumbled by, barely visible in fog that made the tall grass slick and damp. There was a break before yet another three trucks approached.

Patrick could hear Dewey grunting. The man already stank from sweat and the little cigar stub he chewed. He could sweat more than any human alive, and now he added the awful stench of Thai chili diarrhea. He had to be the vilest human on earth. Patrick crawled away.

Trucks were close now. Engines clattered and Asian music wailed from a radio. When they were just yards away, the lead truck slammed on brakes and juddered to a stop. There, in the foggy headlight beams, Dewey Block squatted, naked and moaning as he squeezed out his Thai chili. His flight suit was down around his ankles, revealing the body of a great white whale. Reflecting against dark background, Dewey's belly might as well have been a neon billboard.

A skinny Asian man in a uniform dismounted the lead truck but left his engine running. He held a large rifle but seemed unsure as he yelled in some shrill sing-song language. Dewey waved back as though saying, "Just a minute." Another uniformed man joined the first.

Patrick was too scared to think. He pressed himself against the wet ground until he could barely see the two soldiers. At least he assumed they were soldiers. They were both shouting now, shouting at Dewey. Patrick almost wished they would just shoot the fool—*well, not really.*

The soldiers were getting bolder, moving closer to Dewey, who was talking to them, loud and slow, as though they might understand if he treated them like children. *What a fool.* Through the grass, Patrick saw an odd movement reflected in twin shafts of truck lights. He slid his hand toward the pistol in his survival vest. *Why hadn't he drawn it earlier?* Gingerly, he raised his head. The two soldiers faced Dewey directly. The man with a rifle was actually poking at him. At least Dewey had pulled his flight suit up.

Patrick saw the movement again. Someone was behind the soldiers, hunched over, scooting around in the shadows. It had to be Lieutenant Lee. Now Patrick Tooney had to act. He squared his shoulders, cocked the hammer of his revolver and pulled his knees under his body, ready to move. It hurt but he didn't have long to wait.

The shadow figure bolted onto the soldiers, dragging one down. The other soldier shouted something and spun but his rifle was long and awkward in such close quarters. Patrick stood and fired at the dark figures. He had done all right in marksmanship training and his aim was surprisingly true. The rifle soldier yelled, dropped his gun and danced in pain. The lieutenant's silhouette came fully into the foggy headlight and slashed the dancing man. Patrick walked toward the scene holding his gun with both hands extended just as he had been taught.

Lieutenant Lee stood over the bodies. He was breathing hard and looking around. There were actually three bodies. Lee had killed one soldier before Patrick noticed. Standing in the dim light, looking down at the corpses, Patrick realized he had been holding his breath. He exhaled in a mix of relief and anxiety and looked up at the lieutenant like a child to a parent.

"What do we do now, Sir?" Despite the darkness, he could see the lieutenant's teeth. He was smiling.

"We hide the bodies. I think we just drastically cut our walking time thanks to the donation of these trucks. We'll make the border by noon."

Dewey came thrashing through the grass as he zipped his flight suit over an egg shaped belly. "What was all that about? I don't think they wanted to hurt us."

"Then you're an idiot. These drivers are North Vietnamese. We're just lucky there were only these three. The trucks might have been filled with troops and your dumb-ass stunt might have gotten us all killed. What were you thinking, anyway?"

"Well you know, when nature calls…"

Lieutenant Lee raised a hand as though about to strike Dewey, but instead he opened that hand and whispered, "Do you hear that?"

Patrick listened. More engines, he heard more engines. He could hear them even over the clatter of the three diesel trucks that sat idling. The lieutenant barked.

"Get these bodies off the road. Patrick, you drive the last truck. Dewey, you drive number two. We'll stay in contact through our emergency radios. Let's get moving. We don't want the next bunch of trucks to come across us or their buddies. Move out now." Patrick ran. Dewey whined and lumbered. The lieutenant was already gone.

The truck's controls were pretty standard and Patrick had no trouble putting it in gear and starting out. Dewey sat grinding gears and revving the engine. Finally, he too lurched forward and the newly formed American-driven convoy was off.

Patrick's truck rattled along. The steering wheel was huge and heavy. Surprisingly, there was no power steering for diminutive

Vietnamese drivers. But then, Patrick was no giant himself. Luckily, the former owners had screwed wooden blocks onto the brake and clutch pedals, making them just right for him. Patrick strained to see the lights from the lieutenant's lead truck as fog thickened. He fumbled with his emergency radio trying to work the controls in the dark.

"*Screech*...Hey Lieutenant, how far are we going in these trucks?"

After a pause, a static-laced voice answered. "Remember the intersection I told you about? It's about an hour ahead at this speed, that is, if I converted kilometers on the speedometer to miles-per-hour correctly. Anyway, once we get there, we'll turn south until daylight. Then we'll stop and take stock."

At least they had a plan. Patrick settled back and concentrated on driving his huge, clumsy truck. It was pretty scary, driving an unfamiliar vehicle in total darkness on a dirt road in enemy territory. This would be a story for his grandchildren... if he lived to have them.

Once again Patrick fumbled with his emergency radio. He tried to steady his voice. "Lieutenant, the trucks we saw coming, they're gaining on me. They're close enough I can see their lead truck's headlights reflecting off the fog. I'm not sure, but I think they're full of soldiers and they're getting closer."

The radio screeched. "Okay Tooney, stay calm. Just tuck in tight behind Dewey and let me think. I'm gaining on the trucks in front of me, getting a little too close to them." Lieutenant Lee seemed to be taking a deep breath before he continued. "When we took out the three solo truck drivers, I think we may have just had a lucky break. They were obviously part of a much larger convoy that got spread out in the fog. You know, I think these might actually be the trucks we were hunting before we crashed. This may be what our secret mission was about. There must be something special about these trucks."

Then the radio was silent. Patrick realized he was breathing too fast… again. He concentrated on driving, constantly shooting glances at his rear view mirrors. The trucks behind kept getting closer.

The night air was humid. It was always humid in this damned place. It felt like a sauna, or at least what he expected a sauna felt like. Back at his Thailand base, they said the monsoon was beginning. One sweaty hand clamped the steering wheel as he reached out the window to wipe condensation off his mirror. *Damn it, didn't they have enough to worry about without this stupid fog?*

The fog continued to thicken. The lieutenant's headlights, two trucks ahead, were getting harder and harder to see, sometimes disappearing completely in the mist. "Hey, Dewey, tighten it up," Patrick shouted into his radio. There was no response. He was about to shout again when he heard the lieutenant's voice crackle over the radio. "I'm turning hard left. Follow me now."

Patrick couldn't see the road as fog billowed around him. He guessed at the time it took to reach where Lieutenant Lee had been when he made the call. Patrick held his breath and yanked the steering wheel. His truck bucked with tooth rattling violence that shot pain from his damaged groin.

Am I even on the road? For just a second, he caught a glimpse of dim headlights ahead. Patrick corrected to follow them. *Stop breathing so fast. This has to be the road.* He was so focused on looking for the lights he almost rear-ended Dewey's truck ahead.

Good, we're all back together. Let's just hope the bad guys didn't follow us. He checked his fogged-up mirrors, nothing. He relaxed just a little, just a little.

Two more uneventful hours. His muscles knotted into kinks. Sweat ran into his eyes. His damp hands welded to the steering wheel. Then the fog became brighter, swirling over his windshield. It was getting light outside.

The first hint of sunrise caught Patrick by surprise. In the dark, he assumed they were still driving through open grassland. The deeply rutted dirt road had consumed his attention as he fought to keep the big clumsy truck in line behind the other two. Now, in the gray light of morning, mountains of limestone rose on all sides. Sheer walls of gray rock plummeted out of the clouds like office buildings stuck into the ground. Some towered a thousand feet, others just a few hundred. These were the karst towers of Laos he heard about. At their foggy bases and again at the crest above, the giants were cloaked in jungle vegetation.

He could see the two trucks ahead of him, but none behind. At least, they seemed to have escaped the rest of the convoy. Patrick tried to stay focused on driving as they wound through empty canyons between cloud-draped monoliths. It was an almost magical looking place that reminded him of Chinese scroll paintings he had seen back at his Air Base in Thailand. It made him feel small, tiny even. It was an overwhelming scene for a kid from Iowa. For a moment, he forgot they were driving stolen trucks deep inside the enemy's territory.

Lieutenant Lee, in the lead truck, came to a stop. Patrick and Dewey pulled up behind him. The three men shut down their engines and gathered as the lieutenant unfolded a soft plastic map the size of a small tablecloth. He looked frustrated.

"We're lost. These roads don't look anything like the ones on my map. I did see route numbers on some metal signs. If they can be believed, we're way south of where I expected. The Mekong River should be just over this next range of mountains."

Patrick and Dewey listened but said nothing. The lieutenant bit his lip. "To cross the river, we're going to have to ditch these trucks and steal a boat. Once across, we'll be safely in Thailand. The problem is that the river's edge is heavily populated. We'll have to sneak down in daytime and find a suitable boat. Then we'll wait for nightfall to steal it. Everybody agree?"

Patrick only shrugged. He had no better idea.

"Okay then, let's see what's in these trucks. Maybe we can find something helpful like food or guns."

Patrick felt a twinge of hope. They were close to Thailand and they had a plan. He went to his truck, lowered the tailgate and threw back the canvas flap. Inside were wooden boxes, dozens, maybe hundreds of boxes. He climbed up to sit on one stack and used his large black-bladed survival knife to pry one open. It was full of papers, like a file cabinet's contents. They looked official, but all in Vietnamese. He tossed that box back and went to another and another. They were the same.

He was about to give up when he saw that the bottom layer of boxes was different from the others, more substantial with metal handles and padlocks. He tried to wiggle one free from the stacks above. It was too heavy. He restacked boxes until he had completely uncovered the bottom box. Then he jumped down from the tailgate and tried to slide the box free. It was still too heavy. He used his knife to pry a board loose. Then Patrick Tooney let out a gasp. He stepped back and stood for a long breathless moment before finding his voice.

"Lieutenant, you got to see this. You're not gonna believe it."

The lieutenant came walking with a handful of papers. He was mumbling. "This is a gold mine of intelligence information, tactical maps, orders, and communiques. I can't read any of it but I'll bet our Intel guys would love to get their hands on it. So what've you got, Patrick?"

Patrick Tooney was quiet but excited. "I've got a different kind of gold mine." He reached into the box and strained to remove something the size and shape of a deck of playing cards. It was metal and felt as though it was being held by a strong magnet. It wasn't magnetic. It was gold. The lieutenant grabbed the bar from Patrick Tooney and the weight of it pulled his hand down.

"Jesus man, how much is there? This has to be worth a fortune."

"Yes sir, this entire box is full. I don't know about the others."

The lieutenant stood with his mouth open. He motioned with his free hand as though about to speak but nothing came. His mind was obviously racing.

Dewey joined them with a confused look. When he saw the gold he inhaled so deep it seemed he might explode. He recovered and whistled. "Uncle Ho is not going to like this."

"Uncle Ho?" Patrick repeated.

"You know, Ho Chi Minh, the communist leader. What we have here is a shit-load of his gold. He could buy a lot of guns with this."

Finally composed, the lieutenant barked. "Check the other boxes. See if they have gold as well."

They did.

THURSDAY

Kelley bolted upright in bed. *Where was he? Who was yelling?* He began to focus. A small Asian-looking woman was standing in the bedroom doorway. She was attractive with delicate features and long silky hair. There was nothing delicate about her voice.

"Who the hell are you and what are you doing in Patrick's bed?"

What was he doing in the bed? Oh yeh, he was in Hawaii in Uncle Pat's condo. It was all coming back.

He cleared his throat. "I'm Kelley Price. I inherited this place from my uncle, Patrick Tooney. Who are you?"

The voice came back even harder and more high-pitched. "Inherited? You *inherited* this place? Are you saying Patrick is dead?"

Kelley was aware that he was wearing only jockey shorts. He pulled the covers around him. "I'm sorry, but yes, he passed away last week."

Her tone turned skeptical like a cross-examining attorney.

"How did he die? Where did he die?"

Kelley felt a sudden pressure. He had to pee and very soon.

"I don't know. His lawyer said only 'natural causes.' I have only been here a few hours. I haven't had time to find out any more. Listen, if you give me a minute to get dressed, we'll talk but I have to go to the bathroom. Please wait outside."

"I go nowhere." She folded her arms and stamped her foot like a two-year-old.

"Well, suit yourself," he said and flipped off the covers to walk to the bathroom. *Where was the bathroom?* He stood for a second getting his bearings. There were three doors. One was open to the main room. He headed for the one on the left—fifty-fifty chance.

The intense black-haired lady eyed him with curiosity but no embarrassment. He tried to ignore her. He considered himself a reasonably good looking man, six feet tall and once quite athletic. He needed to drop a few pounds but he looked presentable in a sport coat. Of course, just awakened, nearly naked and unwashed for two days and five thousand miles, he probably looked pretty ragged. But then, she didn't seem to be evaluating.

He found the bathroom. It was bright, very modern, white tile and glass. Pat must have had a decorator. There were fake plants, palm trees or something. It seemed to have a woman's touch, something Kelley would not have expected of his uncle.

He sighed with relief as he finally let go a high-pressure stream but was startled when the woman suddenly appeared standing beside him. Some things, once begun, can't be interrupted. He kept peeing.

Her voice softened. "You are sure, Patrick is dead?"

Kelley turned slightly away from her but kept splashing. "All I know is what the lawyer told me. How and where Pat died I have no idea. So, who are you and what is your relationship with my uncle?"

"I'm Aelan. Patrick was my friend, my good friend."

Her voice faded as she slipped away. Kelley stood for an eternity before he was able to finish and shake the last drops. As he went back into the bedroom, he saw the third door standing open. It was a walk-in closet and Aelan was there, running her hand along the rack of Pat's clothes. There were tear streaks on her cheeks but no other sign of emotion.

He grabbed his pants from a chair and stood in the closet door. "Tell me about my uncle. I hardly knew him."

She leaned her head toward her shoulder. Her voice was softer now. "People didn't give him enough respect. He was a good man, very smart. After he got shot, he had the shakes. He didn't go out much after that. People stared and it embarrassed him."

"How did he get shot? I didn't know he had been wounded."

"I don't want to talk about it." She took a breath, shook her long hair and seemed to compose. "Did Patrick have a funeral?"

Kelley remembered his conversation with the lawyer. "No, there was no service. I have the box with his ashes right here in the condo."

Her voice was flat, resolute. "Good, we must offer the proper respect. I will make arrangements and call you with details." And, with that, she brushed by him and was gone. He heard the front door click closed and breathed easier.

Later, showered and dressed, he spent half an hour figuring out how to work the coffeemaker. It was Italian and had no directions but he finally brewed a cup. He took it to the balcony and stood feeling the ocean breeze. Strange birds chattered nearby and he could see the surf just a few blocks away. He could even smell the salty blue water that filled the horizon. He took a long, deep breath.

Less than forty hours ago, he thought his life was a complete mess. Now he found himself the owner of this magnificent condo and two income producing properties, not to mention a bank account that could wipe out all his debts. He even had a sports car...if he could find it. Kelley decided to go for a ride.

He fished the car keys from the stack of papers the lawyer gave him. And there on the table was the brown paper wrapped box. The lawyer had called it a dragon box. What could it hold? Surely, there was no more money. He tore away the brown paper wrapping to reveal an incredibly heavy, very Asian looking polished black lacquer box inlaid with mother-of-pearl dragons and other beasts. It was beautifully crafted and probably expensive. It was also locked and there was no key.

Perhaps, it held jewelry. With effort, he held it to his ear and shook. *Damn, this thing's heavy, must weigh twenty- thirty pounds.* It didn't sound like jewelry, more like paper. All right, now he had a mission. He would take the car and find someone to open his mystery box. It was a good day for a drive, his first full day of a new life in paradise.

The Audi was in an underground garage in a spot with the number that matched his condo. He smiled—*his condo.*

It wasn't new, but it was still a flashy little car. A round nosed silver two-seater, he struggled to squeeze into a seat better suited for his five foot five uncle. He turned the key and felt instant love for the throaty rumble of the engine. He just had to squeal tires as he pulled out, had to do it.

Sun and wind and the ever-present smell of coconut tanning lotion. He didn't even mind the New York City style traffic on Kalakawa, Honolulu's main drag. He found an Interstate- *how could there be an Interstate Highway on an island?* Accelerating, he climbed up into the Pali, the mountainous backbone of Oahu. The forest of concrete high-rise buildings gave way to a real tropical forest. The little car was nimble and fun.

Beyond the jungle mountainside lay wide fields of flat red earth and neat rows of deep green plants. He stopped in a small roadside restaurant. It was crowded and noisy with locals, no tourists. After scrambled eggs with spam and pineapple, bad coffee and directions to a local jeweler, he was back on his way.

The jeweler turned out to be a withered little Japanese man with a sour attitude. He grabbed Kelley's box, inspected it and mumbled something about Mainlanders. It took him only seconds to open it with a small tool. Then the held the box in tight fists, looked up and pronounced "fifty dollars."

Kelley laughed. "Twenty."

The old man put on a fish mouth. "Forty."

"Twenty five or you can lock it back up."

The jeweler slid the box toward him with a sneer and Kelley dug out a twenty and a five. *Who did this guy think he was, anyway? Nobody from New Jersey pays tourist rates.*

He had guessed right about the contents, paper certificates, fancy gilded certificates. Kelley unfolded one. It was a stock certificate for General Motors preferred shares dated November, 1973. He started to fold it back up when he noticed the name on the certificate wasn't Tooney, it was Block. *How strange.*

Once back at the condo, Kelley spread the papers and tried to make sense of them. Among the certificates he found a plain white envelope. Inside was a letter. He opened and read.

My Dearest Nephew Kelly,

If you are reading this, things have gone badly for me. Please do not despair. I have made choices that led to my current situation and I must deal with the consequences.

First, let me say that I always admired you and wished we could have come to know each other better. But I honored your mother's wish and stayed away. She was always a fine woman and I miss her. It was more than a tragedy when her life ended so abruptly. She had so much to give. Now, I too, am gone. You are one of the last surviving members of the Tooney clan and I am depending on you to carry on.

But first I must tell you my story. More than forty years ago I, along with two others, hijacked a cargo from the North Vietnamese. I feel no guilt about it. They stole it from the Lao people and we stole it from them. That cargo was raw gold, truckloads of gold, enough to ransom many kings.

We got it as far as Thailand but it was impossible to get most of it out of the country. We were able to smuggle only a few tons to Hawaii."

Kelley stopped reading for a moment. *Only a few tons?* Back to the letter.

"My two co-conspirators, Eli Lee and Dewey Block cheated me, as thieves are wont to do. I was able to hold onto a small amount of gold which I invested, and rather well I might say. You are now the recipient of my very prudent efforts. I hope they bring you a comfortable life. This is but a teardrop in the ocean compared to the gold that is somewhere here in Hawaii and an even larger cache in Thailand and Laos.

The enclosed stock certificates were drawn on all three of our names. It was an early effort to launder our wealth. I have only recently recovered them and I don't know if they have any value. Do with them as you wish. If you are able to discover what these scoundrels have done with my gold,

I ask that you return, at least a goodly portion of it to the people from whom it was taken, the Lao.

Be careful. Do not trust Lee. He has led a disreputable life and is certainly dangerous.

In closing, I ask that you live your life deliberately with both passion and compassion. Do not mourn me. I have felt joy and I have few regrets. I hope you do the same.

Excelsior!
Your Uncle,
Patrick Tooney

Kelley held the letter and sighed. He wished he had known the man better. Just from the letter, he sounded more interesting and certainly more literate than Mother had led him to believe. But why was he chosen to represent the Tooney clan? What did Uncle Pat know about his two brothers?

He remembered from an old poem, the word excelsior meant "onward and upward," a nice touch. Kelley gathered the certificates and the letter and shoved them in a desk drawer.

Then his thoughts drifted. *Tons of gold, could it be true?* He tried to make a mental calculation. A ton was two thousand pounds he thought. Sixteen ounces in a pound made 32,000 ounces. He hadn't kept up with gold prices but he thought it was over $1500. That would be forty eight million dollars a ton... *Wow.*

Back at the condo, Kelley decided to spend a leisurely afternoon playing tourist and trying not to think about the gold. He walked among the crowds, roaming the endless booths and shops of Waikiki. He tried to pace himself. After all, he had nowhere to go and nothing to accomplish. He watched the endless parade of giggling bikini girls and Muumuu matrons. All the men wore identical uniforms, cotton short sleeved Aloha shirts that differed only in color and flower pattern.

The weather was Hawaii perfect, mid-eighties with a gentle trade wind breeze that barely moved palm trees and flags. He walked the beach sidewalk like an official bikini inspector. Sprawling coconut-oil-lathered girls seemed so young, so childish. He squinted, eyes irritated by sun reflecting off water and sand. That same sand infiltrated his leather shoes and settled between his toes. Tired of the grit and glare, he took a stool in a thatched roof beachfront bar and ordered a Mai-Tai in a coconut shell, quickly deciding he didn't like fruity drinks.

A deeply tanned man with a red-flowered shirt, mirror sunglasses and narrow-brimmed straw hat slid into the next seat and grinned, "Just another shitty day in paradise, huh, pilgrim?" Red shirt began a rambling tale of his background that devolved into a sales pitch for oil exploration partnerships. It was a completely inappropriate conversation but Kelley imagined the fellow had no other topics in his portfolio. Vacation or not, he was a perpetual salesman.

By late afternoon, Kelley was bored. He went back to the condo to watch the sunset from his balcony. Perhaps he would see the fabled green flash. In the elevator, two men in ill-fitting suits seemed nervous. Maybe it was because they were the only two men in all of Honolulu wearing suits, with the possible exception of Mormon missionaries. The men shifted weight and cleared their throats repeatedly. He checked them out. They wore laminated ID badges on lanyards around their necks. Bulges under coats suggested guns. They had to be law enforcement of some kind. He hoped crime was not going to be a big problem here in his new Hawaii home.

The men got off on his floor and walked ahead of him down his hallway. They stopped in front of his door and, to his amazement, knocked. The older of the two squared his shoulders and pounded again before yelling, "Immigration and Customs Enforcement, open up."

"Excuse me," Kelley offered, "This is my condo. Can I help you?"

The older, fleshier of the two men spun. He took a deep breath and tried to look tough. He was a heavy breather. "Mister Patrick Tooney, I'm Homeland Security Investigations Special Agent Diggins. I have a warrant to search the premises."

Kelley smirked. "Homeland Security, what on earth does the ICE want with my uncle? Never mind. Step aside and I'll let you in. You don't need a warrant. I have nothing to hide. Just try not to break anything."

"Mister Tooney…"

Kelley cut the man off. "It's Price. I'm Kelley Price. Patrick Tooney was my uncle. Tell me about this warrant. What do you suspect my uncle of?"

Special Agent Diggins lifted his chin and sounded authoritative. "We received an anonymous call indicating that Mister Tooney is involved in the slave trade."

Kelley almost laughed. "Slave trade, what does that even mean?"

Diggins was defensive. "There is a sizeable traffic in Asian immigrants who pay to be smuggled into the islands. Here, they are sold to wealthy clients who use them as sex workers, housekeepers, gardeners and such. They are virtual prisoners without rights or options. Some are even killed."

Kelley looked skeptical. "So how does my uncle figure into any of this? As far as I know, he has no connection to anything like what you describe. He invested in real estate and stocks."

Diggins was curt. "Here is the warrant. Now, tell me where we can find Mister Tooney."

Kelley grinned. "He's right there on the table." Both agents looked confused.

"Right there, he's in the cardboard box. He was cremated a few days ago."

Diggins scowled. Kelley began to read the warrant. "Say, this authorizes you to search the home of Patrick Tooney. Since I inherited the place, this is no longer Patrick's home. So, is this warrant still valid? Like I said, you're welcome to look around but I'm not sure of the legality, if you know what I mean." He put on an innocent-looking smile. Normally quiet, Kelley could come out of his shell when the situation called for it.

The two agents stepped aside for a quiet huddle accompanied by some animated gestures and muffled grunts. After a pause, Diggins turned back. "Mister Price was it? We'll have to take this up with our supervisor. In the meantime, don't leave the island. Here's my card. We'll be in touch."

"No problem," Kelley said in a cheery voice. He waved as they left. "And a great big Aloha to you."

When they were gone, he went looking for a phone number for Aelan. Maybe she could shed some light. There were no address books or lists in Patrick's desk. There was a computer. Kelley turned it on and was confronted by a flashing box that demanded, "password."

Where would he find a password? Patrick, it seemed, was a conscientious man. He wouldn't leave such a detail uncovered. He must have left Kelley a clue. But what? He tried several words that came to mind. Nothing. He tried the condo address, the ZIP code, the phone number. Nothing. What about the letter in the dragon box?

Kelley smiled and typed in "Excelsior." The screen changed to a picture of rocky surf with an airport in the background. A voice spoke. It was his dead uncle, Patrick Tooney. It had been years since he heard Uncle Pat's voice. It sounded calm, confident and almost fatherly.

"Hello Kelley and welcome to Hawaii. I'm sorry we meet under these circumstances. I regret even more injecting you into a drama which might turn out to be more than you bargained for. You will find information on this machine about my search. It will provide you names, dates, contact numbers and background on my research. You will find many references to Dewey Block. He is no longer a factor. Eli Lee is the other key player. He is in San Quentin serving life without parole, but don't count him out. The man is devious, intelligent and resourceful. Beware of him. Aelan is a dear friend. She will help you. Good hunting, nephew. Excelsior."

The audio ended with a laugh. Kelley wished he had known the man better. *Now for the address book.* There were dozens of icons on the start-up screen, none labeled addresses. He began the search just as his phone rang.

He answered and Aelan began a rapid-fire speech. "The funeral is all set up. We need to be at the temple by nine tomorrow. I'll meet you at eight thirty. You probably have nothing but Howlie clothes so I went shopping for you. Please tell me you have some shoes other than the black leather ones I saw on the floor. This will be a Hawaiian funeral and you don't want to look like an accountant from New Jersey. I have invited the guests, arranged for flowers and the priest. There will be a small afternoon gathering after. Any questions?"

Kelley could only manage a long, "Uh-h-h."

JUNE 7, 1969

"This changes everything. Uncle Ho has just given us a great gift for which we thank him." Lieutenant Lee squatted beside an oversized truck's tire and grinned. "I say we forget about rescue. We are no longer distressed airmen. We are now soldiers of fortune, entrepreneurs recovering a fortune in gold. More than forty boxes we've counted so far. Most weigh about 180 pounds. At least, that's my guess. Others are much larger, coffin size. I can't even guess what they weigh."

Patrick spoke almost compulsively. "But, if we forget about rescue, how do we get back safely, gold or no gold?"

The lieutenant's face took on the devilish look of a teenaged boy planning his next bit of delinquency. "We wing it."

"Wing it?" Patrick didn't like that.

"Yep, just like a special ops mission, we sneak out of the country in a bold, audacious move, figuring it out as we go. Are you guys in?"

"Hell yes," sputtered Dewey. He seemed intoxicated by the thought of so much gold.

Patrick saw only disaster. He started to protest but Dewey and the lieutenant were already walking away. He had to hustle to keep up with the now energized pair. Lieutenant Lee was lecturing.

"First, we have to get off this road and consolidate the gold into one truck. We'll be more maneuverable and harder to detect. We'll take only the smaller boxes. The bigger ones are just too difficult to manage. Those we'll hide to recover after the war. We'll still be rich. With just the one truck we can make a dash to the river and find a ferry. War or no war, gold will buy us passage." He stopped and looked at them with boyish enthusiasm. "All right then, we need to find a hiding place that will hold the largest boxes of our loot for a couple of years." He clapped his hands. "Let's move." The lieutenant had just become a general.

After another fifteen minutes of driving in hazy fog an explosion shattered a stand of trees two hundred feet away. The concussion shook Patrick's truck and made the doors rattle. Seconds later, a big jet roared over the tree tops so low and so loud Patrick instinctively ducked behind the steering wheel. The lieutenant abruptly turned hard into a shallow stream bed and the others followed. Thick vegetation overhung the dry bed. Branches banged against the front window. Patrick could barely see the truck in front of him and had no idea where they were headed.

They bumped along for half a mile and then pulled up sharply onto a narrow rocky path that led around one of the karst towers. At one point, Patrick saw Dewey's truck ahead with one of its dual rear wheels actually hanging over the edge. Dewey overcorrected and metal on the other side of his truck made sparks against sheer rock. Finally, their caravan came to a stop on the very crest. For a long moment, no one got out. Engines off, there was an overwhelming stillness. Patrick exhaled and released his steering wheel death grip.

They were on a plateau where tropical plants flourished. Thick with vines and giant trees, everything dripped from condensation in the steamy air. Strange bird calls and the buzz of insects welcomed the sun. There were no other sounds. Patrick took a deep breath and turned back to take in the dramatic view. The fog below continued clearing to reveal a fantastic landscape. All around, sheer canyons and valleys cut through soaring karst knobs. Waterfalls plunged into the abyss of lingering mist. Beyond the most distant hills, the air was clear enough to see a great brown river, probably the Mekong.

For a moment, he indulged in the sight and felt tension drain from his body. A strange thought popped into his mind. *This is probably where I'm going to die.* He felt a clarity and calmness he had never known. *It could be worse.* He spread his arms and turned full circle, taking in the panorama. Soft wind rustled the trees like some exotic, alien music. *Everyone has to die. At least I shall be in a wondrous place, a magical place.* He stopped. *But what will they tell my parents? Their son was a thief, killed in a foreign land because he let greed overcome responsibility.* His moment was over.

Lieutenant Lee was enjoying his role. "Okay, let's scout. We need to find a hiding place for the gold accessible by truck but safe from discovery. Tooney, go east. Dewey, you head north over the ridge. I'll follow the path to the west. Move out."

Patrick nodded and stepped out as directed, stumbling along over crags and boulders. Everything was wet. Grass, leaves, mud, everything was slippery, even slimy. *How could they possibly drive anywhere in this mess?* He lost his footing on a shiny rock, gasped and nearly slid over a cliff edge, saved only by a desperate grab of vines. He hung, dangling halfway over a sheer drop-off. Bits of dirt fell and took several seconds to hit bottom. He was afraid to look down. The strain of holding himself on the tangle of lifesaving vines made it hard to breath. But still, he twisted his neck to look. There, in a relatively flat area below, ancient stone buildings had been overgrown by jungle.

He clawed his way back up onto flat ground and caught his breath. Then, composed, he backtracked and found an old path downward. It was wide, nearly a road, and almost invisible under the brush. It led to the ruins he had seen. He walked carefully, oh so carefully. *This looks like a perfect place for snakes.*

When he reached the site, it seemed truly ancient. Crumbled stone walls were pierced by crawling vegetation. Hoary statues that resembled Siamese dancers lay half-buried under moss in the carpet of dense, tangled greenery. A troop of monkeys screamed at him from sun-dappled treetops. *A real wonderland, this must have been a fantastic place when it flourished hundreds of years ago.*

He explored, poking into broken doorways and collapsed walls. Beyond the main structures lay a field of large, flat, vine-covered stones laid out in neat rows but now almost invisible. *Burial vaults probably.* They looked just about the right size to hold the large gold boxes. He ran back to tell the others.

Halfway up the overgrown road he stopped in mid-stride as a shiny black form glided smoothly through underbrush. Silent and sleek, it slithered through debris without disturbing a twig. He stood frozen in-place with one foot raised, having almost stepped right on it. In Jungle Survival School he was taught that most tropical snakes were deadly. After a deep breath, he continued, but more cautious now. *Even Eden had its serpent.*

After inspection, the lieutenant agreed the crypts were perfect. For the next three hours the men struggled to get a truck through the jungle growth to the graveyard. In its equipment box, along with a jack and lug wrench, were pry bars, hooks and chains. They would be useful.

After hooking several chains together around a slab crypt cover and attaching them to the truck frame, Dewey drove slowly forward. The massive rectangular stone began to move. It was badly weathered and overgrown but you could still see intricate carvings. Warriors battled dragons, bare-breasted women in elaborate costumes struck strange poses, figures with snake-like fingernails and animal faces looked on from carved thrones.

Once the crypt was fully exposed, Patrick approached to peek down into the chamber. He didn't know what to expect. There was a stale smell of damp stone, moss and dust. He gritted his teeth and leaned forward to see deep inside.

There was nothing, no body, no bones. It was empty. He exhaled in relief.

The men fashioned a ramp from fallen wood, anchored the chains to a stump and wrapped them over the first of the large gold boxes. Then, they inched the truck forward. The chains tightened. The box straightened and began to slide off the truck bed onto their makeshift ramp. It tilted, wobbled and then fell perfectly into the empty vault with a crash that sent dust billowing. The men cheered like sports spectators.

They worked all day and into the sunset, sweating in the greenhouse atmosphere. Dewey complained constantly of hunger. Water was no problem. It dripped and trickled from every leaf and branch. You had only to hold a wide leaf to your lips and just let pour. By dusk, they had only one large box to hide. Now, it wasn't just Dewey complaining. They were all starving. Brightly colored fruit hung all around but who knew if it was poisonous.

Patrick remembered seeing a bedroll in the cab of his truck, the same kind he had seen in newsreel scenes. Vietnamese soldiers wore them strapped over a shoulder like an ammo belt. He retrieved his and spread it in the truck bed.

"Rice," he yelled. "I found a bag of rice. Look in your trucks. I'll bet you have one too." *It made sense. The Vietnamese soldier-drivers were self-contained with food, sleeping gear and whatever.*

They made a small fire, a risk in enemy territory, but they took it without regret in order to have hot food. The Vietnamese soldier's helmets became bowls to boil rice. Exhausted and fed, they slept like zombies, safe from snakes inside their truck cabs.

Patrick dreamed of paradise and it looked just like this place. He saw beautiful dancers in ornate costumes just like the statues in the ruined temple. He saw animals laughing in the trees and he heard the wind singing in its beautiful foreign language. He felt at peace.

At the first gray hint of sunrise, Patrick awoke to distant shouts. The language was shrill with lots of rolling "L" sounds— Vietnamese. He moved quietly, grimacing from muscles strained moving all that gold. *Where was the driver's rifle? It didn't matter. He had his own gun.* He drew the pistol and inched his door open. The damned thing creaked as though in pain. Patrick cursed, squeezed himself through the partially open door and ran through wet, dripping jungle to the lieutenant's truck. He rapped furiously on the window. The Vietnamese voices were getting closer.

Lieutenant Lee sat up, stretched and smiled at the face of a very tense Patrick Tooney. Immediately, he sensed the situation and swung into action. His door didn't squeak as he got out and drew his pistol. Together, they listened to the approaching voices. Then he grabbed Patrick's arm and drew him close. "Get Dewey. Try not to make too much noise. Bring the fat bastard over to the ruined temple or whatever it is. We'll have good cover there and several escape routes."

He slapped Patrick on the shoulder. "Go."

It was no easy task to rouse Dewey Block. He had found whiskey in his truck and now snored like a bull, resisting all Patrick's tugging and poking. Finally, in desperation, Patrick pinched off the bigger man's nose and held tight. Dewey exploded to life swearing and swinging.

Patrick put a finger to his lips and pointed furiously toward the advancing soldiers. Dewey shook his head and then lumbered out with the wallowing effort of a drunk. Grunting all the way, he allowed himself to be led to the ruined temple. Inside it was dark and damp and soundless.

They waited for the lieutenant but he didn't come. Patrick checked his watch. Minutes passed. Dewey was snoring again. There were no sounds outside. He eased his way to the entrance and peeked out—nothing. He stepped into tree-filtered sunshine and looked around—nothing. He cocked his head and listened—nothing but birds and monkeys. He relaxed slightly.

Where was the lieutenant? Patrick scouted the ruins, climbing rubble piles and scanning as far as he could see. There were no soldiers and no lieutenant.

What to do? He went to the trucks. They were undisturbed. He straightened and was about to go back to Dewey when he heard a low, deep-throated growl. He turned very slowly and saw Lieutenant Lee crouched motionless, holding a rifle with a bayonet and staring intently into the jungle. There, in deep shadow, was the hulking shape, the huge head and glowing eyes of a tiger, a real live, wild tiger. With each growl, the tiger showed dagger-like fangs.

All the air went out of Patrick. He slowly drew his pistol and realized his gun arm felt weak. The lieutenant didn't flinch, didn't move, didn't even seem to breathe. The tiger breathed enough for all of them, rumbling exhalations like sounds in a cavern. They all stood for an eternity, men and beast, neither giving an inch.

Then came a bleary voice, "Hey man, what the hell? You wake me up, drag me into a cave and leave me there." Dewey clomped through the brush like a water buffalo.

The tiger rose on its haunches, made a sound like ripping canvas and then, in a single motion, turned and leaped back into the undergrowth.

The lieutenant stood and leaned for a second with one hand on his knee and the other on his rifle. He drew one deep breath after another.

"You okay, Sir?" Patrick asked. The man nodded and stood straight. He turned and smiled at them.

"Dewey, I never thought I would be so happy to see you."

The fat man looked confused. "What? What did I do? What's everybody talking about?"

FRIDAY

Kelley sat turning a hot coffee cup in his hands as he watched his second sunrise over the ocean since he arrived in Honolulu. Seagulls flapped and danced on the balcony rail watching him for any hint of dropped crumbs. He heard a click and turned to see Aelan breezing through the door with dry cleaning bags over her shoulder.

"You could knock, you know."

She stopped and made a sarcastic face. "I have a key. Why should I knock? It's not like you have any secrets."

He shrugged and sighed. "Do you want coffee?"

"Sure, but we don't have much time. You need to get dressed."

Another sigh, "Can I ask why?"

She put a hand on her hip. "Didn't you listen? The funeral is this morning. I bought you some clothes instead of your Howlie outfit."

"Howlie, that means foreigner, right?"

She made a face. "Yes, in the same way Spic means Hispanic. I'm told that it's from an old Hawaiian word 'haole' that means no breath. The Polynesians thought white people had no soul, no breath."

She took her plastic covered clothes hangers and held them up for his inspection. A blue and white flowered shirt and white linen pants, he looked them over.

"Definitely not Howlie. How did you know the sizes?"

"I have a good eye for men's sizes. I also have sandals and socks. Ordinarily, no one here would wear socks but I'll bet your New Jersey feet are paper white."

"Well, thanks for helping out the poor, clueless Howlie."

"No problem, we have to stick together. My father was white and back in school, they used to call me a half-a-Howlie."

He laughed. "I don't know anything about you. You seem to know all about me and I don't even know your last name."

"Come on, get dressed. We'll be late." He took his new clothes and went into the bedroom. She spoke loudly through the wall, not quite a shout. "My last name is Comer, rhymes with Homer. Your Uncle Pat helped my mother get into the States. I was born here in Hawaii. Never knew my father. Patrick was a friend to my mother and a kind of father figure to me. She died in my first year of high school and he became an even bigger part of my life. He put me through college and helped me get my job as a staffing manager for a cruise line. Is that enough information for you?"

Kelley looked in the mirror. The clothes fit well and felt expensive. The cloth lay smooth and comfortable on his body. He came out and paraded for her. "What do you think?"

She looked him over and nodded approvingly. He liked this girl. Brash, saucy, even abrasive, she interested him. On top of that, she was attractive in a grown up way. How long had it been since he had a grown up relationship? *Maybe, just maybe…*

They drove the little Audi up Route 61 into the rain forest heights of the island. Aelan gave directions and Kelley followed. Wind in his hair, twisting his sports car through the winding mountain road, he felt good. Better than good, he felt free.

The funeral, at some sort of small temple, was anything but normal. Kelley didn't understand a bit of what was going on. The very Hawaiian looking priest chanted and then spoke in English, praising Patrick Tooney for his good works. Incense burned and people gathered to tie strings around a pole. Then they sang, again in some strange language. He wasn't even sure what religion this ceremony was, maybe Buddhist?

The attendees were an odd mix of Anglo school-teacher types and Asians of many different stripes. Attendees wore flowered shirts or Saris or yellow robes. Some of the women had on elaborately woven hats covered with gold coins and chains. It was all very bizarre. At the end, at least what he thought was the end, they gathered, pressing close in a circle and raising their arms to reach up toward the string pole. He felt a little claustrophobic pressed into the mass of flesh.

Then, with a great cheer or chant, or maybe just a shout, they all broke up and spread out. Without comment, they went outside where a table of drinks and hors d'oeuvres had been set up. There, they gathered and chatted with cocktail party abandon.

Aelan pulled him aside and whispered. "Come, we must go now." She dragged Kelley with some force and he almost stumbled. Moving quickly, she picked up the box with Patrick's ashes and continued away from the temple on a path.

"We must hurry." She sounded serious. Kelley didn't understand but then, he hadn't understood much of anything about this woman or this place. She picked her way along the path until it disappeared and then continued on through the thick brush finally stopping at a clearing of moss and ferns.

"Here," she announced. "Help me dig." Kelley shook his head and knelt to help her claw into the ground until they had a foot-deep hole. She sat back, spread her arms and spoke to the sky. It was, of course, some strange sounding foreign language. Then she dumped Pat's ashes into the hole and used her foot to pack dirt over the hole. She whispered, "Time to go, but we must be quiet. The phi—evil spirits—must not know where he is buried."

"Evil spirits?" He stood and brushed dirt from the knees of his new white linen trousers. "Seriously, evil spirits?"

She took his hand and, again, pulled him after her. In a hushed voice, she half whispered, "I made a promise to my mother that I would bury Patrick in the old way. It was her last wish. Evil spirits or not, I have been a good daughter. I have kept my word."

He allowed himself to be dragged through jungle undergrowth and finally asked, "Aelan, you seemed much closer to my uncle than I ever was. Why did I inherit his property rather than you?"

She didn't turn to look at him but kept trudging straight ahead. "I don't know. He must have had his reasons."

"How do you feel about that? It must make you a little angry."

She stopped abruptly and Kelley's forward momentum made him bump into her. They stood inches apart but suddenly there was a great distance between them. She spoke to his chest. "He had his reasons. He was very generous to me in life. He paid for my school, got me a good job and bought me a small condo. I have no reason to complain. I loved the man and I respect his decisions."

Kelley reached to put a hand on her shoulder but she turned and moved swiftly through the wild growth. He had to almost jog to keep up. When they reached the temple she didn't look at him but he could see she had been crying. He spoke softly. "Come on, let's go to the reception."

She shook her head no. He wanted to take her in his arms but didn't. She bypassed the crowd and went to the car, head down and suddenly looking frail.

Kelley offered to drive her home but Aelan insisted on going back to his condo—*his condo*. She didn't say another word until they parked in the designated garage spot. Finally, she looked at him with puppy dog damp eyes. "Buy me a drink but don't even think about hitting on me. I'm in no condition to make sound judgments."

He started to argue but thought better and simply nodded. She led him through a series of hotel underground parking lots avoiding tourist-crowded streets and then took a side entrance to a dark hotel bar. It was filled with fake palms, paintings of tropical plants and a trio playing Hawaiian music. After just two days, he was already getting tired of steel guitars and ukuleles.

The dim lounge was crowded with large, overstuffed booths in wild floral patterns. Each booth was overhung with fake palm trees that provided privacy. It seemed a perfect place for an extra-marital affair, perhaps a holiday tryst. It was mid-morning but plenty of people were already drinking. She ordered something he had never heard of. He had a beer, a breakfast beer. No one spoke for a long, awkward time.

Finally, he couldn't stand it. "Evil spirits… really?"

Aelan chuckled quietly, still head down. "It's what she believed. I kept my promise."

"Tell me about your mother."

She exhaled and did not take another breath for a long time.

"She led a hard life before she met Patrick during the Vietnam War. He helped her get to the States but, as far as I can tell, there was never any romantic involvement. She would never tell me about my father. I have no idea who he was except that he was an American military man. Patrick told me only that he was basically a good man but had no self-control and asked me never to try to contact him. I honored his request but I never stopped wondering."

"But you were born here. What does your birth certificate say?"

"The original was lost and the duplicate I have says only 'father unknown.' My mother went by Gina but the certificate had her Asian name, horribly misspelled."

"So what did your mother do here?"

Aelan's face scrunched. "Oh hell, I've seen you naked, why should I keep secrets. I think she may have started out as a prostitute but later Patrick got her a job as a bartender in Pearl City. That's what I remember. She was very strict, tolerated no error, no bad behavior. She was always religious. We had a little Spirit House on our balcony to honor ancestors. She took her religion seriously."

"But you don't?"

She made an exaggerated shrug. "No, not really. I tried, but it seemed kind of—I don't know—weird. I guess I'd say I am one of the Nones."

"Nuns."

"You know, religious preference—none."

"What about Uncle Pat? Was he religious?"

Another shrug. "He was open-minded. He always lectured me on tolerance for people's beliefs. He was really a good guy." Her head fell again. After a time, she shook her hair and breathed deep. "Thank you for helping me. I think you might turn out to be a good guy, too."

He sipped and smiled. "Do you know anything about Pat's business dealings?"

Her tone was now matter-of-fact. "I know everything. I did his books."

"Do you know about the old stock certificates?"

She thought for a moment. "No, I guess maybe I don't know everything."

"No problem. Back to your mother, she was Thai?"

"Not really. She belonged to a very small group, a tribe really, who lived on the Thai/Lao border. They are a strange group with lots of odd customs. They wear hats that display their age and status in life. It's really bizarre, almost like military uniforms. One look at a GI and you see his whole story. His rank, his medals, his badges—they tell you everything he's done in his career. My mother taught me that. Her people are the same. Their hats tell their life story once you understand them. I know a little of the language but not enough to really have a serious chat. I've been there twice to see her people, once with her and once after her death."

"What did she die of?"

"Stroke—dropped dead in mid-stride. No one notified me. When she didn't come home that night, I went to the bar looking for her. The people there were distant, evasive. No one wanted to tell me. When I finally got it out of them, she was already processed at the morgue, already filed away like some old document. I called Patrick and he took care of everything. I felt as though my whole world had ended but Patrick took me under his wing. He told me I must honor her and become a success. God knows, I've tried."

Kelley reached out to place his hand on hers. She flinched away as though his touch burned.

Her voice cracked. "Now, Patrick has died and again, no one bothered to tell me. Why, I wonder, am I so trivial, that when the most important people in my life die, no one bothers...?"

With a quick, "I've got to go," she swept out of the room. He started to stand, to go after her, but hesitated and sat back. *Maybe another time.*

"Mister Price? This is Clayton Sheppard calling for..."

'Yes, yes, I know. What did you find out about the stock certificates?"

"Yeah well, that turns out to be more of a challenge than I anticipated. I found only two people on the island who do that kind of research on these old certificates and they don't come cheap. They're both working on it but have only validated two documents so far. Those two certificates have active CUSIP numbers so it was easy to calculate their current value including all splits and dividends over the last forty years. Between them, there's about $300,000 worth of paper. Many of the others, I'm afraid, are going to be worthless except as collectable wall decorations."

Kelley sat back and bit his smiling lip. "Another three hundred grand, that's great news."

"Well, possibly. Neither of the two certificates is in Patrick Tooney's name. One was issued to an Eli Lee and the other to Dewey Block. I don't know how, or if, we can establish your ownership. Do you know these men?"

Kelley wasn't smiling now. "I have heard the names but don't know them. I believe the Lee guy is in prison. The other man...I know nothing about."

"Well, okay Mister Price. I'll keep them working on these certificates and keep you advised. Anything else you need?"

"Yes, Clayton. Do you have any idea why two ICE agents visited me with a search warrant? They said Uncle Pat might be connected to human trafficking." There was a long silence. "Clayton, are you still there?"

The lawyer's voice changed completely. No longer light and chatty, he was all business. "What exactly did they say to you?"

Kelley repeated everything he remembered from the visit. Clayton listened with occasional questions. He was obviously taking notes. Finally done, Kelley asked, "What does it all mean?"

"Well, Mister Price, I never thought these allegations would go this far. They're absolutely false, but these Immigration and Customs Enforcement people are dangerous. They have powers far beyond normal law enforcement. They can seize property and imprison people for the most trivial suspicions. Let me see what I can find out. In the meantime, get rid of any files, cell phones or devices Mister Tooney may have left. There's no telling what these ICE creeps might infer from whatever they find."

He paused for a second. "Tell you what, bring them to my office. I can safeguard them under client privilege. That's shaky when the client is dead but it will work until a judge orders me to turn them over and, even then, I can argue that your inheritance makes you the client."

After another pause, Clayton added, "Do it today—right now if you can. These clowns scare the shit out of me. I helped Pat bring many deserving immigrants into the States. I know how capricious and irresponsible the INS and its demon child ICE can be. I'll be waiting here. Please, do this quickly."

Kelley hit 'end call' and sat back. *What exactly was going on here?* There was only one person...Aelan kept Uncle Pat's books. If anyone would know, she would. He had to find her number. He checked his recent calls. Her number was blocked.

Back at the computer, he began a slow search of files. Uncle Pat had said everything needed was there, but where? Endless spreadsheets and database files looked like gibberish to him. This was pointless. In desperation, he Googled Aelan Comer and was rewarded with a flashy website for the Pacific Voyager cruise line. Beside pictures of giant boats and Hula girls in grass skirts a sidebar listed key employees. He hit "A. Comer" and got a pop-up which included a 'contact me' button. That gave him an email and a phone number. He dialed.

A cheery recorded voice made a pitch. "A big Aloha to you and thanks for visiting Pacific Voyager, the premier cruise line for your ocean adventure. I can't come to the phone at the moment but if you leave a detailed message, I'll get right back to you. Thanks and have wonderful thoughts of palm trees and sandy beaches and far-away, exotic kingdoms just waiting for you…beep."

"Aelan, this is Kelley. I need to talk to you. It's about the ICE and Patrick. Please call quickly."

He hung up and began a search of the condo. It only made sense that Pat had other computers or a cellphone at least. He began with the desk. There were lots of file folders. All were neatly labeled and organized. Kelley stacked them on the floor, ready to move. There were supplies and a box of loose photographs. He'd look at them later. The box went on the pile. Once the desk was empty, he started to move on but hesitated.

Every junior detective knows about secret compartments. He pulled out the drawers, one at a time, and felt around behind them. He was about to put the top left drawer back when he noticed that the bottom was thicker than the others. After a lot of pressing and squeezing, he was able to tease out a false bottom panel. Underneath was a small leather ledger no larger than a man's hand. *Well, move over Sherlock Holmes.*

He thumbed through the book. Dates, names and amounts were neatly entered without explanation. Transactions of some sort were documented on a roughly two-week schedule. Numbers were paired with letters in some seemingly simple code but Kelley had no idea what they represented. He shoved the book in his pocket and continued to search.

In the closet, he found a semi-automatic pistol and shoulder holster under a sport coat. *Add that to the pile.* In the same coat there was a smart phone. The battery was dead. Behind the clothes, a wall safe was open and empty. Searching the clothes yielded twenty seven dollars and some loose change, an unpaid parking ticket and a hand-written note that read, "You were right, call me." There was no name or number. *One more thing for the pile.*

Kelley found several cloth grocery bags, the kind you bring to the store if you're trying to save the planet from plastic or paper, and loaded them with his stack. He lugged it all to the sports car and filled the passenger seat. Adding the computer made it difficult to reach the gear shift. But it was a short drive. He'd probably never get beyond third gear. He could manage.

Clayton was waiting, still looking ridiculous. He was the only man ever to wear a bow tie with a Hawaii shirt. He helped carry the files and computer upstairs and locked them in a storeroom. Finished, Clayton turned to Kelley. "Aelan just called me. They have subpoenaed her and alleged she is an illegal alien. These guys are going full bore. We have to be careful."

"Why are they doing this? What do they want? Surely Pat wasn't involved in anything illegal...was he?"

Clayton motioned for Kelley to sit. He paced and chose his words. "You uncle was a good friend to Aelan and even more to her mother Gina. Her family back in Thailand and Laos were members of a minority that have been severely persecuted over many, many years. Apparently, Mister Tooney felt he owed them some great debt. At first, he tried to bring them here to Hawaii legally as political refugees. That didn't work. He was a clever man and he found other methods. He found them jobs as farm workers and housekeepers. I helped him establish documentation. In confidentiality, I tell you that many of the source documents were forged... but very well forged, I must say."

He paused checking for reaction. Kelley offered none. "After the first generation, it became easier. With an established support network, we were able to create believable birth certificates and American lineages. Mister Tooney set up English language and culture classes. The people, Ankha they call themselves, were adaptable and generally very bright. They blended well in Hawaii. Today, hundreds of them, now with Polynesian names, are living successful lives, working, saving and building a future."

"But ICE is after them?"

Clayton made a painful expression. "Well sadly, not all the immigrants stayed on the straight and narrow. A very small minority may have become involved in criminal activity. I think that may be the reason ICE picked up their scent. Now, the bloodhounds may be out in force. I don't know. For now, just be careful what you say and do."

Kelley took it all in. *So Uncle Pat was a smuggler. Never would have expected it.* "What about Aelan? Is she involved?"

Clayton nodded slowly. "Up to her ears, but she's very careful. I don't know what they might have on her." He fiddled with his hands for a minute, looked pained and asked the question. "What do you know about the gold?"

"The gold?" Kelley sat back. "Uncle Pat had a message on his computer saying he had an enormous stash in Thailand and that he and two accomplices brought a large quantity here but it was somehow lost or stolen."

"Okay, so you know. The gold colors everything about this case. Many people have heard the rumors but no one except the original three know much more. Those men had a falling out back in 1972, just before Aelan was born. I have no reliable information about what happened to the gold but I do know that Eli Lee was charged with killing Dewey Block. Much later, Mister Tooney was wounded. Lee's in jail. Block is dead. Tooney spent four decades looking for the gold. Personally, I think it's like the Lost Dutchman's mine. It will never be found, if it ever existed at all."

JUNE 8, 1969

When the excitement of the tiger encounter passed, Patrick asked, "What happened with the NVA troops?"

The lieutenant chuckled. "I spied on them from atop the big pile of rocks. There were six. The sergeant in charge was one of those tough guy types who yelled constantly. I think one of the troops wanted to climb down the hill to see what was in the ruins but tough guy wasn't having any of it. He kept them on the road, or path or whatever. They never set foot in the jungle."

"Maybe he was afraid of snakes," offered Patrick.

Lieutenant Lee chuckled. "I'll bet the tiger would have made him shit his britches." Then both had a rare chance to laugh. Their adventure so far had been pretty serious.

By noon, they had all the large containers hidden in stone crypts. They siphoned gas from two trucks into the remaining gold-laden one. Then, they rammed the two soon-to-be orphan trucks as deep as they could into the jungle and left. The lieutenant drove the remaining overloaded gold truck and they began the stomach-tightening, smoking-brakes descent back to the main dirt road.

After an hour without seeing any soldiers, they crested one last row of hills. The wide Mekong River valley stretched out before them and their environment changed completely. Instead of largely uninhabited mountains, they entered an endless village of huts and buildings alongside rice paddies that clustered the river. Motor scooters putted and honked, crowds in straw cone hats jammed the road. The air was full of strange shouts and calls. All along the road, villagers stopped to gawk at the Americans, finally crowding so close the truck was overwhelmed and had to stop.

Children piled on the fenders and hood, laughing and pointing. The lieutenant got out, held up his hands and tried to be the spokesman. "English, anyone speak English?"

The chatter continued. People crowded closer, touching his flight suit, fingering his patches and even rubbing his skin. They were pressing closer, getting more aggressive, pushing the lieutenant back against the truck in their curiosity.

"English," he shouted. "Who speaks English?"

They ignored his words, pressing, pushing and laughing. Patrick felt panic. Things were quickly getting out of control. Without really thinking, he stepped out onto the running board, cleared his throat and yelled. "*Parlez vous Francais?*" The commotion calmed and faces turned toward him. A shy boy, probably a teenager, stepped up and replied, "*Un peu*"

Patrick fought to remember his French. "*Pouvez-vous nous aider a?*" The lieutenant's mouth fell open.

The shy boy clutched his arms and rocked. He said nothing and looked away.

Patrick tried again, slowly pronouncing each word. "*Nous devons traverser la riviere.*" He whispered to the lieutenant. "I told him we need to cross the river."

The boy shook his head. "*C'est impossible.*"

Patrick gained confidence. "*Nous devons. Nous avon l'argent.*

He spoke quietly out of the side of his mouth. "I told him we must get to Thailand and that we have money."

Dewey was now standing beside them. He whispered, "So where did you learn that French shit and how come these gooks speak frog?"

Patrick looked at the fat man with disgust. "I had to take a language in high school. And this place used to be called French Indochina. It seemed worth a try."

The boy disappeared into the crowd and returned leading a stooped, elderly man with a wispy white beard. They spoke and the old man approached to hold out a bony hand in silent demand. His eyes were clear and steady and patient.

The lieutenant went back into the truck and pulled his big knife. He returned with a slice of gold the size of a chewing gum pack. He placed the gold into the old gentleman's hand and stepped back to bow deeply with his hands together in front of his face as though praying. The old man fingered the gold and then duplicated Lieutenant Lee's bow.

The old man shook his finger and spoke in a gravelly voice. "*Vous devez rendre a Monsieur Chang.*" Patrick whispered. "He says we must go to see Mister Chang."

The shy boy faced the old man and bowed. He turned to the lieutenant and bowed. Then he jumped on the truck's running board and beckoned with a cupped hand. He would be the guide.

The crowd parted and they drove where the boy pointed. The truck cab was tight with four people. The boy seemed excited, waving and laughing at people through the window. He jabbered and Patrick struggled to understand.

"He has never been inside a truck before. He thinks it's fun being up so high and moving so fast. He says we honored his grandfather and he thanks us. He will take us to a town called Khon or Quan or something. There is a woman there who speaks English. She will take us to Chang."

The boy giggled and squirmed as they hit a pothole and bounced high. Patrick continued. "He says Chang is a very bad man. I don't really understand what he is telling me. Maybe Chang is a gangster or something. Anyway, he says to be careful."

The boy began to rock and sing, almost forgetting to signal a turn. Finally, he became more excited, pointing enthusiastically to a very large bungalow with a thatched roof and wraparound porch. The boy held up hands to signal them to stop. Then he jumped down from the truck and ran off yelling.

"Now what?" the lieutenant asked Patrick.

"Not sure. Maybe he's going to get our English translator."

Another curious crowd began to gather. No one said it but the three Americans all had the same thought. If this kid skipped out, they were screwed, big time.

"Patrick," the lieutenant said. "Without making it obvious, I want you to take one of the bars we kept on us for emergencies and start slicing it into strips."

Patrick nodded while keeping his eyes on the crowd outside. "How big do you want the strips?"

"About a quarter of an inch thick—I think that's about the same weight as a fifty dollar gold piece. Cut up a whole bar. We might need to do a lot of bargaining. Use your knife and be careful to keep them an even size. The gold is harder than cheese but softer than wood. Make smooth slices and don't cut off a finger." Patrick set to work.

The crowd was growing bold but then there was a commotion. A woman in a wraparound skirt and odd square cap embroidered with colorful stitching, gold coins and small chains pushed her way through, shoving and shouting. She confronted the Americans defiantly, hands on hips. Her voice was loud and biting.

"What you doing here GI? You're a long way from home and you got a Vietnam truck. You steal it?"

Lieutenant Lee opened the door and stepped down. She laughed and stepped back, looking him up and down. "You're a flyboy. What happened Sky Pilot, get your ass shot down?"

"Actually, yes. Now we need help. I can pay you. We need to get over to Thailand and the boy here says a Mister Chang can get us across the river but we need a translator."

"Translator?" She threw her head back and laughed. "You go to Chang, you need coffin, maybe wind up in river. How much money you got flyboy?"

"How much do I need?"

She put on a mock sneer. "For me," she considered, "a hundred dollars U.S." She looked a little more serious. "For Chang, who know?"

"I will pay in gold," the lieutenant sounded casual.

The woman scowled and folded her arms. "Show me."

Patrick reached an arm out the truck window and displayed a slice from the gold bar. She jerked it from his fingers, turned it, touched it to her tongue and then bit lightly. Satisfied, she stared at the lieutenant. "My price, three like this."

He didn't hesitate for a second. "Two."

"Three piece. No bullshit, Flyboy."

Lieutenant Lee thought it over. "Two now, one more after we see Chang."

She nodded with certainty. "Okay, deal. Come now. My mother make you food before trip."

"Thank you, but we must stay with the truck."

She shook her head. "Don't be asshole. Nobody steal your stupid truck. These are good people. Besides, you can see truck from window." She extended an arm. "Come on. It is insult to my mother if you don't come. *Bai Lao*, Let's go, GI."

They laced up the truck's canvas cover and went inside, but with long looks back at their gold-filled truck. In the large house, Patrick was surprised that they were treated as honored guests. A man in a Nehru jacket showed them to an enclosed atrium where two four-foot-high clay water pots were surrounded by wooden benches and towel racks.

Patrick stripped down, cupped water in his hands and drenched his face. It was cool, relaxing. They all disrobed and washed, dancing around, splashing each other and laughing like kids. He was just grateful to be clean after days of sweat and dirt. For a moment, the truck was all but forgotten. *Maybe things would work out.*

After they toweled off, a small man in a white coat bowed and presented them with robes and sandals, both a couple of sizes too small for everyone but Patrick. Then, white coat whipped a mug of shaving cream and, one-by-one, expertly shaved off grizzled beards. Patrick had never had a steaming towel put over his face. He felt like a big shot. The barber, or whatever he was, took away the towel and splashed scented water on Patrick's cheeks.

Clean and refreshed, it was like being reborn. The barber ushered them into a large, open room where a banquet was being set up. Another crisp man in a white jacket and slicked back hair offered cigarettes or a clay pipe from an ornate box. Patrick declined. They sat, awkwardly cross-legged, on bamboo mats. It was difficult to position their robes for modesty. The meal was sumptuous, spicy and strange. Patrick grinned. *We're a really long way from Sunrise City, Iowa.*

The translator woman wore an embroidered silk jacket and sarong. Her tone was very different than at their first meeting.

Now she was gracious, bowing and making introductions in English and whatever language she spoke. Patrick asked her, "Please, what is your name?"

She smiled. "You can't say my name. GIs call me Gina. They make many jokes."

"You work with GIs?"

"I am bar girl at the American Air Base in Udorn, Thailand. I make enough money there to take care of my family here. It is honorable profession. You Americans treat me like whore but here, I am honored as good daughter." Her smile was almost sweet.

Patrick pressed. "Why were you so rude at the truck?"

"You're American GIs. Got to talk tough to GI flyboys. Take no bullshit. Got to be tough or get hurt from drunks." She smiled again. "Please, I wish you meet my mother. This is her house."

They ate and drank some alcoholic concoction and laughed with people they couldn't understand. Gina and her mother smoked small pipes. The smoke of these pipes was sweet, definitely not tobacco. Later, Patrick collapsed onto a reed mat and slept as though in a coma.

JUNE 9, 1969

In the morning, freshly washed flight suits, socks and underwear appeared beside polished boots. Patrick and the others dressed, checked the truck and ate watery rice with hot tea. The three men bowed and thanked the mother, their hostess.

Gina announced, "We leave in one hour. I sent word we are coming. It is good to leave mother's people a tip. One U.S. dollar for three people is good, okay?"

Clean, rested and ready to take on the world, they marched back to the truck only to notice the Vietnamese writing had been painted over and a large white star was emblazoned on each door. Gina made an offhand comment. "Vietnam truck get you killed. This is Royal Lao country. White star is for U.S. Everybody in Royal territory like U.S., at least U.S. money."

A quick check to make sure the gold was still there and they were off to see Mister Chang.

Thunder rumbled and a drenching rain began. Their big truck bounced along a road of slimy mud and deep holes. Gina pointed directions but seemed tentative. "This way—I only go here one time. It is bad place with bad people but this is the way." She hesitated. "I'm pretty sure."

The windshield wipers slung water but sheets of monsoon rain came faster than could be swept away. Patrick, at the wheel, could barely see. Gina looked intent as she pressed her face close to the windshield. Then she exploded in relief.

"Here. Here. Turn here. Only a little way to go." She turned to the lieutenant and sounded businesslike. "Okay now, when we get there, you talk only to me. I talk to bad guys. You keep gun close. If they want hurt me, you kill 'em, okay?" Her voice was louder than needed, even over the hammering rain.

They entered a village of tin and thatched-roof houses and stopped in front of the only cement building in town. A blinking neon sign flashed squiggly Asian characters through a curtain of rain. Patrick watched Gina rub her hands on her face, straighten her back and then crawl over the men's knees to jump down from the truck into the deluge.

Two bulldogs of men in short sleeved shirts stood under the awning. It was hard to see clearly through the downpour but it looked as though the men were shouting at her. She shouted back at them. One grabbed her arm and yanked her toward him.

"Okay, everybody out, guns drawn," the lieutenant commanded. Patrick dismounted the truck into a lashing rain and tried to follow Lieutenant Lee. It was hard to see, even harder to hear. He couldn't be sure who was who until he was under the awning and able to shake water off his face.

The lieutenant stood there, gun cocked and leveled at the face of the man holding Gina. Patrick extended both hands to steady his gun and walked up to the second thug. Dewey emerged and added his gun to the standoff. The two thugs glanced back and forth. Gina spewed high-pitched invective and shook her fist in her assailant's face.

After seriously considering the situation, the first thug let her go and raised his hands in a conciliatory gesture. Gina pounded his chest with both fists still screaming in her strange language.

The thug backed up. Unfazed by Gina's assault, he kept his stone face. Then both guards turned and went inside.

Lieutenant Lee was breathing hard. Rain water ran down his face and off his nose. Ringlets of hair stuck to his forehead. Gina paced, arms folded tight. In less than a minute, thug number one reappeared, held the door open and motioned to enter. The lieutenant led the way but paused. "Dewey, stay with the truck. Kill anyone who tries to climb in. If we hear shooting, we'll fight our way out. Got it?"

Patrick squinted as they entered a dimly lit bar room of bamboo furniture and small Formica tables. Girls with dark, round faces wore imitation Playboy Bunny outfits and stood around smoking on a listless, rainy morning. It could have easily been midnight. This was obviously a twenty-four hour operation. Smoke hung in the air, a mix of tobacco, incense and marijuana. American rock and roll wailed somewhere in the background.

Thug one led them behind a curtain, through a damp storeroom and into a dungeon of an office. It reeked of mold and bleach. Rain hammered on the metal roof. A single overhead light cast a cone of light onto a table stacked with paper. Behind that table sat Mister Chang.

They needed no introduction to this man in a black silk tunic. Thug bowed and backed away. Chang did not acknowledge. No question, this was the man in charge. Taller than most Laotians and paler than any they had yet seen, he looked as though sunlight had never touched his face. His unblinking eyes were black marbles. His white beard was wispy and his hands almost feminine with unnaturally long fingernails. A perfectly straight pillar of smoke rose from a cigarette in his right hand. Otherwise, the man was motionless.

Gina whispered. "I make introduction." She bowed and began a quiet speech while keeping her eyes downcast. She looked up. No reaction. Chang was absolutely still. She tried again. Nothing. Now, Gina became animated, gesturing toward the Americans and back to Chang.

Finally he drew on his cigarette and exhaled a stream of smoke. When he spoke, his voice was different than the others. His was distinct, precise. Even though Patrick had no idea what the language might be, he thought this man was educated, cultured.

Gina listened closely, nodding and bowing. She turned to the lieutenant. "He say he can get you across the river but not the truck. I told him truck must go. He say he wants only American dollars. I tell him you have gold. He say to show him."

Patrick fished in his survival vest pocket and produced a slice of the gold bar. He started to hand it to Lieutenant Lee but Lee nodded toward Chang. Patrick felt awkward as he walked up, did a clumsy little bow and laid the gold on the table.

Chang shouted a single syllable and a man appeared out of the room's dark recess. He had a balance scale like the one Lady Liberty statues in front of courthouses always hold. The measure man fingered the gold, bit it and rubbed it. Then he put it in one hanging pan and began trying small weights on the other pan. Satisfied with the weight's balance, he made a pronouncement and handed the gold to Chang.

There was another long silence before Chang made a speech. He spoke into the air with no eye contact. Gina leaned close to Eli Lee and Patrick. "He will get you a boat for truck but he wants one thousand taels of gold."

"How much is that?" Lee asked.

Gina nodded to the table. "What you give him is, maybe, one hundred tael."

"Tell him I will give him even more than a thousand."

Gina shook her head. "Oh no, you must not. That would be insult. That make him seem poor and you rich. You must offer less. Make him be generous, not you. It is for honor, understand?"

"Okay, offer five hundred...whatevers."

Gina flicked a momentary smile at the lieutenant and then turned back to Chang. They argued for ten minutes before settling on eight hundred. Patrick handed the measure-man pieces of gold and he weighed them until he was satisfied. A nod and it was done. Lieutenant Lee reached out to shake Chang's hand but the deal maker ignored him, staring into space.

Gina spoke to measure-man and got directions. As they walked back through the bar, Patrick asked Gina, "Why are these girls here so early? No one goes to a dive like this for breakfast."

She made an off handed shrug. "Girls live here. They have little rooms behind bar, where they take men. They never go outside. Mister Chang own them. He buy them very young."

Patrick considered that. "So they're slaves. What happens when they get older and men don't want to pay them anymore?" Gina just shrugged.

It took only five or six minutes driving to reach the ferry, a good-sized flatboat with two pontoons and several logs lashed underneath. Large wooden ramps on the front and rear allowed drive-on loading. A small control station was offset near the front so it did not block the ramps.

The storm had lessened but rain still came steady. A barefoot man stood waiting in ankle-deep mud. He was brown and wrinkled as a date fruit and naked except for a black turban and matching black cloth wrapped around him like a diaper.

The black turban man began shouting even before they pulled to a stop. He walked along the truck, bent to see underneath and shook his head. He pushed down on the fender and watched it recover. He reached underneath and felt the springs. Then he shouted again.

Gina followed him. She called to the Americans. "He say it is too heavy. It will sink. He wants more money."

Patrick spoke to the lieutenant. "That makes no sense. How will more money keep it from sinking?"

Gina called again. "He say men go in other boat. Truck go on ferry. Boat will cost you more."

Patrick looked worried. "Boss, if we get us separated from the truck, they could steal it."

The lieutenant got down from the truck and confronted Ferry man. "Tell him we'll go in the boat, but the boat must be tied to the ferry, understand?" There was an argument but finally an agreement that required one more gold slice.

Loading the truck was an adventure. The front wheels went on easily but the rears spun on the muddy river bank. The lieutenant and Patrick tried shoving wood under the wheels. When Dewey applied power, the truck wheels just spit out the wood. Ferry man yelled, pulled out a thick rope and fastened it to the truck frame. Then all four men groaned at a manual winch. It didn't budge. After three attempts, they fell back breathing like sprinters.

Between breaths, Patrick asked, "Dewey, when you left the truck, did you set the parking brake?"

Dewey thought, then suddenly seemed to find something in the river water fascinating. He stared down into the muddy, storm-driven torrent without answering. Patrick waded back to the cab, released the parking brake and took the transmission out of gear. He sloshed back and motioned to try again.

This time, the truck did come aboard, inching its way up the ramp. As it did, the ferry boat sank deeper and deeper until water actually washed over the ramp. Lee was still huffing from exertion. "I guess he wasn't kidding about it being too heavy."

Ferry man started his boat's diesel engine. It rattled and belched evil black smoke. He motioned for the Americans to wade back to shore as though he was concerned about something. When they were clear, he nodded approvingly, quickly cast off mooring ropes, and ran back to the controls to gun the engine.

"Hey, the bastard's leaving. Where's the boat for us?" the lieutenant bellowed and shook his fist.

Gina was yelling. Dewey was yelling. They were all yelling. Ferry man ignored them as the partially submerged ferry labored to pull away from the muddy shore.

Ferry man had not raised the loading ramp. Gina was closest. She splashed her way to belly flop onto that ramp. Patrick and the other men followed. Ferry man abandoned the controls and ran screaming back toward Gina. He raised a machete but lost his balance as the pilotless boat wallowed. The American men just made it to the ramp. They were hanging on for dear life unable to save her.

Patrick had grabbed a loose rope and held on tight as the overweight boat plowed deep. A huge rooster tail of muddy water blasted him directly in the face. He pulled hard on the rope but the torrent was unrelenting. With one hand on his pistol and the other clamped onto the rope, he thrashed back and forth in the violent wake. The ferry was picking up speed and the gush of water was like a fire hose in his face threatening to drown him. He strained, strained with all his might, but couldn't pull himself up. The blast of water was just too strong.

He was still flopping and flailing when the ferry picked up enough speed to rise up out of the water. The awkward boat was now skimming the surface. Patrick held the rope like a water skier's tow rope, gasped for air and pulled himself to his feet. He had a clear shot. Ferry man had recovered his footing and now stood over Gina, blade raised.

One second to aim and shoot, Patrick didn't hesitate. Two quick pops and Ferry man jumped, looked down at his bloody chest and tumbled backwards overboard. Gina still cowered with arms curled over her head. She seemed unharmed but shaking as she peeked and then unfolded. Patrick fell back on the ramp, exhausted.

He saw the lieutenant and Dewey still clawing their way up the ramp. They were safe. They were all safe. *But who was driving the boat?* Still weak from exertion, Patrick gathered himself and worked his way alongside the truck and took the ferry boat's controls. He steadied the craft against the current and breathed easier, but where was he going? He had no idea.

He called back to the others, "I don't know how to drive this thing. Somebody help me."

Dewey waddled up. "Get out of the way. I've had boats since I was a kid. Hey Lieutenant, where're we headed?"

There was silence. Lieutenant Lee unfolded his plastic map and spread it on the wet deck. Gina stood over his shoulder. She was still shaking as she pointed. "You here… I think."

He looked up to scan the shore. Then he sprang to his feet and pointed behind them. "There's a boat chasing us." The lieutenant stood like Washington crossing the Delaware. "It's a long-tail motorboat. They're fast. They usually have car engines and with long drive shafts to the prop, very maneuverable."

Patrick was more and more impressed with this man so many people dismissed as a drunk. "Sir, how do you know so much about these boats?"

He continued to focus on the boat behind them but Lieutenant Lee's voice was calm and controlled. "Boats like that carry North Vietnamese troops and cargo on the Mekong and other rivers. We hunt and kill them in our gunships. You're new to the business but that's our job, killing enemy trucks, boats and troops traveling the Ho Chi Minh Trail. You have to know your enemy to kill him."

The long-tail boat was closing. Lee kept his focus but asked Patrick a matter-of-fact question as though nothing special was going on. "Do you know what brand of truck this is? No? It's a Ford. American companies sell trucks to Yugoslavia who, in turn, sell them to Russia. The Russians supply these trucks to the North Vietnamese. When the Defense Department complained, the U.S. car companies made a concession. They put something in the ignition systems to generate electrical noise. Then they sold us a detector that lets us see where every American-made vehicle within ten miles is operating. They build the trucks and sell them. We shoot and burn them. Win-win, except of course, for the fourteen guys who died on our airplane three days ago."

The lieutenant squinted hard. "The men in that boat have guns." He turned and shouted, "Dewey turn into the current. Go directly upstream, full speed. Got it?" The ferry turned slightly and the engine accelerated.

Staring back again, the lieutenant spoke to Patrick. "That long-tail boat sits one man behind the next. If they are following us directly, they'll have to shoot over each other. Patrick, go get one of the rifles out of the truck. We're going to have us a turkey shoot."

Lieutenant Lee took the long gun, worked the bolt action to be sure it was loaded and knelt on the rear ramp. He aimed but the ferry boat was bouncing and the rifle barrel seemed to wave up and down. The lieutenant was patient, accepting the rhythm of the waves and waiting for a null spot where all motion was momentarily still. He fired. Patrick looked back at the speed boat as though his eyes could follow the bullet.

He was still staring at the long-tail boat when the lieutenant fired again. This time it was a hit. The chasing boat careened, digging a deep swath in the water as it spun and overturned. Patrick felt the lieutenant's hand on his shoulder. They were both transfixed on the overturned boat as its former occupants bobbed and splashed around.

"I had to hit the helmsman sitting in the rear. The others were just shooters. He controlled the boat. When he went down, he let go of that long drive shaft tiller and the boat went wild." With a deep breath, it was back to work. "Now, let's figure out where to land in Thailand. Our adventure is a long way from over."

The day turned bright after storm clouds drifted into the nearby mountains. Blue sky looked down on the wide, muddy waters of the Mekong River and the ferry boat as it clipped along. Little villages passed on the shore where fishermen hung nets and playful children scurried along flimsy bamboo docks. Patrick smelled the scents of river bank vegetation, cooking fires and even the dank Mekong water.

He felt alive, delighted to be alive. The threat of ferry boat captain turned assassin, long-tail pirates, North Vietnamese troops and Chang's thugs seemed far behind them. Ahead lay Thailand, which he had been told, meant "Land of the Free." Dewey played ship's captain at the wheel while Gina and Lieutenant Lee stood up front enjoying cool spray in their faces. Despite the sauna-like heat, everyone seemed refreshed. Patrick joined them just as Gina spoke.

"Okay, here's the deal. I been thinking about you and your truck. Why so important to take truck over river? You could get three guys over easy. Truck cost you much gold. And why you have gold, Lao gold? Why truck so heavy?" She looked the lieutenant square in the face. "Gina think you steal Viet Nam truck full of gold. So, here's question. What you do with gold in Thailand? Just go to bank and say, 'Here is truck full of gold.' I don't think so."

The lieutenant scowled. "You trying to shake me down?"

She shrugged. "I don't know what means shake down, but listen, please. Gina can help you. I know people in Udon. I can hide gold or sell. If you try to do that, you go to jail."

"How much do you want for your help?"

"Fair share. I think you are man with honor. You treat me fair. I treat you fair. What you think, Eli Lee? We all get rich."

"How did you know my name was Eli? Oh, never mind." Lieutenant Lee laughed and started to hold out a handshake. "Okay deal, Dragon Lady. We all get rich." Gina ignored his offered hand and bowed with praying hands directly in front of her face. Patrick had been told in his "Welcome to Thailand" briefing that where someone holds his hands when greeting shows relative status. Gina was bowing to the lieutenant as an equal. *Interesting.*

Dewey broke their moment with a shout. "I see a landing. It looks like a road leads right down to the water. Do you want me to dock there?" Sure enough, tire tracks led down a muddy slope right into the water. Other boats had beached there.

The lieutenant answered with an enthusiastic, "Go for it." Then he turned to Gina and grinned, "Sound okay to you, partner?" She nodded with a slight smile.

Patrick was concerned. "We're going too fast."

The lieutenant looked back at the approaching riverbank. "Jesus Dewey, slow down."

Patrick turned to see an anguished look on Dewey's face. The fat man's voice was strained. "I...can't. The throttle cable must have broken." Dewey desperately slapped the throttle lever back and forth without effect.

"Shut off the engine," Patrick screamed. The land was close and getting closer by the second. "Shut it off." Patrick felt helpless.

The lieutenant yelled, "Jump, everybody jump." He grabbed Gina's hand and dove off the side, pulling her along. Patrick hesitated just for a second to look for Dewey but he was already gone. That second delay was disastrous. When he finally started to jump, the boat bucked and Patrick slipped. He hit something hard just as the ferry boat slammed into the shore at full speed and splintered as though it had exploded.

Stunned and helpless, he felt himself go airborne, cartwheeling in slow motion. For a long moment, blinding sun, dark water and deep green foliage flashed as he tumbled. Then, a hammering impact knocked the wind from Patrick's lungs and jangled his brain. He felt the cool water on his face. Limp arms and legs floated and all was quiet. His mind was still, peaceful, shutting down. It seemed to be getting darker and darker, and he didn't really care. He didn't care. Everything faded, sounds, sights, sensations...and he just didn't care.

MONDAY

"All rise. The regular Calendar Session of the Immigration Court of Honolulu, Hawaii is now in session, the Honorable Bernard Phillips presiding."

The judge gathered his robe and sat. "Call the first case."

The Clerk of the Court announced, "Yes, Your Honor, first docket item- the Office of Chief Counsel versus Alien Comer."

The judge motioned with an impatient wave.

The prosecutor, Michael Ellis, stood. "Your Honor, Ms. Alien Comer was properly served but has failed to appear."

"If it please the court, I am Clayton Sheppard, her attorney. Please note that her name is pronounced 'A'-'lin' not 'alien.' Urgent business prevents Ms. Comer from being present but I believe the USCIS charges will be easily shown to be without merit and filed in error and should be dismissed immediately without requiring her testimony." There was a moment of silence in the court.

The room was paneled in exotic wood with marble and brass statues built into alcoves. High ceilings housed slow-turning fans with wide palm-like blades. The judge sat behind a towering bench backed by a larger-than-life painting of King Kamehmeha. He leaned forward and looked at the Immigration Control Enforcement/Homeland Security Investigations prosecuting attorney who immediately jumped to his feet.

"Your Honor, a legitimate NTA, Notice-To-Appear, was issued allowing plenty of time. The individual claiming to be Aelan Comer is an illegal alien. In light of Ms. Comer's failure to appear, I request that you order her immediate arrest and initiate ERO, Enforcement Removal Operations."

The judge forced a thin smile. "That's what you want, Mister Ellis? Well, let's just hear the evidence shall we?"

The ICE/HSI attorney, in a white short-sleeved shirt and tie, started to sit. "I meant now, Mister Ellis." The two men didn't appear to have a close relationship. Clayton Sheppard suspected that would work to his advantage.

Ellis half stood. "Your Honor, our proof will show that the lady in question used a forged birth certificate to obtain a U.S. passport. She is not a United States Citizen and should be immediately detained to face removal proceedings. This court has the authority to issue a deportation order in absentia."

"Thank you, Mister Ellis, for reminding me of my authority." The judge turned and raised his eyebrows at Clayton who rose with a confident smile.

"Your Honor, the only true thing my colleague has spoken was that Ms. Comer's birth certificate is improper. Given the fact that it was officially filed only a month after her birth, I don't think she can be held responsible for that error. In fact, ICE obtained that birth certificate through an illegal, warrantless search. I believe it should be suppressed as inadmissible. Further, the ICE investigative unit has no evidence whatever that Ms. Comer was born anywhere other than the United States."

Ellis, the ICE attorney raised a hand. "Your Honor, despite any impropriety in obtaining the document, it is clearly a counterfeit, and we request strongly that Ms. Comer be taken into custody while the investigation continues."

The judge did not look up. "It sounds to me as though we're getting a little ahead of ourselves, Mister Ellis. Before we begin to deal with the status of this Ms. Comer, we need to find out about this birth certificate. Was it obtained legally? Is it a forgery? If so, what is the nationality of the lady in question and how did she come to be here with a U.S. Passport. Can you answer those questions, Mr. Ellis?"

"We're investigating all those issues of course, Sir."

The judge scowled. "Investigating, you're just investigating now... *after* you've brought charges?"

Clayton Sheppard was quick. "Your Honor, I believe we can clear this misunderstanding quickly if you will allow me to call one witness. He is on the prosecution's list and he is present in the courtroom."

"I object, your honor. I should be able to call my own witness in his turn." Ellis sounded rattled. The ICE attorney looked uncomfortably at Special Agent Diggins sitting in the first row of spectator seats. "I'd like to discuss this first..."

Now the judge was impatient. "A minute ago you were asking for detention and possible removal through deportation. Now you want to huddle and plan your next play? I'm inclined to dismiss your motion completely since you seem unprepared to move forward. Now are you going to present your witness or shall I do it as an adverse witness?"

Ellis tucked his tail. "We have no objection to Agent Diggins being called. I assume he is the witness Mister Sheppard wants to question." Clayton nodded and the judge called Agent Diggins to the stand. After the oath, the man sat back in the witness chair, surly and defiant.

"Agent, how did you obtain this birth certificate?" Clayton was confident, on his game.

"It was given to us by an anonymous third party."

Clayton walked to his table, picked up a document, flipped a page and read aloud. "The passport and birth certificate were found during a search of the suspect's home." He smiled. "So, what was it, a search or a third party thief?"

Diggins glared. "I wouldn't call him a thief. He is a confidential informant whose identity must be protected."

"So, when this man, your CI, broke in to Ms. Comer's residence and stole these documents, he was operating under your direction?"

"Objection, Your Honor," Ellis bolted from his chair. "He is leading the witness and assumes facts not in evidence."

The judge leaned forward. "Mister Ellis, I am familiar with the rules of evidence. I remind you that, as an adverse witness, the defense is allowed to ask leading questions. And…I want to hear the answer. Do you have a problem with that?"

Ellis clenched his teeth and nodded consent.

Diggins fairly hissed. "As I said, he was assisting us in a case but acting on his own initiative."

Clayton Sheppard came back confident and at ease. "Wow, initiative, not the word I expected. Are you aware that his illegal search was recorded on a home surveillance system? You might want to keep your CI anonymous but my client does not share your desire, and the pictures are clear." Clayton spoke loudly to the whole room. "His name is Tongay Apu, a gangster the Honolulu Police have had under scrutiny for years. Never expected him to be working for ICE."

Ellis bolted. "Objection, Your Honor. This is intolerable. The defense lawyer has just revealed the identity of a confidential informant. He must be censured."

The judge was unemotional. "On what grounds, Mister Ellis? If the thief was caught on the woman's security camera he has no reasonable expectation of anonymity. Now, what he was doing there? That is another question and one that is drawing my interest. Please explain."

Diggins growled from the witness chair. "I can explain, Your Honor. We work with this man on human trafficking cases. He's slime but he is effective. He has contacts. I told him we were interested in Ms. Comer and asked him to check her out. He brought us the passport and birth certificate and I paid him. I should have asked more questions."

The judge steepled his fingers, waiting.

Clayton Sheppard saw an opportunity, "Sir, I think it might be of value to ask why ICE is interested in Ms. Comer and how much they investigated her *before* leaping to prosecution."

The judge just stared. Diggins squirmed. "All right. All right. We had an informant we trusted. We should have been more careful. No real harm done."

Clayton approached the witness stand. "No real harm done? An illegal search, a preposterous charge, a clear violation of the law, and you say, no real harm done? All right Agent Diggins, answer me this. Why are you so anxious to get Ms. Comer into your hands? What about her interests you? Not ICE, what interests you personally?"

Lawyer Ellis took a breath and plunged back in. "Your Honor, I didn't know all the background in this case. At this time, I'd like to withdraw all charges. We'll apologize to Ms. Comer."

The judge began sifting through papers. "You'll do more than that, Mister Ellis. You'll turn over all your files to the Honolulu Police Department and take your lumps for possibly condoning an illegal break-in and theft. This hearing is adjourned and all charges against the defendant are hereby dismissed."

Clayton turned away from the seething Agent Diggins and began to whistle a cheerful little tune.

JUNE 13, 1969

Patrick Tooney woke terrified and gasping for air. He felt a tube down his throat. *Where was he? What was going on?* He coughed and the exertion brought jolts of pain to his chest and leg. Every movement hurt. He lay back in his bed. *He was in a bed.* Slowly, he focused. The bed was in a bare, unadorned room. It was beige or maybe tan. Whatever the color, everything was painted the same. Ceiling, walls, floor- even the metal bed under him- everything was the same dull color. At least his sheets were white.

His chest was wrapped in cloth bandages and just touching them made him groan. He was hurt, and pretty bad he thought. *And that damned tube in his throat…What happened?* He couldn't remember. *Where was he?* He looked around but there were few clues. His back stuck to the damp sheet. It was suffocating, hot and humid. *He was probably still in Southeast Asia but where? And how did he get there?*

A nurse passing by the door stopped as he moaned. She was a corn-fed Midwestern lady with a grandmother-warm smile. She touched his arm with a light, comforting hand.

"Airman Tooney, can you hear me?"

Patrick stirred and tried to answer but coughed up phlegm and began gasping into his breathing tube.

"You just lay there and relax. I'll get you a doctor. I'm so happy you're awake. I was worried about you." She sounded sincere and her voice was comforting. After she left, he worked at slowing his breathing to minimize the pain.

A team of white coat doctors and technicians in green scrubs rolled in and set to work removing machines and the tubes in his nose and arm and even one in his penis. *That was no fun.* No one really spoke to him. It was as though he was just some piece of meat they were working on. Finally, the activity subsided. The doctors scribbled on his chart and left. The corpsmen dwindled until he was, again, alone with the nurse. She listened to his chest and then flipped her stethoscope over her neck and looked around as though checking for doctors. Seeing none, she whispered.

"I think your lungs are clear enough to remove the last tube. This will be a little uncomfortable." She was gentle but it still rasped. Once it was clear he sucked in air like a drowning man.

"Where am I?" His voice was hoarse.

She patted his arm. *She had to be somebody's grandmother.* "You're in the hospital at Udorn Royal Thai Air Base. You've been here for three days. It was the strangest thing. You arrived in a taxi with a Thai lady who didn't seem to speak English. She dropped you off at the main gate and the guard called an ambulance. Do you know what happened to you?"

Patrick thought for a long while. He remembered everything up to the ferry boat crash but nothing after. What he didn't know, and needed to, was what story the lieutenant had concocted to explain their actions after the crash. *He had better play it very carefully.*

"I remember my airplane being shot down. There was a fierce fire and I bailed out. After that…it's pretty much blank. I have no idea how I got here."

She did her Grandma smile. It really did make him feel better. "Oh, don't worry. Your memory will come back in time. Amnesia after trauma is quite common but it's almost always short term. Physically, you're doing quite well. The doctor will give you a complete run down but I can tell you that you have several broken ribs, a puncture wound in your left leg, torn ligaments as well as a concussion."

She hesitated. "And there is damage to your…scrotum." She had trouble saying the word "scrotum." Patrick didn't need anyone to tell him his balls had been smashed. Every step he took, every bounce of the truck had reminded him constantly. The nurse forced a smile and continued. "These things are all treatable but I'm afraid your flying days are over. No one can be on flight status after a concussion."

Patrick forced a weak smile and drifted off to sleep.

Sometime later—he didn't know how long—he was awakened by a sweaty man in a tan uniform that perfectly matched the room's paint scheme. "Your dog tags say Airman Patrick Tooney, is that correct?"

Patrick cleared his throat. It was much easier to speak now. "Yes, I'm Patrick Tooney."

"I am Major Driscoll, 555th Tactical Fighter Wing Intelligence. Can you describe the events that led to your injuries and your arrival here at Udorn?" The major sat and positioned a yellow legal pad on his lap.

Sure hope he buys this, "Well, not completely. I was training as an AC-130 gunner. It was only my second mission but I was getting the hang of it. The hardest thing was working in the dark by just faint red light. It was exciting and dangerous working around all that machinery, guns spinning at 6000 rounds-a-minute, spent shells flying, deafening noise and all of it in a big airplane that's maneuvering violently."

The major scowled. "Yes, yes, but what about your injuries? What happened?"

"Well, what I remember very clearly is the explosion. It was in the rear of the plane, probably the flare launcher. I don't know what caused it but, in just an instant, the whole rear end of the plane lit up like a giant sparkler. We were trained to bail out from the ramp at the back of the plane but that was impossible. I heard a lot of shouting and then a continuous bell. People were yelling 'Bailout, bailout, bailout.' I didn't react. I guess it just seemed too unreal. Master Sergeant Block grabbed me and pushed me out one of the side exits right behind the props."

Patrick took a breath remembering the terror of that night. "I went from all the noise and chaos of the burning plane to almost instant silence. I was floating under a parachute in near-total darkness. It was unreal. There was no sound but the air flowing through the parachute. I watched my airplane hit the ground and burn. Then I hit the ground. It knocked me out. I vaguely remember someone, maybe several people, helping me but that's it. The next thing I recall is waking up here."

The major's thinning hair plastered against his sweat-shiny scalp. He had a built-in sneer and an attitude of superiority. Patrick didn't like the man.

"Are you telling me that you have no memory of the last six days? I don't see how that's possible. Someone dressed your leg wound and made a rudimentary splint. How could you not remember that?"

Patrick made a show of shifting and moaning. The pain was real. The drama was for effect. He made his voice sound strained. "You would have to ask the doctor about that. I have no memory of the...no mem..." He closed his eyes and sagged.

The major made an exasperated sigh and stood. "Well, that was a complete waste of my time." He sniffed, closed his pad and left. Patrick opened one eye to make sure he was gone and then made a small laugh. *Oh man, did that hurt.*

SECOND TUESDAY

Kelley used the address on the website to find Pacific Voyager Cruise Lines, LLC. It occupied the top floor of a residential condominium building just off the Ala Wai canal. He waited for the elevator in an unattended lobby and watched the numbers above the door descend until the door opened with a cheerful chime. Stepping inside, he pushed sixteen, the top floor. The elevator door did not respond. He pushed repeatedly but with no effect.

He had to lean over to read the small words etched beside the button, "Limited Access." He laughed. *Since when does a cruise line need that kind of security?* He pushed fifteen and the doors obediently closed. Floor fifteen opened into a hallway shared by several businesses. Kelley walked the hall offering a happy, "Hi, how ya' doing," to everyone he passed. They all nodded pleasantly and rushed by. Apparently, anyone in a flowered shirt fit in well enough to go unnoticed.

At the far end of the hall, he pushed into a fire escape stairway and climbed to floor sixteen. That door was locked. Ever the boy detective, he produced a combination screwdriver, corkscrew, flashlight key ring and used the screwdriver blade to remove the lock faceplate and open the latch. The door opened to a deserted hallway.

There was a flashy white marble reception desk flanked by palm trees but the chair behind that desk was empty. The whole place was deserted, a high rise ghost town. He walked and read names on doors until he found "Aelan Comer, Director of Offshore Employment." He took a breath and entered without knocking. Six cubicles were outfitted with computers, printers, wall calendars and in-boxes. All were empty.

A small, polite voice inquired, "May I help you, sir?" Kelley looked around for the speaker. He was looking too high. Beside him stood a diminutive lady he took to be Japanese-American, although he wasn't that good at guessing ancestry. She stood less than five feet tall in a prim business suit with sensible shoes. Her hair was iron going to silver. Her unblinking eyes were polished black Kukui nuts. *He was getting into this Hawaiian stuff.*

"Yes ma'am, I'm looking for Ms. Comer. Is she in?"

"Oh, I'm so sorry. She's not. May I take a message for her?" The lady sounded as pleasant and about as sincere as a recorded phone message.

"No, seriously, I need to speak with her. I'm Kelley Price and this is personal."

The lady almost smiled and folded her hands softly as though holding a trapped firefly. "I shall inform her of your visit at first opportunity, Mr. Price. I am sure she will be in contact quite soon. And thank you for visiting Pacific Voyager…"

Kelley let his aggravation show. "Where are your employees? What is going on here? Is this even a real…?"

A disembodied woman's voice came from a speaker somewhere. It was Aelan. "Mrs. Adachi, please tell the jerk I'll be right out."

The tiny lady, Mrs. Adachi he presumed, looked amused as she dipped her chin and motioned to a soft chair. "Well, I guess she is in—for you. Please have a seat. I don't know how well the two of you are acquainted but you might be in for an interesting conversation. I'd offer you coffee but we just had the carpets cleaned."

An enormous floor-to-ceiling picture of a looming cruise ship clanked and rotated to become a doorway leading into a second office, this one fully occupied. Inside, a bank of desks hummed with activity. Six women, all young, all Asian, all smiling, worked computers and headsets obviously dealing with clients.

Aelan came, arms tightly crossed, shoulders hunched, chin forward, ready for battle. Her voice was shrill and her eyes intense.

"What are you doing here? This is not your place. You may have inherited Patrick's things but you did not inherit me and you have no right to intrude into my business and my life. I'll tell you when and where I want your company. You have already meddled and made my life complicated. I don't know how much you know or how you know it but you are a threat and I don't allow threats to go unanswered. Do you understand me?" Her voice got louder and louder. Mrs. Adachi nodded approvingly.

Aelan moved uncomfortably close. Kelley could smell her hair and almost feel the warmth of her body. He backed up a step but she kept coming. Her face was inches from his even though she was a head shorter. She hissed through clenched teeth and he felt tiny droplets of her spit. "Get out. Never come here again. Never."

They stood for a long, cold moment. Kelley realized his mouth had dropped open. He started to mumble something when she whispered, "Coffee shop across the street in fifteen minutes." She stepped back and pointed to the elevator. Kelley went like a whipped puppy.

As the big picture door closed, Mrs. Adachi trilled, "Aloha and have a nice day," with a sweet smile. Apparently she found his humiliation entertaining.

The coffee shop bustled with tourists and workers from the hotels that towered all around. Kelley got two cups of the most normal sounding brew on the chalkboard menu and took a back table. *What in the world was going on? Aelan seemed to have gone completely psycho.* He sipped and watched the crowd. The talk was mindless and the mood light.

Aelan appeared suddenly, slipping into the seat beside him. She took the paper cup that sat waiting and held it like a shield in front of her face while deliberately scanning the crowd.

"ICE has me under surveillance. You must never be seen with me, never."

Kelley didn't know quite how to act. "All right, but what was the big show of hostility back at your office? What did I do to deserve that?"

"Oh yeah, I'm sorry but I have to keep up appearances. This is a cutthroat business and I need to make sure people respect me."

"The cruise line business is cutthroat?"

She straightened and looked around before whispering, "I thought Clayton Sheppard told you more about the family business. Did I misunderstand?"

Kelley felt confused. "He told me you helped disadvantaged people immigrate to the US. Is there more?"

"Hell yes, there's more. We are in constant conflict with the slave traders. The gangsters who run human-smuggling-for-profit operations do their best to disrupt our business. They threaten, they hijack and they might even kill to stop what they see as competition. And now, now we have these ICE idiots breathing down our necks. My people have to believe I'm tough enough to protect them and our clients. And, like it or not, you're involved. It came with the inheritance."

He leaned forward. "I don't really see that I am involved with the 'family business' but I do feel I am involved with you. And, to tell the truth, I would like to know you better."

She drew back. "You can't be serious. You know almost nothing about me. Worse, you know nothing about the world you are skirting. I have many enemies and you know the old Chinese proverb, 'The friend of my enemy is my enemy also.' You must not be seen as my friend."

Kelley gave her his most winning smile. He had been told it was his best feature. "I think you may have turned that proverb on its head. And I don't see any armed guards. If you're really fighting gangsters, is it safe for you to be sitting here with me?"

Her gaze softened. "So you think you're calling my bluff, huh, tough guy."

The prize-winning smile. "A guy's got to do what a guy's got to do."

Her posture relaxed and her eyes met his. "Oh Kelley, you're a child really. You're adorable and seem so earnest, but you're a child. I'm afraid for you. Tell me something. Why do you think Patrick trusted you so much? It wasn't as though you grew up together. He barely knew you."

He shrugged. "I guess I haven't really thought about it. You're right, it doesn't make much sense."

She didn't seem pleased with the answer. "All right, tell me about yourself. You said you lost your job and divorced your wife recently. Tell me."

He gave an uneven sigh and held his coffee cup in both hands. "My wife became pregnant while I was out of the country. I had been in Bulgaria for almost a year. I offered to stay with her and keep the baby even though I was not the father. She said no. Said she never really loved me. Said I was a humorless 'joy straw,' that I sucked the joy out of life. She did want to stay married until the baby was born so my medical insurance would cover…" His hands were crushing the cup. He forced himself to relax. "I was a program manager for a pharmaceutical company testing a new cancer drug in Bulgaria," he explained. "The FDA won't allow human tests until years of animal experiments have been evaluated and anyway, animals don't show the same types of cancer we were working on."

"So you used human guinea pigs?"

"Oh, don't make it sound that bad. We gave the drug to people with liver cancer, a hopeless disease. It gave them a chance, admittedly slim, but a chance.

She leaned back, skeptical. He went on. "Then an American lawyer sued on behalf of one subject's family. The test was curtailed and I was terminated. It's too bad. The drug had promise."

"So you're a scientist?"

"Not really. I'm a statistician. I design and evaluate experiments. My job was to determine which effects were real and which artifacts."

"Ah," said Aelan. "Your job was to find truth in a clutter of distractions. Just the skills a treasure hunter would need." She seemed quite satisfied with her pronouncement.

Kelley was troubled. "Do you really think Uncle Pat gave everything to me just because I might help find his gold? That seems kind of cynical."

She looked him directly in the eyes. She had the deepest, warmest eyes of any woman he'd ever known. Until then, he thought of her as a reasonably attractive woman. But now, this close, she seemed absolutely beautiful.

She smiled and raised her eyebrows. "It would honor his memory and fulfill his cause. This would be the act of a noble son."

"A noble son." He thought of his own parents. He was the oldest of three over-achieving boys. The other two were already wealthy. A cardiologist and a commodities trader, they were polite to him at family get-togethers, steering talk to sports rather than their real estate ventures or the stock market or their dean's list children. His mother always asked if he needed any help. She would put her hand on his shoulder and tell him that she and his father were quite "comfortable" and would be happy to loan him whatever he needed.

The half-crushed cup of coffee had grown cold in his hands.

"Mister Price, I think you'll find this interesting."

"Clayton, I think you can call me Kelley by now. You've made enough money from me that we should be on a first name basis."

"As you wish. I have quite a bit of information for you. I've been going through the files that you brought me and found three communications that were paper-clipped together. I think they are all from the same time frame and I thought you'd find them interesting. The handwritten note is the most intriguing. It is clearly an attempt to communicate in a very cryptic way—to say something without saying it."

There were two typed pages with curled edges, fragile with age. Kelley read the first.

First Lieutenant Eli Lee June 29, 1969
16ᵗʰ Special Operations Squadron
Ubon Royal Thai Air Base, Thailand

Dear Lieutenant Lee,

I have been airlifted to Hickam Air Force Base, Honolulu, Hawaii. I am currently an outpatient of Letterman Army Hospital. They tell me that you and Msgt. Block were the only other survivors of the tragic crash of Specter 30. I regret that I did not have the opportunity to know the rest of the crew better. I am sure they were all fine men.

The intelligence people said you assisted me and probably saved my life. I have absolutely no memory of events after the crash. I would appreciate any information you could provide on what happened in Laos and how I came to get to Udorn Air Base. This information could be helpful in both my physical and mental rehabilitation.

I have made a significant recovery and will soon be assigned to the Hickam AFB aerial port squadron. You may contact me through general delivery Hickam.

Thank you, in advance, for any information you can provide and for any assistance you rendered during our escape and evasion from Laos.

Patrick J. Tooney, Sgt, USAF

The next letter read:

July 11, 1969

Dear Sergeant Tooney

First, let me congratulate you on your promotion from Airman First Class to Sergeant. I always thought you showed initiative and self-motivation. I hope you have a long and productive career ahead. The Air Force needs men like you.

Now, to answer your question: You and Msgt. Block met me on the ground after our bailout. It has now been officially declared there were no other survivors. The three of us evaded capture for several days and eventually commandeered a North Vietnamese Army truck. In the process, it was necessary to kill several NVA soldiers. You performed courageously and I have nominated you for a bronze star for bravery. You were wounded in the knee and will receive a purple heart.

We drove the truck through enemy territory engaging in several conflicts with NVA and Pathet Lao forces. Our survival radio batteries all went dead before we were able to establish contact with friendly forces. Eventually, we contracted a ferry boat to cross the Mekong River. The operator attempted to hijack us and our truck and, in the ensuing fight, the ferry crashed. You were badly hurt and knocked unconscious. It took a great effort to

get the truck out of the water and we feared for your life.

A local villager spoke a few words of English. We pooled our money and hired her to bring you to the American base at Udorn for treatment. I felt it necessary to stay behind with the truck since it was full of Vietnamese documents that might be useful for our intelligence people. After two days, Msgt. Block and I managed to get the truck running and drove to the US Army outpost at Pak San. We were right about the truckload of documents. It was a gold mine of Intel. Now, it is all safely protected for later analysis. Thanks for your outstanding work.

Eli Lee, 1Lt, USAF

The note looked torn from a tablet of lined paper.

Petunia, This note is being hand carried by a friend on R&R in Honolulu. The previous letter was for public consumption. Gina helped us cash in on our good fortune and make provision for delayed gratification. Don't you worry. I'm looking out for your interests. My own Hawaii R&R is planned for August. I'll look you up so we can trade war stories and talk of our plans for the future.

Get yourself well.

EL

Kelley looked at Clayton and raised his eyebrows. "So something was probably worked out during Lieutenant Lee's visit in August 1969. I wonder how we can find out what happened? Uncle Pat's letter said Lee was in San Quentin prison. It would really be something to go talk to him. Do you think that's even possible?"

Clayton Sheppard looked at the ceiling for a minute and then spoke very slowly as though still carrying on a mental debate. "Tell you what, I'm not too busy right now. Ms. Comer's case is pretty much quashed. I'll go with you as Mr. Tooney's attorney. He turned to look at Kelley. "All except the flight time will be billable hours, you understand. They'll let me see him...if he's still alive."

Clayton then pulled out another of his many manila file folders and handed Kelley a summary sheet. "And let me bring you up to date on the stocks. As you can see, all the stock certificates have been authenticated. It turns out that most were, as I anticipated, worthless. The companies have gone under without transferring value. Still, as the sheet shows, the estate of Mister Block can redeem approximately $242,000 from several valid stocks. Mister Lee, when we see him in jail, will be owed almost $300,000. You, as heir to Mister Tooney's stock, will be eligible for about $320,000." Clayton made a theatrical grimace. "It's a good thing, too. My tax guy advises me that you are liable for some heavy inheritance taxes. The new laws are just brutal. You're going to need all the money you get from these stocks and then some. I'm still working on the Haida Corporation lease for your Kona property. The beach house is pretty much a done deal."

Kelley sat back in his chair with a shrug. "This being an instant millionaire has its complications doesn't it?"

Clayton handed him an elaborately scrolled paper. "This last certificate is a puzzle. All the rest are perfectly valid, even the ones for bankrupt companies. This document is completely bogus. As far as my researchers can determine there has never been a 'Khoa

Industries.' Moreover, the other certificates are all from the early '70s. This one was printed within the last year. It looks believable but it's a complete fake. Patrick Tooney was not a playful man. There has to be a reason for including it among the other stocks. He wanted you to get it, wanted you specifically to get this in his 'dragon box.' It has to mean something."

Kelley took the certificate and inspected it. Intricate gold lettering looked very official. It showed Patrick Tooney as the owner of six shares of Khoa Industries. Fine print at the very bottom read, "Payable upon presentation at the following address," but there was no address, only a blank space followed by a certificate number.

"Do you suppose Uncle Pat was losing it? This seems awfully detailed for a joke."

Clayton shook his head, "Well, he certainly had some issues after being shot in the head. He had a continuous tremor in his right arm and an intermittent tic that made his head jerk. His mind, however, seemed to be as sharp as ever. He was a surprisingly tough businessman. He trained Ms. Comer to take over his many enterprises and taught her well. She's every bit as sharp."

Kelley broke into a grin. "Tell me about it. She treats me as though I were a runny-nosed adolescent. I went to look her up. We hadn't spoken since the funeral. I just wanted to be sure she was okay considering the ICE investigation."

Clayton shrugged. "I think she'll be all right. They found a forged birth certificate and, while that was thrown out by the judge, it really got the bloodhounds sniffing. It could be disastrous if they turn over too many stones in our immigration operations. Hundreds of decent, hard-working families could be deported and we could all go to jail. I'm trying to make sure your name isn't linked to anything that could bring suspicion. To that end, I think you should stay away from Aelan's office and really... from her."

Kelley shook his head in an almost playful way. "Not a chance. I like her and I want to see if there's any future between us."

"Mister Price—Kelley—that is a very, very bad idea. You seem like a decent enough fellow but these are pretty rough waters for an inexperienced swimmer."

Kelley still grinned. "You don't have any idea where I've been swimming, Clayton."

MAY 23, 1970

Eli Lee had left Gina, his new wife, and was headed into a war zone, but not in a tank or battleship. He was going on an aging, overcrowded train with wooden bench seats that would have been just the right size for elementary school children. He spent long hours watching out the window as lowland rice paddies and villages of Thailand gave way to foothills of alternating tall grass and gigantic trees.

The train rocked and clattered on ancient tracks. Black, gritty smoke from a wood-fired steam engine drifted by the coach windows leaving an acrid charcoal smell. Successive wooden bridges groaned under the train's weight. Inside, everyone swayed in unison as the train navigated mountain passes, snaking higher and higher.

Eli shifted position constantly. His long legs cramped from hours sitting on the too-small benches alongside a crowd of diverse but serious-looking brown faces. Someone in back had a wooden cage full of chickens that cackled and sent feathers drifting. Another man threw the hindquarter of small pig onto the overhead rack. A woman beside him heated a witch's brew of Oriental spices on a tiny portable alcohol stove at her feet.

The windows were closed to keep out bugs and smoke from the engine. That turned the passenger compartment into a tropical oven trapping odors of sweaty dense-packed humans, spicy food, cooking oil, chickens and that pig on the overhead shelf, which was now beginning to drip slightly.

From their clothing styles, Eli concluded his fellow passengers were of many tribes or cultures. There was little conversation. There seemed a general air of mistrust as eyes darted constantly and people clutched their possessions tight.

An oversized westerner, he was an object of curiosity but no one spoke to him. It was just as well. He knew only a handful of Thai words and none of the other languages of the area. Luckily, all the train station signs were printed in French so he was able to track his progress on the plastic map he carried.

At Udon Thani, he disembarked and stretched, grateful to finally stand straight. Beside the depot, a red dirt parking area was jammed with waiting tricycle "samlor" pedicabs. One driver waved and chattered. "Heh GI, I give you good deal. Twenty Baht to hotel. Come with me. I am good driver. Okay?"

Eli fished a five Baht coin from his pocket and held it before the English-speaking samlor driver. "Grand Hotel, go straight on big roads, understand?" Eli knew it was common for the drivers to take newbies into alleys and rob them.

This driver grabbed the coin and motioned with his head for Eli to load his gear and get in. They bounced along a rutted road crowded with brightly dressed Thais. Many of the women wore ankle-length skirts of red and gold with intricate embroidery. Most men wore simple shorts, sandals and cone straw hats. Some carried pots hung from the ends of long poles they balanced on their shoulders. They were an attractive people, generally cheerful and polite. But then, Thailand billed itself as the "Land of the Smile."

Eli leaned forward to the driver, who rose and fell with each pump of the pedals. "How much English do you speak?"

The driver looked back with a wide toothy grin. "I have good English. I work for many American pilots and soldiers. I learn very good."

"Okay. Tomorrow, I want to go to Vientiane. I will pay one hundred Baht. Can you help me?"

There was a long, very concerned sigh, a standard negotiating tactic. "Oh no, Vientiane is very difficult. It cost maybe…one thousand baht."

"Two hundred."

"I think, maybe, eight hundred."

"Two fifty."

"Oh no… I tell you what. My brother has car. He will take you for two fifty a day…as long as you want." The deal was done, two hundred and fifty Baht a day, equivalent to ten dollars.

The next morning the car arrived at dawn, just as promised. It was an ancient Citroen that might once have been maroon with black fenders. Now, it was the same red dust color of everything else that moved on rural Thai roads. Water buffalo, elephants, pushcarts and human travelers all wore the same dull, rusty color.

Nguyen, the driver, was a stick figure of a man, skinny as a concentration camp survivor. He bowed, clasping his hands in a "wai," the prayer-like Thai greeting gesture. His English, though cheerful, was kindergarten level.

Eli wore a tan safari outfit with matching broad-brimmed hat and mirror lens sunglasses to make it obvious he was not one of the thousands of military men from a nearby base. He tossed two duffle bags onto the back seat. Then he and Nguyen were off with a painful grinding of gears.

In early afternoon, they boarded a ferry over the Mekong. The feel of cooler, more humid air over the water and the distinct smell of wet clay and shoreline vegetation instantly brought memories of his ferry ride almost a year ago. Very near this spot, he had been chased by riflemen in a motorized long-tail boat. He smiled and watched the river flow. A shouting vendor tied his canoe-like craft alongside. Iron cooking vessels trailed wispy smoke from the vendor's boat. Eli bought meals of rice and fried fish.

He took out his map and showed Nguyen the town where Gina's mother lived. There was another long exhalation and solemn head shake. "Oh no, mister. You must not go here. This is bad place. White man get killed in this place."

Eli stood beside the car, tall and threatening. "I need to go. Can you find a way?"

The driver waved his arms in pantomimed anxiety. "Oh no. This is no good." Then he looked at the sky, thought hard and seemed to brighten as an idea formed. With a sly look, he said, "Mister, can you speak French?"

"No, I don't know any French. Just a little Spanish." Nguyen grinned wide. He looked as though he had a plan.

The first hour in Laos was uneventful. They honked and putted their way through one overcrowded village after another as crowds of farmers and merchants pushed along the road, grudgingly letting the Citroen pass. Many shouted. A few banged on the fenders and shook fists. Eli tried to slump down in the seat. Nguyen traded insults with practiced fluency.

Then they left the heavily populated river side to drive up into a cloud-masked world of sheer limestone cliffs. Eli felt a childlike exhilaration in returning to the scene of his adventure. He remembered every vivid detail of the scenery. The smells, the dampness, even the jungle sounds brought him back to the great escape, the great gold caper.

But an NVA checkpoint shook him out of any reverie. Nguyen slowed and almost whispered. "I talk only. You say that Spaney thing, okay?"

A skinny North Vietnamese soldier in a green pith helmet and uniform two sizes too large held up a hand for them to stop. He leaned down and scowled at the western passenger. Nguyen rattled excitedly and pointed to Eli. They argued. Nguyen almost screamed. Finally, the soldier took out a small pocket tablet of lined paper and wrote '100B'. He tore off the sheet and thrust the paper past Nguyen toward Eli, who took it and made a disgusted face.

Eli looked at the soldier and made a "give me" wave. When there was no response, Eli snapped his fingers impatiently and repeated the motion. The soldier reluctantly handed his pencil through the window and Eli jerked it away. He crossed out 100B and wrote 20. The soldier became angry. Nguyen shouted. Two other soldiers gathered to watch the fun. Eli said something in Spanish. He wasn't sure just what but it sounded enough like a demand.

A thick, round-faced soldier pushed the skinny one aside and took the note. He produced his own pencil, scribbled 50, showed it to Eli and then crumpled the paper with a defiant glare.

Sensing the negotiation had run its course, Eli reached over to his bag on the back seat and found a leather case. He fished out a fifty Baht note and handed it over Nguyen's shoulder. His other hand slid deeper into the bag to grip the handle of a .38 revolver. Thick soldier inspected the money and made a surly nod. He waved once and the red and white striped road barrier raised. Nguyen gunned the car and they motored on. The soldiers watched them until the road bent behind a stand of trees.

There was silence for a few miles as Eli thought over the incident. Then he turned to his clever driver. "You're not Thai are you?"

"Ah...I live in Thailand."

"But you're Vietnamese, right?"

"Yeh, okay, I was born in Vietnam. But good thing, yes? I can talk to Vietnam guys good. You pay only fifty Baht. Thai boy maybe get to pay two hundred. Maybe get kill. Maybe both get kill, yes?"

Eli sat back with a grin. "Yes, you did well, very well." There were no more checkpoints before they rolled into Gina's village. It seemed different than he remembered. There were fewer people about. Many houses looked deserted. The remaining villagers acted suspicious until they saw Eli step out into the sun. Then they came streaming to him, touching his shoulders and patting him. They jabbered with excited news he could not understand.

When a man with slicked-back hair and a black Nehru jacket appeared, they grew silent, bowing heads and drawing back. The man spoke English slowly as though drawing from a collection of long neglected words. "You are Captain Lee? You marry my mistress' daughter?"

Eli stood military straight. "Yes, I have come to bring your mistress to America."

Nehru jacket gasped, drawing air through his teeth. Then he recovered and, despite a pained expression, bowed and extended a hand toward the house. Eli started to walk to the steps but paused. "Please, will you take care of my driver?"

Nehru sneered. "Vietnam driver? He can sleep with the pigs."

Eli was patient. "No, please treat him as a guest."

Nehru glared but spoke quietly. "As you wish."

They entered the dark house and Nehru tugged at Eli's sleeve to remind him to remove his shoes. The old lady sat on an intricately carved chair in a room with no other furniture. Eli did an awkward bow and she began speaking. He didn't understand but it didn't sound friendly. Nehru kept his eyes on the floor but whispered. "She say, why go to America?'

Eli looked her directly in the eye. She didn't appear to like that at all.

"Her daughter, my wife, wants her to come. We want to make a baby soon. She wants her mother to be there."

Apparently, that needed no translation. The old woman snapped open an ornate rice paper fan, pursed her lips and began to fan herself furiously.

Eli was about to speak when there was a commotion outside. All heads turned toward angry shouts. He recognized Nguyen's voice. It sounded as though the man was pleading. Eli turned to Nehru and asked, "Where is my bag?"

Eli went to unzip one duffle. He drew his revolver and stepped barefoot out into the glaring sun. Three soldiers had followed from the NVA checkpoint. The skinny guard and one other held Nguyen by his outstretched wrists as he knelt, head down. The thick soldier stood behind and kicked the helpless driver. There was a lot of high-pitched screaming.

When they saw Eli, all three soldiers released their victim and stepped back. Thick made a guttural sound and pawed at the flap of his holster. Eli shot him square in the chest. The other two stood motionless, panic in their faces. Thick had been the leader. Without him they seemed unable to act.

With no more emotion than squashing a bug, Eli shot them with one well-placed bullet each. Nguyen still knelt, sobbing and shaking.

Gina's mother emerged from the dark interior and surveyed the scene. She drew herself up in a haughty, almost imperial pose, waved a hand toward the bodies and made a pronouncement. Several villagers emerged from hiding like Wizard of Oz Munchkins approaching the dead witch. Reluctantly, they set to work hauling away corpses. Eli and the mother stood silently.

He should have felt revulsion at the limp bodies being dragged, limbs trailing, heads akimbo. Thick soldier's empty eyes stared at the sky and his tongue hung out the side of his mouth. Eli should have felt something. If not horror, he should have felt, at least, a rush of relief, of victory. He had, after all, just saved his driver and perhaps others. But he didn't. He felt nothing at all.

Then the old woman took a deep breath and spoke with a voice of great authority.

Nehru was attentive and bowed when she finished. He tried to keep a stoic expression but his chin grew weak, almost trembling. "Mistress say you do great thing. You are good man. If you say go to America, she will go to America." Then he turned and hurried away. Eli thought the man might cry.

MAY 24, 1970

Gina's mother insisted on riding alone in the back seat. That meant most of her "absolutely necessary" items had to be packed in burlap bags and tied to the Citroen's fenders and open rumble seat. When done, it looked like the Beverly Hillbillies leaving Appalachia.

Nguyen, the driver, was worried. "You kill Vietnam guys yesterday. I think for us to go back like we came is maybe... difficult. This man tell me other way but it is slow. I think maybe you pay me more than two hundred fifty Baht, okay?"

Eli smiled at his entrepreneur of a driver. "If you get us to Bangkok, I will make you rich."

Nguyen lit up. "Okay deal. But if you want to get lady to America, is better to go to Sattahip. It is easier to buy ride on ship. Not so many open hands there."

Eli held out his own open hand and, after a moment's hesitation, Nguyen shook it. Neither realized that this was the beginning of a forty-year friendship and business. Not only would Eli make Nguyen rich, the driver would help them launch a smuggling operation that spanned two continents and a half-dozen nations.

The route they traveled was more jungle trail than road. People in small villages gathered to stare. Obviously, not many motor vehicles ever used these paths. Eli worried. The old woman in the back seat chattered in a never-ending but unintelligible harangue. Nguyen reassured them both, constantly shifting from English to some other language. He alone seemed confident and cheerful.

It had taken two hours to get from the ferry landing to the mother's house. It would take six to return through the jungle. Eli stayed alert, pistol ready, but no threat ever materialized. As they drove under dense, overhanging trees, he imagined drivers on the Ho Chi Minh Trail.

He visualized how the overloaded Citroen might look like to a marauding American plane like the gunships he had flown. There were few breaks in the overhead canopy. No wonder it was so hard to find the thousands of trucks that streamed out of North Vietnam daily bringing supplies to the Viet Cong and NVA troops in South Vietnam.

At one point, the jungle road gave way to an open landscape of grass and low shrubs. It had been cool in the forest but under the open sun, it was baking hot. In the distance, Eli saw huge Karst towers, the same mountains where his hoard of gold lay buried. If he could only get it he would be a modern King Midas. But one man alone could never hope to transport so much out of the NVA occupied area and, besides, there was no one here he could trust with such a treasure.

Like a sad-eyed dog waiting for its master's return, he stared for a long time. The gold would have to wait, but he swore to himself that he would be back. No matter what, he would be back. One day, he would reclaim his prize, no matter how long it took.

After three hours, the mother became even more insistent. Nguyen tried to calm her but it was hopeless. He turned to Eli and seemed sheepish. "She wants to eat. There is no place. She is…unhappy."

Eli considered and said, "Tell her that if she waits until we get to Thailand, I will buy her the grandest meal of her life."

Nguyen seemed happy with that. "And me too?"

"Yes, you too, Nguyen. If you get us there, you will deserve it."

"No problem, Boss. I know many people. I will get you to the big boat in Sattahip. I will make deal for you and lady to go to America. My price is very good. You will see. All is good. You will see."

Nguyen was true to his word. They emerged from the jungle well downstream from the ferry landing where they entered Laos. After an energetic negotiation, a small ferryboat operator agreed to take them across to the Thai side of the Mekong River. Their boat trip to a sleepy fishing village was uneventful.

The ferry docked at a ramp made of bamboo poles lashed together with wood strips. It didn't look substantial enough for a loaded car. Eli remembered the accident with the gold-laden truck at a similar shoreline. He frowned and asked, "Why here? Why not closer to Vientiane?"

Nguyen seemed very pleased with himself. "I bring you here because no Thai police. At Vientiane crossing, many police, many hands open for money. Here, nobody care. I do good, yes?"

"Yes, you did good." Eli felt a surge of confidence. He was, by nature, a worrier but somehow Nguyen made him feel as though everything was going to be okay. It wasn't, of course.

The old lady was growing louder and more insistent. The sky was filling with tall thunderheads and they had a three-day drive ahead where every Thai checkpoint required a bribe. Still, Eli could relax for the moment.

In the town of Chai Buri they found a restaurant that met the mother's demands and paid two hundred baht for a four course meal served by three overly attentive young girls who made it a point to spend time hanging on Eli's arm. That is, until the mother ordered them away with a sharp command.

Nguyen spoke to the owner and after a fierce negotiation that included arm waving, fist pounding and finger wagging, made a deal to rent the restaurant's delivery van along with a driver. It was a Volkswagen mini-bus, old and noisy, but big enough to hold the mother's household goods. The van was a clunker but it would get them to the port at Sattahip. The Citroen would attract less attention without cargo strapped all over.

In the days that followed, roads and towns all looked alike. The rain never stopped and neither did the old woman's complaints. Even ever-cheery Nguyen grew tired of her incessant voice made more irritating with windows rolled up. The car became a sweat box. Condensation dripped on the windows. Wipers banged away like a metronome counting seconds in some Chinese torture device.

Sattahip was a dirty industrial cargo port but it looked like heaven to Eli. They found the best hotel in town. Even as they checked in, the old woman ranted. The desk clerk eyed her with suspicion. Nguyen had enough. He pulled her aside and hissed something in her ear that she didn't like. She folded her arms and grew taller, even more stubborn.

Eli knew the clerk spoke English although he pretended not to. "This is my mother-in-law. Please give her the best room in the house and give her anything she wants. Otherwise she will make my life hell."

The clerk grinned, pulled a large brass key from a slot and presented it to Eli. "Top floor, three rooms, good breeze. I will have girl bring fruit and tea. She will be very happy there."

"Thank you," said Eli with relief.

Outside, the sun broke through and the whole world seemed to brighten.

In the morning, Nguyen made inquiries accompanied by one-hundred Baht notes and then led Eli to the docks. They walked up the ramp of a rust-bucket freighter being loaded by cranes that looked too small for the ten-foot wooden boxes they hoisted. No one questioned the two men.

On the bridge they found a weather beaten derelict of a man in a captain's cap standing at the rail. Nguyen approached him and started talking. Eli interrupted.

"Good day, sir. We were told this was a good ship to travel on. We are seeking passage to Hawaii."

The old man sipped coffee from a paper cup and stared down at the loading operation. "You have papers, of course." His English was good but heavily accented.

Without hesitation, Eli replied, "No sir, we have cash."

The old man looked at them now. "I am Captain Villanescu. I don't take many passengers but those I choose are well cared for. My fee is ten thousand American dollars per person."

Eli liked this codger. The negotiation had begun.

Nguyen pulled Eli's arm. "I must go too. Without me, you cannot talk to old lady. It will be very bad. I will be big help. I promise."

Of course that made sense. Why hadn't Eli thought of it before? He turned back to the captain. "Six thousand American dollars for three people if the quarters are acceptable."

The captain never blinked. He just sipped his coffee and said, "Nine. The quarters are the best of any cargo ship in port and I won't kill you and dump your bodies in the middle of the ocean like some of these other devils. Take it, you won't do better."

And so it was done. They were going to America. Gina would have her baby with her mother beside her. Eli could get his life together. Nguyen could forge a new life for himself. Everyone would prosper and be happy. Why didn't Eli feel more relief? Everything was working out better than he hoped. Why did he still stare at the horizon? What was it he needed and how could he ever find it?

THURSDAY

The flight into San Francisco was bumpy and overcrowded. Clayton wanted first class but Kelley bought business class tickets. The lawyer sulked but he'd get over it. "Okay, tell me what you know about Eli Lee."

Clayton opened his valise and pulled out a folder. "Well. I understand his military record says he served with distinction on the job but seemed unable to stay out of trouble. Washed out of pilot training shortly before graduation because of some infraction, he was sent to navigator school and graduated top of his class despite two DUIs and a civilian assault charge."

Kelley thought about taking notes. Clayton rambled. "Sent to Southeast Asia to fly AC-130 gunships, he volunteered for extra flights and was described as having a 'unique' ability to find trucks under the Ho Chi Minh Trail's jungle canopy. Apparently, his drinking was tolerated there. After being shot down, along with Misters Tooney and Block, he was hailed a hero, but that was short lived."

"Then what became of him?" Kelley asked.

"Well, it looks as though he was assigned to Travis Air Force Base, California as a transport navigator but couldn't stay out of trouble. Multiple assaults and insubordination charges. In light of his war service, he was allowed to take extended 'medical leave.'

He moved to Hawaii in 1970 and disappeared off the radar. He reappears in 1988 arrested for the murder of Dewey Block."

"Do we know the story there?"

"Dewey Block's body washed up on Waikiki beach at high noon. It made headlines, but only briefly. The Coast Guard picked up Eli Lee operating Dewey's boat. It looked to them as though he was making a getaway. They found a .45 Colt pistol onboard that seemed to match Block's wound but it couldn't be confirmed. Unbelievably, Eli was given bail. He jumped that bail and fled to California. There, in 1990, he was arrested for another murder. A Mister Phan Vang was stabbed to death in San Francisco's Tenderloin District. It was a pretty brutal affair and California refused to extradite him back to Hawaii, a non-death penalty state."

Kelley took it all in. "Okay, California wanted to kill him decades ago. Why is he still alive?"

"His conviction was overturned on appeal in 1999, but he'd killed another inmate in the meantime. Now, he's rotting in San Quentin, life without parole as a career criminal."

Kelley just sighed. "I wonder what went on in those eighteen mystery years between '70 and '88?"

It would have been a short drive from San Francisco International without traffic, but this was California. They spent twenty minutes on the Golden Gate Bridge alone. San Quentin, when they finally made it, seemed pastoral and quiet as a college campus. Clayton Sheppard outlined the plan.

"Okay, I've scheduled our visit online using the California Penal VPASS System. We have a two-hour, no-physical-contact meeting. You'll need your drivers' license but it's best to leave everything else in the rental car. Keys, wallet, even loose change, leave it all."

From the Disneyland-sized parking lot they, and a hundred other visitors, crowded into a cramped entry hall, picked up laminated badges on lanyards, got hand-stamps and entered a labyrinth of metal cage hallways that buzzed and clanked as barred doors opened and closed. Loudspeakers barked instructions and stern guards hurried them along. Kelley jumped at every noise.

Finally, they came to a cafeteria-size room full of tables with glass partitions in the middle. It didn't look that secure. All around them, orange-clad inmates were freely embracing friends or shaking hands before seating themselves on opposite sides of the glass. Kelley counted only four guards. That wasn't enough to stop a riot. Luckily, there was no riot.

At some point, Clayton had been given a number like the ones car repair shops put on your car's roof. Eventually, a guard led a tall man in an orange jumpsuit to them. The guard pointed at a huge clock and spoke in clipped English. "You have one hour, forty five minutes before visiting hours are over. Plan to be done ten minutes before. Okay, Eli, here's your visitors."

Clayton rose and reached over the glass to offer a handshake. Eli Lee looked pretty good for a convict in his seventies. A big man, prison tough, he wore his orange sleeves rolled up to reveal sinewy, well-muscled arms covered with tattoos. Thin, gray hair barely hid good-sized scars. His neck was all cords and his eyes looked skull deep. He might be old but he'd scare the hell out of you in a dark alley.

Eli shook hands like he was strangling a snake. "Okay, who the fuck are you?"

Clayton pulled free and shook his crushed hand with accompanying facial drama. His voice strained. "I'm Attorney Clayton Sheppard and this is Kelley Price, nephew of Patrick Tooney. We have some questions to ask you."

Eli Lee grinned wide. There obviously weren't many dentists in this prison. "Patrick Tooney. I haven't heard from him in a while. How is my little buddy?"

"Dead, I'm afraid. He passed away almost two weeks ago and Mister Price inherited his estate. You, Eli Lee, also came into several hundred thousand dollars but we'd like to talk before I explain."

Eli Lee deflated and shook his head. His sadness seemed genuine. "Petunia's gone? He was my last link to the world. I should have known something was wrong when he quit writing. Damn." He looked away and pressed his lips tight. Then, with a sigh, "What's this about money? How could I come into money?"

Clayton produced a copy of the certificates. "It's from stocks. We found the certificates in Mister Tooney's effects. The value is almost $300,000."

Prisoner Eli Lee looked all around. "Swell, maybe I'll redecorate. What do you think, pastels maybe?" His face wrinkled. "What the hell do I want with money now?" Then calming, he sat back. "Tell you what. Somewhere out there is my little girl. Patrick used to update me. She's all grown up now and I've never been much help to her. Truthfully, I didn't want her to know anything about me. Please find her and give her that money. It's the least I can do. I've sure as hell never been much of a father."

Clayton took out his pen. "Sure, Mr. Lee What's her name?"

"She was born Eileen Lee, at Letterman Army Hospital April 9, 1972, although she may have married by now, probably has. Sweetest, most beautiful thing you've ever seen." He looked into space. "Tiny little fingers—didn't look real. They were so tiny and so perfect. I cried when I first saw her, my perfect little Gomer."

Kelley spoke for the first time. "Your... Gomer?"

"Yeh, that's what I called her. Gomer's what we used to call the locals. Actually, it's what we called the enemy. It made my wife Gina furious when I called her that."

"Wait a minute. Your wife's name was Gina and your daughter was born April 9, 1972 at Letterman. Holy shit."

Eli drew back.

Kelley held up his hands like a magician's, *ta-dah*. "Eileen, you called Gomer. Eileen Gomer, Aelan Comer—that's your little girl. She thinks her name is Aelan Comer. She lives in Honolulu and runs a cruise line, or part of it, anyway. She has been very successful. Uncle Pat looked out for her. We'll make sure she gets the money."

Eli nodded without emotion or surprise but kept silent. Clayton went back to work.

"Mister Lee, we have a lot of information about the gold. Can you provide more?"

"The damned gold. Of course, you're here about the gold. Oh, what the hell, I'll tell you all I know. You won't find it. If Patrick couldn't, you sure as hell won't." Eli Lee leaned forward on his elbows and began his tale.

"While Patrick was laid up in Thailand and then later in Hawaii, Gina let us store a truckload of gold in her bungalow in the little town of Udon. All those towns sound the same, Udon, Udorn, Ubon. Anyway, she knew a jeweler who took a couple of hundred pounds and made fancy dragon boxes. We shipped those back to the States so we'd have some walking around money while we worked out how to get the rest. The boxes breezed through customs and later, we melted a couple of them down."

Eli paused and smiled. "Patrick Tooney was the smartest guy I ever knew. That man could do magic. How, I don't know, but he got himself assigned to the records section of the Hickam

Air Force Base Cargo Operations. He had everything worked out when I met him on my Hawaii R&R. He lined up a couple of Marine Corps helicopter engine containers in Thailand that needed to be shipped back to Kaneohe Bay in Hawaii. That's how we moved the gold."

Eli bit his lower lip and relived the adventure. "Dewey had his twenty years of service so he retired right there in Thailand. He became our point man. Patrick had him pay off a couple of GI drivers to bring those engine cases to Gina's bungalow on a flatbed truck with a built-in mini-crane. I joined him there and, between us, we loaded more than four thousand pounds of boxed gold inside those two cases."

Eli was obviously enjoying himself. "Then, the genius part, Patrick got me a set of courier orders. As the courier officer for this phony 'classified' shipment, I escorted the two containers so they could bypass customs. They looked like diving bells, each about the size of a bread truck. I watched them load onto an Air Force C-141 plane and then flew with them. We arrived at Hickam Air Force Base, Hawaii at three in the morning on a beautiful star-lit night with light wind in the palm trees. I'll never forget it."

He smiled as though feeling that breeze. "Patrick was waiting with a commercial flatbed truck and a driver he trusted. An Air Force lieutenant from Patrick's squadron got the two containers onto the truck for us. As a courier, I had to ride with my 'classified' cargo. We drove to the Hickam Yacht Club dock and used the boat crane to move the containers onto an old barge Patrick bought. By daybreak, the truck had been returned to the rental yard, the containers were covered with tarps and the barge was heading out to a dredging area for the new Honolulu airport runway. There were a lot of beat up barges there. One more created no interest.

It was a safe holding place. We used an inflatable motorboat to head back to the dock."

Kelley and Clayton were leaning forward, hanging on Eli's words.

"Dewey flew in on a Pan Am Clipper. We met up and worked out our next move. That night we took the inflatable out to the barge. That is when things started going bad. First of all, we couldn't open the engine cases. We used huge wrenches to get the bolts off one case but the three of us couldn't lift the damned cover. It was just too heavy. So we decided to take the barge back to the Hickam dock and use their crane again."

"That barge was old and underpowered. Its small engine was really just for local maneuvering. We couldn't take it out in the main channel. Dewey played captain, another mistake. As we tried to jockey our way through a flotilla of other barges in the darkness, he built up too much speed. We slammed another barge—rammed it hard. We were stuck. Our engine wasn't strong enough to break free. Worse, we were taking on water. There was a lot of screaming and name calling but it didn't matter. Our barge groaned and tilted backwards. It began sinking. I'll never forget that sound, like it was dying."

Eli grinned. "It was dying, just like our dreams of wealth. It sank into the water with a huge wash of bubbles and a bizarre moaning sound. None of us knew what to do. We stood there helpless as the water reached our ankles and kept coming. When it was waist-deep, we finally waded back to our inflatable and watched the last great gulp of air escape as the barge went under. No one on shore, or anywhere else, even noticed what was happening. We stayed watching bubbles rise till daybreak and then started putt-putting back to the dock."

Kelley chimed in. "So the gold's still in the water by the airport?"

Eli shook his head. "Naw, not any more. The engine case cover that was too heavy for us to lift trapped enough air to just float the cover away. The rest of the case—and a ton of gold inside it—sank like a rock. The other still-sealed engine case floated like a cork. Once we saw it bobbing, we turned our inflatable and chased it. We caught up, tied a rope and tried to tow the damned thing. Our boat had a tiny motor. All we could really do was to guide it a little. We herded the thing into the Pearl Harbor inlet with the whole world watching from the shore. I thought any minute the Coast Guard would come roaring after us but they didn't."

"So, the gold is in Pearl Harbor?"

"Naw, not any more. We were pulling at full power when Patrick shouted. I remember it clear as yesterday. 'Holy shit,' he screams. 'There's an aircraft carrier coming into the channel.' Sure enough, this gigantic boat is coming right at us. The thing looked to be eight, maybe ten stories high, wide as a football field and it was bearing down on our dingy—and fast. Worse, the floating engine case wasn't floating so well any more. It was getting lower and lower and, as it sank, the drag increased.

'We're bogging down,' Dewey yells, 'get over to shallow water. We'll drop it and come back with a bigger boat.' This makes sense, so we turn toward shore. Then the case rolls and goes completely under. Our little boat upended and went down with it. So there we were, treading water in Pearl Harbor with an Aircraft Carrier coming. I swam like an Olympic athlete and made it to an overgrown area on the west shore.

I'll never forget the feeling as that giant boat passed. Its shadow was as big as a city and the water around me throbbed from its engines. Its wake tossed me and I went under, churning head over heels in water full of sand. When I finally surfaced and got my breath, I lost sight of the other guys."

"So the gold *is* in Pearl Harbor?"

"Naw, not any more. Dewey made the east shore and took off."

"And Patrick?"

"Patrick drifted far out into the channel and then, after the carrier passed, washed up somewhere near the Pearl marina. Someone fished him out and helped him get ashore. After he got his shit together, he sent a boat back to pick me up. It took more than two hours. In the meantime, Dewey completely disappeared. We didn't hear from him for two years." Clayton took notes, trying to create a timeline.

"It took us a couple of more hours back at the Pearl Marina to hire their largest boat. Then we went back to the spot where our inflatable and the case sank, but there wasn't a trace. We thought the wake of the aircraft carrier might have tumbled them back into the channel but some serious searching turned up nothing. I figure that while I was on the far shore and Patrick was floating around, somehow Dewey managed to get a boat, come back and drag the case away."

Eli shook his head. "Anyway, I flew back to Thailand to finish my Air Force tour and marry Gina. Patrick took up SCUBA diving and, over a six-month period, retrieved almost a thousand pounds of gold from the sunken half-case before construction of the new runway buried the rest. Today, the Reef runway at Honolulu sits on top of a thousand-pound stash of gold."

Eli shook his head slowly. "Patrick divided his rescued loot evenly among us. He even kept a share for that pig, Dewey. That's probably where these stocks came from. We didn't realize then that the fat bastard had stolen the rest of the gold. And that, gentlemen, is all I know."

Eli Lee sat back and folded his arms. His story was done.

Kelley said, "Where were you between 1970 and 1988 when Dewey was killed?"

Eli hesitated and considered. "I brought Gina to Hawaii. Patrick helped. He set her up with a bar in Pearl City. I was assigned to a California Air Force Base but not for long. I came to back to Hawaii to be with Gina and we had a baby." He paused with a wistful smile. "Gina wanted her mother to come to America. Patrick wanted the rest of the gold we left in Laos. I was restless. The Viet Nam war was going badly. I went back to Thailand. Getting the rest of the gold out was hopeless. The North Vietnamese fully controlled the area. I spent years trying. In that time, I got to know a lot of people. Eventually, we set up a smuggling operation to get most of Gina's extended family out. I stayed there working with Air America and the CIA fighting and smuggling people in and out of Southeast Asia. It was important work. I'm proud of what I did."

"Did you visit Gina and your daughter?"

"Oh sure. I came back a couple of times. Then the war ended and my contracts expired. By then I was fully involved with the guerilla war. I tried to stay home but I just couldn't. I had gone too far, gone too native, fighting alongside Gina's people against the Royal Lao, the Vietnamese, and the other tribes. Eventually, I got most of her tribe moved to Thailand and many of them on to the States. I was a hero to them. I just couldn't leave. Not until 1988 when everything went to hell."

"Is that when you killed Dewey?"

Eli Lee's eyes and lips narrowed. "Well, if I had killed that piece of shit, it would have been because he murdered my wife."

Kelley was taken aback. "I thought Gina died of a stroke."

"A stroke? There was no stroke. She was murdered. I'm sure of it. I don't know how Dewey fit into the picture but I'm sure he was involved. Whoever it was that got Dewey Block, I thank them. But it wasn't me."

Eli pushed back with an angry glare and started to stand. Clayton jumped in. "Before we leave, I'd appreciate it if you look at this one stock certificate and see if anything about it rings a bell with you. It's a fake and we think Patrick was trying to tell us something by it."

Clayton tried to pass it over the glass partition. Eli yelled, "Guard, I'm taking a piece of paper here."

The guard walked over, took it, sniffed it, snapped the paper and handed it back. Eli scanned and shrugged. "I don't see anything."

"How about the serial number? It's not like the others."

Eli read it aloud. "TG330100, TG330100—naw, it doesn't mean anything to…" Then he paused, looked hard at the numbers and broke into a grin. "Tango Golf three three zero, one zero zero. Hah, GeoRef coordinates. I think it's the GeoRef coordinates for the main gold stash in Laos. Find yourself a map with a GeoRef overlay and you'll be set. The letters give you a quadrant. The first three numbers give you the east measure and the next three, the north."

He tossed the paper back. "Well, boys, there's your gold. Go get it if you can."

Kelley reached over to shake hands. "Thanks Eli."

The prisoner's voice was low. He looked away into the distance. "You know, for years I dreamed of getting out and going back to live a normal life but gradually I realized there's just something wrong with me. When everything starts to go my way, I find some way to fuck it all up. I'm not cut out for the normal life. I belong here. I'll die here." His whole body sagged and he sighed and looked down. "Just take care of my little girl, okay?"

Kelley almost whispered, "I promise."

FRIDAY

The flight back to Honolulu was delayed four hours. Kelley upgraded to first class so he would have internet and phone access en route. He was troubled by the visit to Eli Lee. Something didn't seem right about Eli's story. Actually, a lot of the story didn't seem right.

Shortly after takeoff, he logged onto the Honolulu Star-Advertiser newspaper archives and checked the 1988 coverage of Dewey Block's murder. There were sensational pictures and extensive copy. Dewey was described as a real estate "developer" for North Shore properties. During the week, newspaper stories worked their way from front to mid-pages. The Chamber of Commerce tourism interests probably had something to do with that.

The arrest of Eli Lee on the day of the murder, was not reported for several days and then it was page two, lost among editorials on tax initiatives. *That seemed strange.* Kelley could find no mention of Eli's bail or his bail-jumping.

Then he tried the San Francisco Chronicle. The 1990 murder of a Mister Vang barely rated mention. The "suspect" arrested was described as a vagrant involved in a drug deal gone bad. Eli Lee's name was never mentioned. There was no coverage of the trial or Lee's conviction. At least, none Kelley could find. *Stranger still.*

Back to the Honolulu paper, he found a birth announcement for Eileen Lee. The parents were listed as Eli and Gina Lee. That was straight forward. *Why the fake birth certificate?* And if the information was that easy to find, why hadn't Special Agent Diggins known? None of this made sense.

For fifteen dollars, Kelley bought a 'guaranteed official' copy of Eli Lee's Air Force record. There was no mention of a 1970 medical discharge, only a "leave of absence." Searches for Lee from 1972 to 1988 found nothing. The man became a ghost.

Kelley tried searching for Gina Lee. She was shown as the "owner" not an employee of the Dragon Lady bar on Kanakawa Drive. After 1973, the owner was Gina Comer. A name change. Okay, that made sense. He checked her business filings but they weren't available before 1999. At that point, the bar was owned by Excelsior Enterprises. Gina Comer's 1988 obituary was generic, no cause of death listed. Kelley was starting to feel as though he had fallen through a rabbit hole. Nothing made sense.

He found Dewey's obituary from the same year. It too, was uninformative. Owner of Blockbuster Realty, survived by wife Ruby Block and sons Billy and Bobbie, it listed no cause of death. Kelley searched for Ruby Block and got a 2011 obit: donations to be given to the Lung Cancer Fund. So she was a smoker. She was survived by son Billy. *Wonder what happened to Bobbie?*

That was all he could stand. Kelley reclined and tried to doze. He imagined a white rabbit. *Where was the Mad Hatter?* Clayton snored as Kelley stared fitfully into the darkened plane. He seemed the only person still awake. Strangely, his frustration gave way to a feeling of comfort. This is what he did. From a chaotic jumble of information, he was usually able to parse out the individual pieces. Then he could mentally wash away the distractions and the emotions to see the underlying truth. His ex-wife, Molly, said he was good at it—good at teasing cold facts from the turbulent avalanche of life's events. He was, as she called him, a joy straw. *Yes, he could suck the joy right out of life...but what was left was truth.*

Just as he was finally sinking into sleep, the captain came over the loudspeaker, "Ladies and gentlemen, we are about to land at Honolulu International Airport. It's a gorgeous Hawaiian sunrise with light winds out of the east. They're bringing us in to the Reef runway, zero eight. Those of you on the right will have a great view of Diamond Head. Those on the left will see Pearl Harbor and the hotel skyline. A great big Aloha to you all and thanks for choosing us for your travel."

The Reef runway. They were about to touch down right on top of a thousand pounds of buried gold, if Eli Lee could be believed. *But where was the other two thousand pounds? And what about the gold Eli Lee said was still in Thailand, or was it Laos?* Kelley was determined to find out. He had a mission, a purpose.

In the cab, he turned to Clayton Sheppard. "I've been rethinking everything Eli told us. If the case of gold sank in Pearl Harbor and disappeared before Patrick and Eli were able to get back from the nearby marina, that means Dewey had only a few hours at most to find a suitable salvage boat and recover the sunken container. He had to get his boat from somewhere really close."

Clayton yawned. "You realize you're talking about something that happened in 1969. Everyone involved has probably died of old age by now. But, never mind. I have an investigator who can check it out. I'll get back to you." He paused for an awkward moment. "You do also realize this will all be billable hours? You know people have been looking for this gold since before you were born. I think a little perspective may be in order. Remember what

Eli Lee said. If Patrick couldn't find the gold, what makes you think you can?"

Kelley couldn't wait. After landing, he headed for his condo. Clayton still had Patrick's computer under lock but he copied its hard drive to an external and gave that to Kelley. Armed with Eli Lee's new information, Kelley began a search. The endless volume of information began to make more sense. Excelsior Enterprise holdings included, not only Gina's bar, but a variety of other buildings including the one occupied by Pacific Voyager offices.

He searched *Excelsior Enterprise, Inc.* The principle operating location was the Pacific Voyager building, big surprise. The CEO, again no surprise, was Patrick Tooney. Board members included Aelan Comer and a half-dozen men he did not recognize. Aelan had not been completely open with him but neither had anyone else. *What did they have to hide? Was it their smuggling operation?* It seemed there must be more.

Kelley had a strange feeling that it was no accident he inherited Patrick's estate. Maybe he had been chosen to fulfill Patrick's lifelong quest. Maybe it was just fatigue clouding his mind but, at the moment, it seemed reasonable. Chosen or not, he was going to give it his all. He was going to find the gold, Patrick Tooney's gold.

The thought made him smile. *Ready or not Mad Hatter, here I come.*

SATURDAY

Oahu's North Shore was different than Honolulu. Largely rural, it had many small, middle class towns crowded along the shore. Cars were older, people racially diverse and shops decidedly downscale. There were still mansions but they were far between. Kelley found the Blockbuster Realty office in a small house of crumbling stucco and tile. Even the sign out front was faded.

Billy Block was a fifty-year-old "senior executive managing director" of the three-person real estate brokerage. He was a loud, fleshy man who filled a room when he entered and dominated every conversation. Kelley disliked him immediately.

"Mister Block, I'd like to ask you a few questions about your father."

"Ha, the old bastard was crazy as a gopher in a clothes dryer."

"That's kind of a strange analogy. What do you mean?"

"He was a drunk, a mean drunk at that. As he got older, I think his brain cells just burned out. He got paranoid, holed up in the big fancy house and became a recluse." Billy swiveled behind his desk and bellowed. "Sylvia, we need some coffee...now, if you don't mind." He shook his head in disgust. "Can't get good help on this damned island. Now, about Dad, he became obsessed with the gold. I'm sure that's what you're really asking about. That's all anybody cared about with Dad. Well, I don't know what he did with it. For all I know, he drank it all away. Mom left us when

I was in college. I dropped out after a year. Waste of time for me—I'm a doer, not a thinker. Anyway, the old man hid his gold. I saw it once. It was in the basement of his Windward House. He built a vault and had a whole wall of stacked gold bars."

Kelley tried to visualize. "How big was the wall?"

"How big? I don't know. I was a little kid, like eight or nine years old. It was bigger than I could stretch my arms." He slapped his hand on the desk and laughed. "Hell of a lot of money for the old bugger to blow, but he managed. By the time I was in high school he was broke. He became a hoarder filling his house with junk until you couldn't walk through. The IRS finally took that house and he went to live on his boat, that ridiculous boat."

Kelley perked up. "Is that the boat he was killed on?"

"I don't know. His body washed ashore. They weren't even sure he was shot. He had a big hole in his chest but after so much time in the water no one could tell what caused it."

Kelley accepted a cup of coffee he had not requested. "Tell me about the boat. It must have been a big one for him to live on it."

"Big? Hell, it was an ocean-going tour boat. Held fifty people, maybe more. He bought it thinking he could start a business taking tourists inter-island. That didn't work. You have to be sober to run a business. Later, when his money troubles made him declare bankruptcy, some old war buddy bought the boat out of sympathy and let him continue to live aboard."

"Some old war buddy?"

"Yeh, the guy had a business—Excellent Enterprise or something. His manager was some Vietnamese or Cambodian woman who used it as a shuttle taking tourists out to cruise ships a couple of times a month and, for those days, Dad stayed in a hotel. He got a real hair up his ass about that woman. I think that had something to do with his murder. I met her once—total bitch."

"What happened to your brother Bobbie?

"Suicide. He had a drug problem and could never keep it together. I tried to help. Hired him to do maintenance work on some of our rental properties but he was unreliable and I had to let him go. Mom got tired of his crap and stopped supporting him. Dad couldn't take care of himself, let alone some whining loser like my brother. Bobby blew his brains out while sitting naked on the beach. That's enough to make any brother proud. Mom died shortly after." Billy sat scowling and quiet for a moment.

"Do you have any other relatives, Billy?

The hotshot realtor spun in his chair and shrugged. "Couple of ex-wives, two non-custodial kids—I'm a free man."

Kelley pulled out one of Clayton's business cards. "Call this lawyer. He has a sizeable sum of money for you. Thanks, you've been a help."

SATURDAY AFTERNOON

Agent Diggins, wearing suit pants and open-necked white shirt, sat alone in an open-air beachfront bar. He turned a cup in his hands but didn't drink. He just stared toward the surf beyond a beach volleyball match.

A leathery-skinned man in a red flowered shirt, straw hat and mirror sunglasses slid into the seat beside the special agent. "Just another shitty day in paradise, huh pilgrim? Say, you don't really look like a tourist. What brings you out to drink with the mad dogs and Englishmen in the mid-day sun?"

Diggins shrugged. Red shirt continued. "Me, I'm here to celebrate fifteen years of non-wedded bliss. This is my anniversary. Fifteen years ago today, I dumped that evil bitch. Cost me almost every penny I had but it was still a bargain." Looking up, he motioned, "Bartender, give me one of those little coconut shell drinks with a parasol but fill it with Jack Daniels not that fruity crap." He grinned from under the twin mirrors of his glasses.

Diggins finally took a slug from his plastic cup—no glass containers allowed on the beach. He grimaced as the liquor bit and spoke while looking straight ahead. "I'm single too. Been married three times but my job is—or was—incompatible with home life. Or maybe, it's me that's incompatible. I don't know."

Red shirt nodded agreement. "My theory is that women aren't supposed to stay with men past child-bearing age. They should go off and live in caves or something where they can trade stories with other hormone-crazed bitches. What do you think?"

Diggins allowed a slight smile to flicker but no eye contact. Red shirt extended a bony hand that had seen way too much exposure to sun. "I'm Bennie, by the way, Bennie Sepatski. I retired here in paradise after my last divorce. Made a fortune in oil well exploration partnerships. I never dreamed it was so easy to make so much dough. You should think about it."

Diggins shook hands and they talked for an hour. Bennie winked at the bartender who knew to refill his coconut shell drink with diet cola not booze. They talked of oil wells and wives and, eventually, of immigration troubles, Diggins' suspension from ICE, and even the case of Aelan Comer. Bennie was careful to remember details. He was skilled at his job, a natural con man. *No, not con man, con artist... yea, that's what he was, an artist.*

Much later that day Bennie made a call. "Why hello Mrs. Adachi, is the good witch there or is it just you and the flying monkeys."

"Why, that's so clever, Bennie and you sound almost sober. I'll see if she's available. Maybe you can pick some poppies and skip down the yellow brick road while I check."

He whistled and jingled change in his pocket while scanning the beach crowd. Aelan's voice came on in just moments. "Bennie, what do you think?"

"Well, hello Sweet Thing. I have just spent my afternoon listening to former ICE Special Agent Charlie Diggins telling me that life ain't fair. I should charge you double for making me listen to that much whining. Anyway, there's something wrong about this guy. His interest in you is based on a misguided belief that you and your people are in the prostitution game. Specifically, he thinks his seventeen-year-old runaway daughter has been recruited as a street hooker. I don't know yet if that's true, but he's convinced she was drugged and kidnapped by 'white slavery' traffickers, specifically by you. The guy is more than slightly paranoid. He wants to find the girl before she gets sold off to some sultan or oligarch."

There was a moment of silence. Bennie knew to give her room to think. She finally came back. "So, it's all about his daughter. Any chance you can find anything on her?"

"Already on it, Sweetness. After I left Diggins nearly face down in his fruit drink drippings, I've been on the street. I talked to a guy named Tongay who, as you probably already know, works for your competitor, Clark Shipping Containers. He's something of an enforcer or body guard, tough guy type. Clark doesn't get actively involved in the day-to-day management of hookers. They resell them to a gentleman named Pak or Pok or something who farms them out to local pimps. If Diggins' girl child is hustling for them I'll find her. I did get a picture of the little darling, somewhat dampened by paternal tears and malt liquor. I'll send it to you. Tonight, I'll see what I can sniff out among the street people. Maybe she's still here on the island. I'll get back with anything I find."

"You're an angel, Bennie."

"Yea, I know. I'll bill 'ya, Sweetness."

JULY 7, 1972

Eli watched Gina say goodbye to her mother. He knew it would be painful but the tenderness of the moment surprised him. Gina, hard edged and combative bar girl turned business woman, was passive, almost shy. The old lady, who had always been a domineering hellcat, was gentle. Gina knelt before her mother and spoke softly in that strange, lyrical language of hers. The mother reached out with a light, affectionate brush of Gina's cheek. It was obvious both thought this to be the last time they would ever be together. The mother, for once, put aside her harsh tone and spoke softly. Eli thought her rhythmic words might be a blessing of some sort.

He had never experienced such emotions. His own mother was a frightened shell of a woman, battered into numb submission by a brutal drunk of a husband. Eli's father was a failure to the world but, in his house with his family, he had been lord and master. A tyrant, he lashed out at every imagined shortcoming or disrespect. In his whole life, neither of Eli's parents ever held him. Neither ever made a single positive statement. Neither ever indicated they cared if he lived or died. Well, his father did often say he wished young Eli had never been born.

Now, watching them, Eli Lee was touched by Gina's gentle sorrow and the proud old woman's obvious love for her daughter. Neither cried. They were too strong for that. Then the moment was over. Gina stood and bowed and that was that. Farewell to her mother and her old life. It was time to go.

Eli led the mother to a waiting cab and the two of them drove in silence to the international Airport where Nguyen was waiting with his ever-present grin. Two years in Hawaii had improved his English and added twenty pounds to his frame. The three of them had arrived in Hawaii like rats on a derelict cargo ship. But now they were leaving with first-class tickets on a Continental Boeing 707 to Bangkok. The passports and documents were fake, of course, but no one paid much attention to who was departing the United States. INS, the Immigration and Naturalization people, only cared who was coming into the country. Once in Thailand, they would have no problem with immigration officials. A one hundred dollar bill tucked inside each passport guaranteed that.

The flight was long with a stop in Guam. The old lady was quiet. Unlike two years ago where she spent the entire car trip from Laos to the Sattahip port berating the two men in the car, this time, she seemed lost in her own thoughts. Sometimes, she actually smiled and closed her eyes as though lost in memories.

From Bangkok, they took the train north to Vientiane, this time riding in a private compartment with padded seats and air conditioning. A servant in a white coat poured tea, fluffed seat cushions and prepared meals with sauces so hot they could strip paint. The old woman was gracious. Perhaps the memory of her new granddaughter's tiny fingers or the little eyes looking up so full of curiosity gave her a new perspective. Perhaps she just saw her life coming to a new phase. For whatever reason, she was different now. She seemed at peace.

They took a modern car ferry across the Mekong River to Vientiane, Laos and there, everything changed. The town was an armed camp. Soldiers, Thai, Royal Lao and mercenary fighters of every nationality, milled about in fatigue uniforms with guns slung over shoulders. The roads were clogged with military vehicles fighting their way through the chaos of pedestrians, pedicabs, pushcarts and motorbikes. It looked like a refugee exodus from some disaster and that is exactly what it was.

The travelers checked into the Erawhon Hotel, the best in town. At the bar, Eli sat alone and slugged back gin and tonics as though he just crawled out of the desert after a week without water. His thoughts were not of the wife and new baby he left in Honolulu. They were not of his mother-in-law and their impending trip back into the jungle and mountains of this strange land. He was focused on the ruined temple that held his gold. For two years he fantasized about the gold, about being rich beyond belief, about the power it would give him. He dreamed of the moment he cracked open the ancient burial vault and saw sunlight reflect off the neat rows of gold ingots inside. Unlike Patrick Tooney, Eli had no real plans to share.

His day-dream was interrupted by a short, heavyset New Yorker who wheezed when he talked. The man wore an untucked short-sleeved shirt with embroidered dragons. He shot a stiff-arm handshake. "Johnny Creech, what brings you to this hell hole? I don't see many fellow Americanos here. You Raven, Steve Canyon or Knife, maybe?" From his days flying gunships, Eli knew these were all covert programs run by the CIA to support the "secret war" in Laos.

"No, I'm just here to bring my mother-in-law back to her home village." He shook Johnny Creech's hand and turned back to his gin and tonic.

Johnny Creech seemed interested. "Where's that?"

"Forty miles east of here."

Johnny shook his head. "You'll never make it. A little less than a year ago, there was a huge battle here in Laos. 'Long Chen' they called it. Didn't get much press back in the States because there weren't many American ground troops involved but it was one hell of a fight, a major turning point in the war."

"Haven't heard of it. What happened?" Eli tried to sound casual.

Johnny seemed to know what he was talking about. "The NVA had always controlled the PDJ, the Plaines des Jars, but the Hmong fighters pretty much kept them on the defensive in the south away from the mountains and the Mekong. Then, last year, the North Vietnamese attacked with division sized forces and a ton of artillery. We fought back using Thai regular army troops, Lao soldiers and the entire force of General Vang Pao's Hmong army. Hundreds of American planes bombed the NVA for a week and we defeated them."

He took a sip of his drink, some strange, dark liquid. "We won but our losses were crippling. The Hmong were decimated. They may have lost as many as ten thousand fighters. The Thai were demoralized and pulled back. The Lao retreated to lick their wounds. And then, the North Vietnamese quietly moved back and overran the countryside. They lost the battle but won the aftermath. Now, they have near total control of the mountains. No way will you make it through on the roads."

Eli wasn't sure how much stock to put in a barroom conversation. "So, how can I get there?"

"Well, you could fly." Johnny Creech grinned. "I work with Air America. I could get you there."

Eli thought for a moment. "I could probably get myself there if I had a plane."

"Really, you're a pilot?"

Eli hesitated. "Well, yes and no. I have a commercial pilot's license but I haven't flown since Air Force pilot training. I had a little run-in with my squadron commander and he made sure I was washed out before graduation."

"Heh, I'm ex-Air Force too. What got you washed out? Was it the formation flying? I had trouble with that."

"No, it was a hot tub."

"A hot tub? I don't get it."

Eli had never shared this story and certainly not to a complete stranger but, what the hell. "My flight commander came home early one afternoon and caught me in his hot tub with his hot wife. It wouldn't have been so bad if he hadn't screamed my name when he walked in. I snapped to attention and stood up buck naked." Eli sighed. "Unfortunately, it wasn't just my posture that was stiff. Anyway, they shipped me off to navigator school and then sent me over here to fly gunships."

Johnny was really interested now. "So, that's how you met a Thai girl and married her?"

"Oh, my wife's not Thai. She belongs to one of the Lao hill tribes, the Ankha. She helped us escape after my plane was shot down."

"Huh. So you have connections to the hill people, you've fought the air war over here, you're a trained pilot and you must have experience directing airstrikes as a gunship navigator. Say, can you wait here for a minute?" Johnny was gone with what seemed some urgency.

He returned two gin and tonics later along with a tall man in a white suit, both man and suit wilted by tropical heat. "Eli, I want you to meet John Dunn. He's my boss." Mister Dunn offered no greeting or handshake. His eyes were skeptical. Johnny spoke in rapid-fire New Yorker sales pitch. "Eli here is the best qualified candidate I've run into in ages. He's got relatives here in the hills and he used to be in the Air Force..."

"Actually," Eli interrupted. "I am still technically in the Air Force. I'm on medical leave undergoing treatment for alcoholism."

Now Dunn spoke. "So here you are sucking up cheap gin in a bar. Well, you'll certainly fit in with the other rascals we employ." Then Mister Dunn leaned back and said, "*Sa bai dee.*"

With Gina's mother around so long Eli had picked up a few words of the Lao language, at least the Lao spoken in Vientiane Province. With a quick sip he replied, "*Kulunaa?*"

Dunn seemed impressed. "Please join us at a table away from the bartender's ears. We want to talk to you seriously." They sat with fresh glasses and Dunn's pitch began. "I don't know you and have no idea what you want of life but here's what I can do for you. I'll pay you ten times your Air Force salary if you give me a three year contract. You'll be working in the field coordinating Air America operations. You will have to contract your own protection forces from the indigenous people but I'll pay for that and any equipment you need. You'll be largely on your own but I'll give you all the support I can...and I have significant assets available. Think about it. After three years, you go home rich and it's all tax-free. You could retire for life."

Eli sat back taking it in. He could be a hero. More than that, he could raise a private army. He could use that army to retrieve his gold. Ten times his salary? Hell, he could bring back thousands of times his salary. His gin had never tasted so good.

JULY 8, 1972

They sat in the luxury hotel's open air restaurant where brightly colored birds sang and flitted over dropped crumbs. Tropical flowers bloomed all around adding their perfume scents to the food. Eli had an omelet and Bloody Mary. Nguyen and Mother had a three course meal of fruit and unidentifiable charred things on top of Saffron rice. The coffee was strong and satisfying. Eli liked living large, living rich. Soon, he could have anything he wanted. Maybe he would buy an island, maybe build a runway for his private jet.

A small, dark man in a white shirt scanned the breakfast crowd, then walked directly to Eli's table and bowed slightly. "Mister Lee? I have your car waiting."

"My car? Waiting for what?"

"To take you and lady to airport. Your plane is waiting. Mister Dunn has sent me to get you. All is ready."

Eli hesitated. The man turned and rattled an explanation to Nguyen and Mother in some dialect both seemed to understand. They were impressed. Eli had a plane at his disposal. It took an hour for Mother to get packed but the man in a white shirt was patient. Once his minibus was loaded, they set off with Mother sitting up front so the whole world could see her. The airport was larger than Eli expected but the driver bypassed the terminal and went directly to a small row of hangars.

There, waiting patiently by his Porter aircraft, was a tall American in jeans, a tee shirt, cowboy hat and ostrich boots. He had a Texas friendly smile and accent to match. "Hi folks, I'm Sandy Vance. I'll be flying you today. The weather's pretty good and the winds are okay. So let's talk about where exactly you want to go." Nguyen and Mother boarded the small plane while Sandy and Eli compared maps.

The Porter was a single-engine tail dragger with an exaggerated long nose and big, fat tires. It held six people or, today, three people and all of Mother's luggage. Once they agreed on a place to land—Sandy called it a Lima Site—they were off.

The plane had barely started rolling when the tail lifted off the ground. A few hundred feet down the runway and the Porter was airborne with a high-pitched droning sound. They climbed over the city of sprawling dirt roads and buildings, some modern but most just shacks. Then into misty mountains and thick green forests that spanned the horizon. Mother glued herself to the window jabbering with excitement at seeing her country from the air for the first time. She grabbed her cheeks in wonder and shouted...in English... "There, there is home." Sandy, the pilot, obliged by dipping a wing to swoop low over tree tops and buzz her village. She gasped with delight, pointed and reverted to her language to describe what she saw.

Sandy pulled up and announced, "We're going to land just over the next ridge. Everybody strap in."

Eli, riding in the co-pilot's seat, saw nothing remotely like a possible landing strip. They slowed, put flaps out and began a steep descent into the valley of dense green. The plane stabilized and Eli realized they were hurtling right at a red mud smear on a fairly steep upslope. This couldn't be their destination. This couldn't be a landing zone.

The trees were getting bigger. He could see individual leaves. They were going to crash into the red smear. Sandy asked, casual as if they were reclining on a beach, "Got your ground transportation set up?" They were closing fast, nose down, dive bombing the muddy clearing. It was much too steep and too small to land on. Eli gripped the armrest and tried to appear cool. He could see people standing around the rectangle of the landing zone. He found his voice just as Sandy pulled the nose up hard and added power. "No, I didn't have time." His voice was a little higher than he intended. The impact was followed by a quick bounce on the big balloon tires. Sandy reversed the prop, hit the brakes and skidded to an amusement ride stop.

Sandy continued the conversation. "No problem. Mister Sattahan here can take care of you. It would be polite to tip him the equivalent of a dollar." He turned and waved to Mother and Nguyen in the back. "Y'all have a good day here in sunny Laos, ya' hear."

The bags and people were offloaded against the propeller's blast. Then, the plane pivoted and took off downhill, humming its way skyward. Eli looked down at the field of raw earth that passed for a landing strip. He couldn't believe the slope. It was more ski jump than airfield.

Nguyen and Mister Satta-whatever were already engaged in serious negotiations but soon they came to some agreement and a jeep appeared. The ride was crowded with three people, a driver and a load of suitcases but somehow, in the ingenuity of people used to cramming people and things onto small vehicles, they made it work. Half an hour later they parked before Mother's house.

It was a ghost town. Her house and all the others were empty. Everything was intact but the people were gone. Only a handful of chickens now populated the once-thriving village. Eli walked around but saw no one. "Before we let this driver go we must decide what to do. Should we stay?"

The old lady had apparently picked up some English during her two-year residence in America. "This my house. I stay." She was as cantankerous and defiant as ever. Eli paid the driver and he was gone. Now it was quiet, eerie jungle quiet. Nguyen stood close to Eli and whispered. "What will we do? This is not good. Something bad must have happened here."

Eli forced a momentary smile. "You heard the lady. This is her house. We stay."

Back in Vientiane, Mister Dunn sat in a second floor office overlooking a hectic open-air market. It was a bedlam of shouting pedestrians, hawking street vendors and gunning motorbikes. A giant floor fan blew gale force wind that threatened any paperwork not pinned under fist-sized jade paperweights. Johnny Creech barged in and plopped a manila folder on the overcrowded desk. Dunn snatched it before the fan could scatter pages. Johnny fanned his face with a hand and shouted. "God, it's hot in here. Couldn't you spring for an air conditioner?"

Dunn sat back and his chair springs squeaked, even over the background noise. "We need to spend the taxpayer's money on combat operations, not civil servant comfort. Our guys in the field deserve whatever we can give them…"

"Jesus, you must have been a Boy Scout. Anyway, here's what I dug up. The hotel recorded all his passport information. Based on that, I discover that Eli Lee, Captain, United States

Air Force, is currently pending medical discharge for substance abuse problems. Ordinarily, he would have received a general discharge for unsuitability but the guy has seven air medals, three distinguished flying crosses and a bronze star for valor so he's getting an honorable discharge without prejudice. He was shot down and spent a week in NVA-controlled territory. During that time, he killed several enemy combatants, stole a truck and escaped to Thailand. He's a regular Errol Flynn. I don't have any civilian records yet, but he sure sounds like a good candidate to me."

Dunn read several teletype messages. The block printing was barely legible but the large "Secret Noforn" stamps were clear. "Okay, so are you looking at him as a pilot?"

"Oh no, we can get all the pilots we need for what we pay. He's a potential ground guy. He married a Laotian girl. He knows the geography and the enemy from his gunship flying and he has experience directing air strikes. You offered him ten times the $7000 a year salary he makes as a junior Air Force captain. I think he can be had. I am concerned about his mental stability."

Dunn squeaked as he rocked and considered. He handed the folder back to Johnny. "Mental stability?" He smirked. "Have you read the job description for this position? It's in the dictionary under 'psychopath.' Send one of our team leaders to give him the pitch. Do it up right. You know, God, country, liberty and justice."

Johnny Creech wiped his brow with a small cloth and grinned. "Absolutely, and I'll be sure to throw in some girls and liquor. Like I said, I think he can be had."

Eli found a machete and cut wood for the house fire pit. Nguyen caught a chicken and picked vegetables from an untended nearby garden. Mother opened an earthen jar the size of a garbage can and found a little rice. She began to cook a meal. There were no candles left in the vacant house so the cooking fire was their only light as the jungle's shadows overtook the sunset. Eli wasn't sure just what was going to happen but he couldn't leave the old lady alone and she definitely was not leaving.

They gathered around the fire to eat but then Mother perked her head. She heard something. Eli fumbled for his gun. The old lady was intent as she held out a hand to quiet the two men. Nguyen drew back into a dark corner. For a long ten seconds, there was nothing. Then a tentative shout from outside. Mother clapped her hands and shouted back with relief and happiness. Several ragged men carrying automatic weapons came inside the house, but warily. The men, probably displaced villagers, checked everything in the flickering light of the fire. Two of them grabbed Nguyen and dragged him out of the shadows. Eli stood tall and Mother made a sharp pronouncement. It sounded like a drill sergeant's order.

The men released Nguyen and circled around her. Then began the telling of tales, excited stories of NVA troops taking away men in chains, beating women who protested and kicking children who cried. The old woman rocked and shook her head in anguish. She shook a finger and scolded. The men protested and held up their weapons as though to emphasize that they did fight back, were fighting back. She folded arms in disgust. Then she pointed at Eli and gave a cold, hard-sounding order.

Nguyen translated. "She says you are a fighter. You must show the men how to fight."

Eli started to protest but why bother. None of them spoke English. But then, the seeds of a plan began to sprout in his mind. *Train them to fight, train them to trust, train them to obey... he could use them to get his gold.* The corners of his mouth began to hint at a smile.

They gathered in a circle, twelve men in odd costume. Small and brown, they were all very serious and attentive. Some wore skirt-like clothes wrapped around their waists. Some wore western pants and shirts. All wore sandals. There were teenagers and men with gray beards. What they all shared was the look. Black glistening eyes with the intensity of polished obsidian, they had come to fight and die.

Eli felt inadequate, an unusual thing for him. He had a translator, the old lady's house man, the one who wore a Nehru jacket. He had the obsequious attitude of a servant. Such men could not be trusted to give bad news. "Sir," he began, "They want to know how westerners fight, how Vietnam man fight."

Okay, Eli could handle that. "Tell them, Vietnamese fight like ants. The big ants stay in the nest and send little ants in a row to fight." He was on shaky ground here. He knew the NVA trained Viet Cong and Pathet Lao fighters in guerrilla tactics but he expected they would use more normal military maneuvers in largely uncontested Laos. In any event, he was just an Air Force navigator and really knew very little about ground army tactics.

The Ankha fighters nodded and murmured among themselves. Eli gained confidence and continued. "Like ants in a line, no one thinks. They are predictable. We must be more like wasps. We must move silently, unpredictably, and then strike silently, kill silently. We will move through the jungle like whispers, careful of each step, alert to the wind and the sounds. Then we become killer wasps, who strike and are gone. We cannot kill all the ants but each one we do kill makes the others more confused. Soon they lose their way and their lines break up. They will gather together for safety and will not attack your villages." Nehru translated.

Eli was really winging all this right off the top of his head but they seemed to buy it. He thought that's what Gina's mother wanted, someone to sound authoritative. As he continued to recite everything he had ever read about guerrilla tactics, he gained confidence and so did his audience. As he translated, even Nehru seemed impressed.

In late afternoon, the troop marched out over a row of hills to where they thought a small detachment of NVA soldiers guarded a road crossing. Eli and the men came quietly though brush, bent and stealthy. The Ankha warriors were good at this, good at jungle hunting. They peered out of the thicket toward the crossing. He counted six soldiers in off-green uniforms kicking around a soccer ball. The men had shirts off to play, obviously fearing nothing. Their rifles were stacked in a tent-like circle.

Eli motioned and his warriors moved into two groups, one on each side to surround the NVA soldiers. Eli and Nehru—he still couldn't remember the man's name—ran for the rifles.

A shout of alarm and the game broke up. The Vietnamese ran for their rifles but Eli got there first. He had only a pistol but three quick shots cut the Vietnamese force by half. The three remaining soldiers simply sat down and raised hands over their heads. The

Ankha fighters cheered and proceeded to massacre the survivors. They slashed and dismembered the three soldiers, cutting off ears, noses and other body parts.

Eli felt a twinge of horror but accepted that this was their way. He was here to help them gain confidence not change their society. When it was done, The Ankha dragged what was left of the six bodies and propped them back to back in a circle where the rifles had been. They stripped all valuables and food and then turned with expectant eyes on their tall American warlord.

What next? With captured rifles, a machine gun, bags of ammunition and a week's food, they had just become a much more capable fighting force. He felt strangely confident, comfortable in his bizarre status as outsider become chief. He knew they accepted him only because Gina's mother had directed it. Still, he had the power. He would try to use it well. He imagined himself and his men sweeping across Laos like Attila into Europe.

"Attila," that sounded right. He would call himself Attila and his force of Huns would grow as they marched through the jungle. His mind raced. He was now an actor in a great adventure play. Shakespeare would love it. A small band of rebels harassing the fierce North Vietnamese Army, humiliating them, destroying them.

He grinned and felt his shoulders pull back and his chest swell. The Ankha started to sing and he joined in, following the tune with no clue about the words. It didn't matter. He was singing a warning. Beware, Attila is coming and no one is safe.

His voice boomed and the Ankha laughed at him. He laughed right back.

APRIL 10, 1973

Many months later, Eli pulled the pop-top on a small metal canister and held it over his head as sulphurous red smoke sprayed out. Little bits of the cloud's hot red powder rained down on his shirtless, tattooed body. A helicopter passed overhead and made two circles around the smoke cloud checking the area before landing. Then, just as the smoke burned out, the chopper hovered to touch down in a windstorm that flattened grass and sandblasted Eli and his Ankha warriors. Two soldiers in unmarked uniforms stepped out of the chopper and scanned the field of tall grass with rifles ready. Finally a man in safari clothes and mirror sunglasses deplaned and wiped his brow.

Eli approached. He had grown leaner and darker after living in the jungle and he knew it made him look intimidating. He also knew that he had developed a downright scary attitude. He liked being scary. Woven armbands and necklaces along with the dragon tattoo on his bare chest just added to the image of a jungle man-beast, a creature to be feared.

"Jesus man, don't you think you're overdoing the Tarzan thing?" Safari suit looked genuinely concerned. "I mean, look at you. That necklace of human ears, what's that about?"

Eli grinned. His teeth had not seen a brush in ages. "The Ankha and many other tribes believe that a man's body must be whole for him to enter the afterlife. When we desecrate the body we condemn the soul. It scares our enemies. Now what do you have for me?"

Safari man's sweat dripped off nose and chin. He gestured to boxes being unloaded. "I have new multi-band radios with better noise suppression and increased range. There is plastic explosive with timers and trip wires. Four boxes have new mines. These are smaller than the ones you've used before but just as powerful. They'll blow a deuce-and-a-half truck ten feet in the air. There's also three full boxes of incendiary grenades. Oh, and the coffee you asked for."

Eli nodded approval. "What about the maps?"

"Oh yeah, there are waterproof large-scale maps printed on silk to be light and durable. I've also included some of those new-fangled satellite photos of targets we want hit." He hesitated. "You didn't ask for any money or gold. Are you sure you don't need financing?"

Eli grinned again. "Naw, just like the guns, we steal what we need."

Safari suit put his hands on his hips and shook his head. "Are you sure you're okay, Eli? We can pull you out any time."

The grin again. "Pull me out of what? I have found myself here. I have a mission, a cause, even a belief system. It doesn't even matter that it's not my belief system. It's something of value, something that makes me feel right. I'm fighting for the survival of a people, for my wife's people."

He looked into Safari's eyes and spoke with an almost contented tone. "Here, I measure time in sunsets and seasons. In the rainy monsoon, the North Vietnamese camp and hide weapons and food for the dry season offensives. Their troops in those sheltered areas are vulnerable. Me and my Ankha, we raid those compounds. We use bamboo sticks to hold down razor wire and then sneak in to kill guards and key officers before detonating bombs. In the dry season, we ambush them on the roads. For every one of my men who dies, I kill fourteen NVA."

He took a deep satisfied breath. "It is an exhilarating life. Always on the run, always hiding, always watching. We are ghosts, elusive but very lethal ghosts. I even join in to the victory mutilations. I have pretty much gotten over all that old All-American 'humanity' stuff. Now I am Attila and I am a killer."

Safari took a breath and looked into the eyes of a man who had grown to look like a full-fledged barbarian. He shook his head and wiped his forehead again. "Well, keep me informed. The new radios will help." He turned and motioned for the helicopter pilot to start up. The two uniformed guards backed up to the chopper's skids keeping an uneasy eye on the rag-tag Ankha band of somber brown faced men in turbans and vests with guns slung over shoulders and machete-like knives stuck in waist bands

The rotors engaged, gaining speed and force until the helicopter lifted off nearly blowing men back but the Ankha stood and weathered the hurricane force just as they weathered everything else.

Eli listened until the whop-whop of the helicopter faded away. Then he turned back to business. The dry season was upon them. Eli knew the NVA would become aggressive, moving convoys and troops across the country like chess pieces.

He and his men, who now numbered in the hundreds, had to hustle to keep track of their enemy. With new radios he could call in reconnaissance support and in airstrikes. That would make him even more powerful. The Ankha would be in awe of a man who could rain down bombs on their enemies. He would be like a supernatural warrior king. He was truly Attila, the killer. He liked the sound of that.

MONDAY

Kelley was settling into his new life as a full-time non-working resident of Honolulu. It had good and bad aspects. He loved the mornings: the birds, trade winds and smells of an ever-present ocean a block away. He hated the music, the crowds and the phony "Aloha" culture of tourist hustling. But, altogether, it was a great place. More than that, he was enjoying the adventure that had been thrust upon him.

Kelley Price, gold hunter, truth seeker, swash buckler—well okay, he hadn't buckled any swashes yet, but he was ready. A month ago, his future looked bleak, almost hopeless. Now, he woke every day ready to jump into action. Or, so he felt.

Today, he was after the boat. Dewey's boat seemed important somehow. An online records check showed that it was owned by Excelsior Enterprises and docked at a private pier on the big island. Kelley ordered a ticket on Aloha Air and a rental car at the Kona Airport.

First, there was a phone call he felt obliged to make.

"Mister Chilton, good morning, or afternoon for you. This is Kelley Price. I don't know if you remember, but I briefed you on the closure of our Bulgarian research operation. Yes sir, it did go well. Everyone got out clean, no suspicion that it was anything other than a straight forward cancer study."

He listened for a moment. "That's great, I'm glad to hear you're adjusting to your recent retirement. Me? I'm a full-time civilian. I came into some money and moved to Hawaii. Say, I have a question about someone who predates either of us at the Agency. I know that in the seventies and eighties we still had people operating in Southeast Asia, specifically Laos. They organized and coordinated local tribes to fight the Vietnamese. Once we washed our hands of that area, some of those people wound up abandoned."

Kelley tried to choose his words. "Sure, I understand that wasn't your area and that you're retired. Anyway, I just thought I'd ask. You always seemed to know what was going on even when everyone else was in the dark." *Always good to butter the toast before the bite.*

"Well, there is a guy in San Quentin for the 1990 murder of a Mister Phan Vang, not sure of the details. The man is Eli Lee, an ex-Air Force officer who disappeared into the jungle for fifteen years. I wonder if he just might be one of our Agency orphans. I can email you an unofficial copy of his military records. Of course, I understand you have no access to the Agency's old records. I just thought it would be worth a shot."

Kelley wrapped it up. "Molly? No, we're not together any more. She traded me in for a newer model. She has a kid already. I'm just a man at leisure, enjoying the tropical paradise. Give my regards to your wife, Maureen. Good talking to you, sir"

There, that's taken care of and now, off to the big island.

The flight was beautiful, passing over jewel-like waters dotted with islands of sandy beaches, and soaring mountains, some thick with vegetation, some bare red earth. The big island of Hawaii was equally impressive with its massive volcanoes and wild, lava-carved terrain.

Kelley picked up his car, set the destination coordinates in his phone's GPS and charged off to find the boat. He wound through a few small towns and subdivisions with tropical trees and grass lawns. Beyond Awakee Bay, old lava flows and barren, black cinder landscapes reminded that this was a very active volcanic island. Finally, he found the gravel road, crested a hill and saw a small harbor of sorts. A craggy wall of rock protected the harbor against thundering ocean surf. Only a small gap allowed access into a shallow cove where the land flattened into a black sand beach. Today, gale winds whipped waves even inside the cove.

He followed the gravel road to a mile-long half circle of chain link fence around a small wind-blown beachfront community. A dozen metal-roofed one-story buildings were geometrically clustered around a grassy common area something like a New England town square. Paved roads to nowhere crisscrossed the small community. Sidewalks ran along the streets with store-front shops. There was even a stoplight hung in front of a small chapel with a steeple bell tower. *Why did they need a stoplight?* A community parking lot held about a dozen cars. There were no people. It looked like a movie set.

Beyond the buildings, a long dock extended over the beach well out into the water. There was the boat. He had expected a fancy yacht but this was a very utilitarian vessel, more like a commercial ferry than a rich man's toy. Perhaps sixty feet long, it had a low, wide hull supporting a glassed-in passenger compartment filled with bench seats. Except for a small viewing deck and wheel house, the roof looked flat and plain.

Kelley stopped at a gate. It was chained and locked. There was no call box. He estimated it to be two hundred yards to the nearest building. Shouting was useless in the constant off-shore wind so he sat and tooted his horn. Once, twice…nothing. He persisted and on the tenth or twelfth blast, someone came out of a building and peered at him. It was an Asian woman wearing a coat with a scarf wrapped around her head. *A coat in eighty degree Hawaii.*

She went back inside but several children now spilled out into the common area, laughing and playing. They were small, preschool he thought. Other than that, he could tell little. Kelley honked no more. They knew he was here. He would just wait. He was a very patient man.

After twenty minutes watching the kids chase and tumble, a man emerged and began hiking up toward the gate. He had a deliberate pace and military posture. As he drew nearer, Kelley judged him to be Eurasian with straight black hair. He wore a sport jacket over jeans and a collarless shirt.

Kelley got out of the car and waited at the gate. The man stopped ten feet short and spoke in a polished, radio announcer voice that might have had a hint of British accent. "I'm terribly sorry, sir, but this is private property and we don't accept visitors."

"Private property, you say. So, whose private property is this?"

The man might have tried to smile, or maybe not. "The Haida Corporation, sir."

Kelley broke into a grin. "Actually *sir*, I am the owner of this property. I lease it to the Haida Corporation. Now, I have no wish to intrude but I need to see the boat, which is not owned by Haida but by Excelsior Enterprises, an organization in which I also have an interest. Please be so kind as to allow me to enter my own property and inspect my own boat." His grin morphed into a male dog dominance stare.

Sport coat turned his back and flipped open a phone. He hunched to talk as wind blew little swirls of grit. The sound of distant crashing surf was loud even over the buffeting wind. Kelley waited. Sport coat gestured into the air and then hung up. He stood for a moment with tight lips and then took a deep breath. He didn't look happy as he turned and fumbled for a key ring.

Unlocking the chain, he opened the gate and motioned to enter. Kelley got back in his car and drove. As he passed, sport jacket scowled and yelled over the wind. "Stay on the road and, please, do not speak to the residents."

Kelley hit the brakes. "Tell me, just who are you and who are the residents?"

The man leaned toward the window. "We are a technical training center. Originally created and funded by Japanese Corporations to benefit Japanese-Americans in Hawaii, we now support all Asian-Americans. I am Charles Hajita, director and curriculum developer. We limit access from the outside world to facilitate complete cultural immersion in an atmosphere seeking to marry Japanese principles of quality with American innovative attitudes. This is a hothouse growing entrepreneurs who return to their communities with a new, positive energy."

He spoke with none of the energy he described. Instead, his speech sounded like a well-rehearsed elevator pitch delivered without inflection. Kelley nodded and drove on. Curious eyes watched from windows as he walked out on the dock. Waves broke all around dampening his clothes and face with sea spray.

Despite its size, the big boat heaved in its mooring. Kelley timed his leap to land on the deck at the top of a rise. He stumbled up from his knees and grabbed a rail. He saw nothing very special. A covered walkway surrounded a passenger compartment enclosed by three glass walls. The aft wall was a bulkhead covered with poster-size pictures of whales. One metal staircase led below deck and another went to the wheelhouse above. This would have been an excellent sightseeing, whale-watching or just general touring boat.

He climbed up to the wheel house- nothing special. The instruments looked ordinary: GPS, radar, compass and radios. He climbed down to the engine compartment- nothing special: two huge diesels, brass gauges and controls. He opened storage compartments. Nothing seemed out of the ordinary. He didn't know much about boats but he couldn't find anything else to inspect. Of course, he didn't know what he was looking for and that made it harder to find.

Dewey Block's son said the man lived on this boat but here were no living quarters. He climbed down a metal stair beneath the engines. There had to be more. He ran his hands over walls- nothing. He tapped his foot on the metal grid floor. It was solid. He found an access door labeled 'fuel tanks,' turned a wheel to open the water-tight hatch and ducked to enter an under-belly plumbing chamber. There was a narrow catwalk forward. There, another water-tight door had long ago been painted over. He strained to break it free. As it creaked opened, the long-closed room exhaled a noxious cloud of dust. Kelley choked and rubbed his eyes. He peered into a filthy dungeon-like chamber.

Everything was covered in a half-inch of grime and dust. A stale, sour vinegar smell almost made him gag. He found a light switch but it didn't work. So, he used his key chain pen light to scan what must have been a windowless cabin deep in the belly of the boat. Books and magazines stacked three feet deep. Under the filth, walnut paneling and furniture of leather and brass must have once made this a comfortable hideaway.

He held his breath but the overwhelming odor still stung his eyes. Several old rear-projection TVs sat side by side surrounded by boxes of VHS tapes. He picked up a few and blew dust off their jackets, pausing to sneeze afterwards. They were porn. He showed the narrow beam of his light around in the fog of dust. A tangle of wires behind the TVs probably once led to Closed Circuit TV cameras that gave an outside view, essential for a paranoid recluse. All in all, Dewey must have been a very sad little man hiding in the belly of his boat, watching dirty movies, drinking and probably cursing the world.

A small hatch behind the TVs was locked. Kelley wiped dirt from a peeling sticker and used his pen light to read "emergency exit only." He didn't bother with it. He needed air, needed to get out of the moldering rot of this tomb and breathe again. The dust was suffocating and the constant motion of the boat brought added nausea. He needed the smell of fresh salt air and sea spray. He needed to be back on deck, back where the sun made him squint and the world seemed alive.

After another hour stumbling around on the tossing boat, Kelley was satisfied. He had seen it all. With another heroic leap, he landed back on the dock, collected himself and walked to his car. The wind was even stronger now. His pant legs snapped like a flag in a hurricane.

As he drove out of the compound, Mister Hajita stared with folded arms and then locked the gate behind.

That damned boat had to fit in somehow. Dewey bought it after he became a hoarder and miser. Why? Patrick bought it when the IRS came after Dewey—even though the man had cheated him. Why? It's moored at this cult-like technology immersion center for Asian-Americans. Why? Dewey was probably killed on this boat and Eli Lee was captured aboard. There had to be more, just had to be. Maybe Aelan could shed some light if she would talk to him.

THIRD TUESDAY

Mrs. Adachi buzzed. "Ms. Comer, that rude man who barged into our office the other day is now on line two. His parents should have done a better job developing his social skills."

Aelan laughed. "You're right, but we must allow some leeway. He's a mainlander, after all. Thanks." She didn't want to admit it but she was actually looking forward to his voice. With a sigh and an amused smile she began, "Hello, Kelley. What have you done now?"

"I went to London to see the Queen. Well, okay, she wasn't in, so I went to the big island of Hawaii to see our boat."

She shook her head, "Our boat? So, have you decided to join the family business after all? I thought you were above that kind of thing." She could almost tell from his voice that he was leaning back with a smug grin, stretching out the way men do when they think they're in control.

"I just wanted to find out more about it. I've always been a history buff. Thought it would be cool to see where Dewey Block met his end. I enjoyed my trip but I'm not sure your friend, Mister Haji Babba or whatever, liked me very much."

She laughed. "That's the understatement of the year. So, you want to know more. Well, I thought you would. To be honest, I hoped you would. All right, I'll meet you at the condo at eight.

We'll go over the operation. But understand this, I'll determine when we have sex and it won't be until I'm comfortable..."

He interrupted, "Wait, you said 'when,' not 'if.' Does that mean...?"

She came back instantly. "Of course. It's inevitable. I find you attractive and interesting. Every time you look at me, I feel as though you're making a mental contour map of my body. I think an eventual relationship is...well, inevitable. Just don't rush it. Things will take their own course in time...are you still there?"

"Yeah, I was just imaging the course and how much fun it will be to navigate."

She suppressed a laugh and shook her long black hair. "You're an idiot. Eight o'clock at your condo." She hung up and spun her chair. The fearsome Dragon Lady was acting like a schoolgirl.

An unlabeled button blinked on her call director. She snatched the receiver and sat back in her chair. "What did you find, Bennie?"

"Hey Sweetness, I've spent a very long night moving among the not-so-rich-and-famous of Honolulu's street society. I'll sleep later. Thanks for asking. Anyway, it turns out, my good buddy, former agent Diggins, lied to me. His story about his poor kidnapped daughter was pure bull shit. I found the girl he called his daughter. Her name is Sylvia, street name Slipper. She wouldn't give me her last name. In fact, she told me Diggins' divorced wife has a restraint order to keep him away from his real daughters after allegations of sexual abuse. The girl Slipper is a seventeen-year-old runaway whose real parents are Navy, stationed at Pearl. She had been living as Diggins' comfort girl for about six months but when he told her she couldn't use drugs in the house, she hit the street as a $50 stand-in-the-alley hooker."

Aelan drummed her fingers on the desk. "Bennie, what does any of that have to do with me? I don't deal with pedophiles or pimps or even mail-order brides. Why is he after me?"

"Well, Diggins thinks you do all of that. The Clark folks have him convinced that you are responsible for taking his little sugar plum from him. I know. I know. You just don't do that kind of thing. But, he thinks you're a coldblooded slave trader. He also thinks his buddy, Tongay, the Clark Shipping Container thug, is helping him. You know how paranoid those Clark people are." Bennie sounded serious. "Now that Agent Diggins is suspended, he's no longer useful to them. Between you and me, I think Mister Diggins needs to be very careful if he wants to collect a federal retirement."

"Bennie, after you get some sleep, I want you to check out a Kelley Price. He paid an unannounced visit to an operation we have on the big island. Find out what he wanted and why he didn't call me first, okay?"

"Yeh, sure, I know the Kelley guy. You had me scope him out when he first got here. I'll pay him a social call. In the meantime, you take care of yourself, Sweetness. It can be a hostile world out there."

She arrived precisely on time and stood at the condo door for a moment, catching her breath, wetting her lips and brushing hair from her eyes. Then she used her key and marched in, chin up and ready. He didn't speak, not even "hello." Kelley Price enveloped her in his arms and kissed her hard. He was a powerful man. She didn't really expect that. She pulled back, breathless and surprised, looked at him, and then wrapped her arms around his neck and pulled him into the deepest kiss of her life.

Things were definitely going to be different now, everything would be different.

He lifted her right out of her shoes, kicked the door closed and walked to the bedroom with her arms locked around his neck and her feet dangling. They tore at each other in unrestrained lust.

They had just begun their second round. She was on top of him, back arched, face straining at the ceiling, body slick with a sheen of sweat, when she suddenly went rigid. "There's someone in the other room."

In a cat-like move she was off, leaving him gasping and unsatisfied. She bent over to peek through the hinge crack just as the door slammed open throwing her back against the wall.

An ox of a man bounded in and made a quick scan. He grinned and spoke in a hoarse voice. "Two people, no clothes, no weapons, nothing to fear."

He looked fearsome enough. An oversized fireplug, he had gorilla arms, no neck and a fifty gallon drum for a body. His hair was curly and oddly thick like black sheep wool. His dark face showed pale scars and a yellow-toothed grin was more animal than human.

"Love birds." His deep voice had an accent. "Sorry to interrupt." He looked Aelan up and down. "Maybe I finish what you start. What you say, boss man?"

Aelan picked herself up. Kelley was standing up straight on the bed, probably to emphasize his height, she thought. "Don't you touch her," Kelley commanded with clenched fists and a reddening face. Clearly his blood flow had been instantly redirected. Buck naked, with a pale white body, he didn't look all that intimidating.

Fireplug laughed and showed the palms of his hands. "I don't hurt nobody." Then, with obvious sarcasm, "I just came to welcome you to the islands. We knew somebody would come to take Patrick Tooney's place. This woman's not strong enough for the business. Now, Mister New Boss Man, maybe we can make a deal. What you say? Wanna come have a talk?"

Kelley leaped from the bed and made a dramatic high pitched Karate yell as he kicked with all his might. His foot thudded against fireplug's chest without noticeable effect. Kelley fell back, bouncing off the bed. Fireplug leaned over him with a look of confusion.

Aelan slipped quietly into the walk-in closet while the two men faced each other. There, on a shelf, was the dragon box. *Damn, the thing was heavy.* She raised it over her head, held her breath and ran at the intruder.

Fireplug turned just in time to take the full force of the box against his forehead. He staggered, touched his head and inspected the blood on his fingers. He grinned and was about to speak when Aelan was distracted. Kelly, still naked, leaped once again from the bed and this time sent a jackhammer kick to Fireplug's chin. The big man's head snapped back and he collapsed in a pile.

Kelley stood over the unconscious body, tight-fisted and breathing through his teeth. Aelan ran to him. Her panic breathing began to subside. He kissed her on the top of the head and whispered in a James Bond imitation, "Actually, I prefer my sex without violence." She sort of laughed and snuggled. Kelley made her feel safe. *It had been a long time since she felt safe.*

After her heart and breathing became quiet, she spoke softly. "This man is Tongay Apu, muscle man for the container company. I'll put on some clothes and we'll deal with him." She pulled apart and looked in his eyes. "Well, you wanted to get involved with the family business. They seem to think you are the new boss. I'd say you're involved now."

Kelley gave her hand a parting squeeze. "Do you have to put on clothes? I like you like this."

Aelan pulled away almost playfully and stepped around the unconscious body on the floor. She had a plan. "There are zip-ties in the bottom drawer. Truss him up and use a dish rag for a gag."

Kelley bound Tongay. "This guy must weigh three hundred pounds. So, what are we going to do with this moron? I'm not going to be party to any murder. And who keeps zip ties in their bedroom drawer?"

"Don't be silly. We help people bypass immigration. We don't murder." She stopped and stared him down. "Did you really think that? Did you think I would kill someone?"

He feigned sheepishness. "Well, we haven't had our talk yet. I don't know what you do. By the way, your shirt tail is out. Hold still and I'll tuck it in."

She slapped his hand away. "Just wait. After we dispose of this rhinoceros we'll come back and have our talk. Then, I'll let you tuck me in.

Aelan turned to the door as Bennie Sepatski knocked four times, then another four and then two separate knocks. It was Beethoven's fifth knuckled on the door. Aelan took a breath, collected herself and let him in.

His mouth fell open at the sight of Tongay's body. "Oh my goodness, girl, what have you done now?"

Aelan tried to sound businesslike. "He broke in, Bennie. What else could we do?" She looked over at Kelley. "You know Mister Price. He's involved. Clark thinks Kelly's the new boss."

"The new boss, huh? We've already met, actually." Bennie grinned. "Just another shitty day in paradise, huh pilgrim."

Kelley, now fully clothed, sounded tentative. "Oh yea, you're the guy at the beach bar who wanted to sell me an oil well or something."

"Oil well partnership, it's a good deal. You should consider…"

Aelan was short. "Bennie, can you get rid of him?" She looked down at the massive figure on the floor.

Bennie exhaled long and slow. "Of course I can dump our friend Tongay, but you know what this means. They aren't going to be happy that you sent their meat grinder to fetch you and you returned him with a bow tied in his hair."

"It couldn't be helped. He broke in on us and tried to drag Kelley off to meet Clark. I couldn't allow it." She crossed her arms and held her head high.

Bennie gave his most insincere grin. "Mister Price, this little lady is the joy of my life but she is going to put me in my grave before she's done. I would advise you to run while you still have the chance…but it's already too late isn't it? I smell sex in this room and I'm sure she has you completely under her spell. So, take this warning. If they really think you are the new power in Excelsior, you'll be their target and you had better damned well be careful."

Bennie nodded with finality and turned back to Aelan. "I'll get a laundry cart from the basement and be back in a couple of minutes. Any place special you want him dumped?"

"Up in the hills, away from any buildings. Search him for cell phones so he can't call. I want it to take a while for him to get back to Honolulu. I need time to think. We can't have an open war on the streets. We have to work something out."

Bennie was gone with a shrug and she turned back to Kelley. "You've been awfully quiet. I think it's time for our talk." She took his hand and he allowed himself to be led onto the balcony. She stood and felt the ocean breeze. "Look down at all the people in the street, normal looking people going about their lives. Some are tourists. Some are hustlers. Some are just trying to make a living. They all came from somewhere. They all probably needed help."

"And you were there to help them."

"You haven't spoken through this little event. What exactly do you think is going on?"

"I'm afraid I'm in the middle of a gang war. Are we about to go to the mattresses?"

"I don't know what that means, but we are under attack. Clark has been involved in the slave trade ever since his father started helping Vietnamese boat people. They shipped in refugees, criminals and ordinary people seeking a better life. All Clark is interested in is money. They charge a fortune to smuggle these poor souls across the ocean locked in cargo containers. A mattress, some water, rice and a portable toilet—the refugees spend a week or more locked in a metal box with no protection from heat and cold. Many die. Many get sick. All are cheated."

She leaned against him and he put his arm around her. "When these people arrive in Hawaii or San Francisco, they are sold to be used up and abused. As illegals, they have no rights and no recourse. Many become unwilling sex workers. More are unpaid laborers. It's a terrible life. They have no medical care, inadequate food and housing. Suicide and murder are the major causes of death."

Kelley finally spoke. "So, how do we fit into this mess?"

"Clark's business is declining. Fewer Asians are willing to pay to come to America. They don't see us as the land of opportunity so much. The idiots at Clark don't get that. They think it's my fault, that I am taking market share from them."

"Market share, just like any other business? So, really, what is it *we* do?"

She breathed deep. "I'll tell you everything I know but there is much that Patrick never told me. Kelley, I'm running a multi-million dollar illegal operation and being hounded by real gangsters—and I don't even know how it works. I am so scared. I don't know what to do. I have nobody to turn to, nobody but you."

"Sh-h-h." He held her tight as she shuddered and sighed. He kissed her forehead and said, "Tell me what you know."

"I run the cruise line and I know every detail of that operation. We use foreign workers on our boats. Over in Thailand and Vietnam, they can get off the boat without visas. Instead, they get shore passes which are not well accounted for. When they get back onboard, our customers mix in with the real workers using fake shore passes. That won't work for entry into the U.S., of course. That's where the tour boat comes in. We take it out to meet the ocean liner in international waters, pick up our customers and sneak them directly to the compound on the big island."

"Yes, the compound where I met your charming Mister Hagi-whatever. Just what goes on there?"

She felt a surge of confidence, almost pride, as she spoke.

"The minute they board the cruise ship, they are dressed in American style clothes and begin learning English. From toddler to elderly, they must speak only English. They work menial jobs on the boat to get them used to being around westerners. They eat hamburgers and fries and watch recorded television. We teach them U.S. laws and customs. At Haida, they are completely immersed in our culture. They live in apartments with microwaves and DVD players. Some have never slept on a mattress before. There are shops, imitations of Starbucks, McDonalds, Pizza Hut and others. They must read menus and order. They learn to drive, attend church and play our sports. They are Americanized."

"Wow," Kelley sounded genuinely impressed. "So that's what Haji-whatsits does."

"Dr. Hajita is an organizational development specialist. He is very good at it. When the customers graduate, we give them jobs and housing in the community. They are paired with sponsor families to ease the transition. Over four decades, we have transitioned thousands of new, productive Americans into our society."

Kelley seemed uncomfortable. "That's wonderful, Aelan, but it sounds like a charity, a non-profit run by selfless saints."

Now, it was Aelan who felt uncomfortable. "Yes, and that's where my knowledge ends. We get paid $20,000 for each customer. I don't know where the money comes from. I don't know who recruits the customers and who brings them to the overseas ports. I simply don't know who runs the Asian operation and I don't know what's going to happen without Patrick. Everything may collapse. We may all go to jail."

Kelley grinned. "Look on the bright side. We might all get killed by these Clark hoodlums and not have to worry about it."

She smiled and felt an unaccustomed calm as she hugged him. Her head fit against his chest and she could hear his heart beating, steady and strong. Her voice was soft. "These are my people, my life. I will not give in to a bunch of crooks. I won't, Kelley. I'll die first."

She felt his hand patting her back. "I won't let you die."

"I couldn't feel more confident. I'm going to be protected from the Honolulu mob by a statistician from New Jersey."

"Come on, who knows the mob better than a Jersey boy? You know, I'm actually..." He let that thought die. "I found a little red book, kind of a coded accounting ledger of Patrick's. Maybe we can figure out what it means."

Aelan pulled apart feeling a spark of hope. "Let's take a look. Maybe we can decipher it. You love puzzles. You said you were fundamentally a geek, a 'joy straw' you said. Well, let's go suck some joy into this mystery."

WEDNESDAY

Kelley worked with her all night on the little red book. Aelan deciphered the dates and numbers of "customers" scheduled for the next two months. She said she understood the schedule for messages providing pictures and descriptions to the document forgers at Haida but could not decode the actual names and addresses. Still, it was a good start.

As the sun broke over the ocean, she complained that she didn't like Patrick's fancy coffee maker, had never liked it. She wanted a stiffer brew from the Kona Coffee shop on Kalakawa Avenue. He rubbed his red eyes, donned his white knight outfit and volunteered to get coffee and pastries. She warned him to use the alley and he nodded like a good little boy. He almost said, "Yes, dear," but that would have been a little too sarcastic after a stressful all-nighter that included a fight with a gangster.

He did take the alley, maneuvering around a belching, clanging garbage truck that left little room. Kelley took a deep breath and had to laugh. Only in Hawaii did the morning garbage smell sweet. Papaya, pineapple, guava and rum gave everything a fruity, exotic scent. He lifted his chin to sunlight visible from above the tall buildings. Morning mist flowing down from the mountains dampened his forehead. After his night with Aelan, the world seemed a brighter place.

The garbage truck's mechanical arms slammed down a dumpster with warning bells and hydraulic noises. A worker in a blue jumpsuit motioned him to step back from the loose garbage cans and Kelley complied, backing up toward a gray van. The van's sliding side door opened.

"Mister Price," a voice called. Kelley had to stoop to see who was speaking from inside. It was a chubby, middle-aged man with thinning hair and a rumpled Aloha shirt. "I've wanted to meet you ever since you came to the islands," the man said. His voice seemed weary.

Kelley bent lower to speak but then two men slammed into him from behind like a pair of tacklers in a football game, propelling him head-first through the open door. His face rammed into rumpled man's lap. He felt his feet being shoved in and kicked but the door was already closing. He drew back, ready to punch with all his might but rumpled guy rammed a pistol under his chin forcing Kelley's face up.

They were in a tangle. Kelley scrunched on top of rumpled guy, arm still cocked but now wavering. Their faces were so close they smelled each other. A second gun touched the back of Kelley's head as the two tacklers took positions in the front seats. Rumpled guy spoke.

"So, how about we relax and have a civilized conversation. What do you say?"

Kelley sat back as much as he could with both gun barrels still against his head. He tried to sound as if nothing special was going on. The awkward body position made his voice sound strained. "Sure, I've got a few minutes to spare." Fear always brought out the smart-ass in him, even as a kid bullied by his brothers.

Rumpled guy nodded to the other gunman. Both lowered their weapons and sat back. "I'm Nelson Clark, Nelson Clark

Junior actually. I'm sure you're aware of my company, Clark Containers." Kelley nodded as he scanned the back seat area. There was no inside door handle. The window was covered with shatter-proof steel mesh. It was like a prisoner transfer vehicle. He sat back and settled in for the ride.

"You appeared on the scene rather suddenly after Tooney's unfortunate death. No one in the business has ever heard of you. Where did you operate previously?"

Without even thinking, Kelley replied honestly, "Bulgaria."

Nelson Clark made a thoughtful face. "Bulgaria, that's pretty exotic. Well, I don't know the circumstances of your involvement but here's the deal. We don't need to fight each other. We need to cooperate. Ever since Patrick started his touchy feely program, I've been losing business. Then, your sleazy lawyer got my inside man suspended from ICE so I'm in a real tight situation. I don't know exactly how you guys bypass customs and immigration but I have containers inbound and no way to safely unload them. I need your help. Whatever you're doing, I want in. I know you get roughly twenty thousand dollars a head for your people. I make barely ten. Tell me how you do it and I'll leave you completely alone."

Kelley wasn't sure of his next move. "Why would I do that?"

"Well, we need to just hit the reset button. My father's dead. Patrick Tooney is dead. That little girl Aelan Comer is in way over her head. Our two organizations have been fighting ever since I was a kid. Every now and then it gets violent and somebody dies. That's no good for business. I'm in this for money and you're hurting my business."

Kelley was stalling. "Why don't you tell me about your business?"

Nelson ran a hand along his jaw and thought. "We started out selling container rides to the Vietnamese boat people who only made it as far as Hong Kong. Back in the seventies there was almost no port security so we brought our containers here to Honolulu. It was easy. We sold the workers to pineapple growers so we made money on both ends. The immigrants paid us. The growers paid us. For twenty years it was a growth industry. But now, demand for our services is falling. ICE is making life more difficult. We supplement our inbound trafficking by finding 'companion' girls for wealthy overseas clients. Our people scout street girls, usually runaways. We take them under our wing and groom them. After two months working Honolulu, if no one has come looking for them, we offer a contract, give them a new identity and ship them off to 'Neverland.' That nets us about a hundred grand per."

Kelley still didn't have an angle and he was getting worried. "I don't see how we fit into your operation."

"Customs, man, you have customs solved. We just lost our rainmaker. He made sure our containers were overlooked by inspectors. Now, here's what I know about your operation. You put your clients on a cruise ship but somewhere prior to Honolulu Port Immigration processing, they disappear. Somehow, you are bypassing the system. I've even tried to infiltrate your operation by signing up informants in Thailand and paying the twenty grand you charge to ship them here." Nelson Clark's voice grew exasperated. "I never heard from any of them. Somehow, you got to them all."

Kelley took another inventory of the car. His options seemed very limited. Nelson Clark still cradled a gun in his lap. The front seat passenger held his pistol steady at eye level. The driver paid no attention. They were out of the city winding though steep hills.

"So," he said deliberately, "if I get your containers by customs, what are you offering?"

Nelson seemed taken aback. Then he grinned. "You got some balls, huh. I'm driving you into the jungle and you're shaking me down." He turned to the gunman in the front seat. "Can you believe this guy?" Then back to Kelley. "You Bulgarians all pricks or is it just you, tough guy?"

Kelley felt his gut tighten but he kept up a bold posture. "I'm not Bulgarian. I'm actually from New Jersey."

"Jersey? Like Tony Soprano New Jersey?" There was a note of admiration in Nelson Clark's voice.

"No, it's nothing like that. The Tony Soprano on that HBO show was a pussy. I come from the real New Jersey, the tough neighborhood." Kelley hoped he wasn't overplaying his hand.

Nelson broke out laughing so hard he wheezed "Okay, I'll give you ten percent, a thousand dollars a head."

"Eighty." Kelley looked out the window. He was sweating hard but audacity seemed his only ploy.

Nelson's laughter stopped abruptly. "Eighty? You out of your flippin' mind? I import these people for ten thousand miles on a boat and you get all the money? You're nuts." He turned to the window and fumed. After a long, tense silence he turned back. "I'll give you twenty, not a cent more."

"Seventy." Kelley couldn't bring himself to make eye contact. He was taking a giant risk but he saw no options. *Bully or be bullied.* He thought he was better off as the aggressor.

Nelson Clark's eyes and lips grew narrow. "Thirty, payable after they are safely out of the customs and agriculture holding ramp." He sounded mean. "And, if they don't make it through customs, you go for an open-water swim. "But it sounds as though you enjoy swimming with sharks." He shouted to the driver. "Johnny, take this asshole back to his place."

"Actually, Johnny, I was on my way to the Kona Coffee shop if you don't mind. And Nelson, I'll be the bigger man here. I'll take the thirty and don't worry about the payment. I'll be by to collect."

The ride back was tense and silent. They dropped Kelley off in front of the coffee shop without farewells. He stood for a moment, noting the license number. Slowly, his Superman was transformed back into Clark Kent. His legs began to shake and he rushed to the bathroom unsure whether he needed to pee, or to just throw up.

WEDNESDAY NIGHT

Aelan called an urgent meeting. With quick welcomes and nods, she herded an odd assortment of ten men into the back offices of Pacific Voyager's headquarters. They sat. She stood. There was no doubt who was in charge.

"I'd like to introduce Mister Kelley Price." All eyes turned to him. "Kelley, this is a working group loosely allied with PASS, the Pacific Alliance to Stop Slavery. Our members include scholars, lawyers, activists, transportation specialists and other concerned citizens who oppose human trafficking but still believe in the American dream. We, the people in this room, are the creators and operators of the Haida Corporation."

Turning back to the group, she continued. "Kelley is Patrick's nephew and has inherited the Haida compound property on the big island. He is new to the operation but Nelson Clark believes him to be Patrick's replacement and that puts him in danger. This morning Clark's goons grabbed Kelley off the street and threatened to kill him if he didn't help get their containers through Honolulu customs. It seems that a Special Agent Diggins, the same man who was harassing me, was on Clark's payroll to make sure Customs overlooked any human cargo. Now, Diggins is suspended and, unbelievably, Nelson has come to us demanding aid. He is trying to force us to help them. I see this as a significant escalation of tension."

She paused to survey faces. There were looks of concern, pursed lips and fierce scowls. Kelley just felt confused. Every day with Aelan revealed some new twist. He felt he was being drawn ever deeper into a dark hole that might just turn out to be a bottomless pit. Of course, it might be a pit filled with gold.

Aelan paced. "During his abduction, Mister Price got away by telling them he could provide assured acceptance of Clark's next shipment. So the question is…how do we deal with this situation without Kelley Price getting killed?"

An older man with a long face raised an equally long, bony finger. His voice sounded strained, even tremulous. "There's more to consider. We must not allow the immigrants in these containers to be enslaved. We must not allow them to be taken by Clark."

Aelan made an exaggerated nod. "That is certainly true, Doctor Peterson, but first—how do we even get them through customs?"

A thick man in a workman's uniform shirt raised his hand. "Actually, with current government cutbacks in staff, the odds of an individual container being opened by customs is about eighty to one. Most inspection is by bomb and drug dogs or by radiation sniffers. If we do nothing, the human cargo will almost certainly get through without incident. I don't think that's the threat."

The old man sounded agitated. "If we do nothing, then it will appear we are in collusion with these bastards. We will be aiding in the criminal debasement of human beings."

Aelan spread her hands. "Okay, let's consider the reality. The containers will probably get through without our intervention. Bobby, if we can get container ID numbers, can you put trackers on them?"

The thick man who seemed to know about containers raised his eyebrows. "Sure, that would be no problem."

Aelan crossed her arms and continued to stare. "How about this? We let Clark think they are home free. We track the containers to the offload and stage a rescue."

The old man was still agitated. "Can't be the HPD. The Honolulu Police Department has shown no more interest in human trafficking than they have in prostitution. They cannot be trusted. ICE, once involved, will simply deport the immigrants."

Aelan had a devious look. "Not if the ICE agents are fakes. What if we imitate agents, rescue the hapless immigrants and put them into our program. Clark will think he was protected through Customs. Then, he pays the agreed fee while we hijack the cargo and leave him empty-handed."

Kelley cleared his throat and spoke. "He'll never buy it. He'll know it was us. Who else is there to suspect? This will spark a war."

A Polynesian looking man with shoulder-length black hair spoke with a steady voice. "Then it should be war. We have tolerated these monsters long enough. I say it's time to put them out of business—for good."

There were murmurs and muttered swearing. Aelan looked distressed. She raised her hands again. "Quiet please."

Kelley stood, took a breath and bit his lip. "Let's analyze the situation. Help me out here. I'm new. How big is Clark and how much muscle does the organization wield?"

It was Bobby, the thick guy in a uniform who began. "Altogether, Clark employs about sixty people. Most are legitimate. They track containers, process orders and arrange forwarding. Only ten or eleven individuals are actually engaged in trafficking. Nelson Clark keeps all that very close to his chest. Everyone in the organization probably knows what's going on but they don't touch the illegal stuff. As for the leg breakers, there is only Tongay and his Micros, about six in all."

Kelley almost laughed. "Micros? I've seen Tongay and that guy certainly looks like a Macro to me."

There were muted chuckles. The professor with the long face explained. "The term Micro refers to Micronesians. They are not really U.S. citizens but, as members of the Compact States, the Federated States of Micronesia, they have visa-free U.S. travel rights and some benefits. They have flooded Hawaii and become a persistent underclass easily led into crime. This all stems from the American nuclear testing on their islands..."

Aelan sounded impatient. "Thank you, John. I think Kelley gets the picture. But back to the question, can we pull off a mock raid?"

A short, muscular man with dark skin and eyes to match spoke quietly. "I can do it. My recent immigrant group would love to poke these Clark hoodlums in the eye. They hate what is being done to their fellows. If you provide a couple of Anglos to play the role of ICE agents, my people will handle Tongay and his thugs."

The room grew quiet. Someone was breathing heavily. Kelley didn't understand. "When you say 'handle the thugs,' what exactly do you mean?"

The dark man's voice remained stern. "I mean to send them to join their ancestors so they may atone for the many crimes they have committed against my people. Their spirits will be exiled to the forest, never to trouble mankind again."

Kelley wanted clarity. "You mean to kill them."

"I mean to do justice."

Aelan looked desperate. "This is a drastic step. We need to be thoughtful and very, very careful about such a move. I don't want to hurt anyone unnecessarily. Isn't there a better way? Please, help me find a peaceful solution."

Dark man said, "When a tiger attacks, you do not negotiate, you defend. Time for negotiation is long past. Time for defending is now. My people are ready."

Aelan stiffened and stood to her full five feet four inches. "Well, I am not. I will not sanction killing even to protect..."

The dark man spoke through clenched teeth. "You do not need to sanction anything. My people are weary of being treated as livestock, as sub-human creatures. This man Clark has been tolerated too long." He stood to his full five and a half feet with chest out and fists clenched. "No more talk. I am ready. When the containers you speak of come, we rescue the souls inside. I will 'handle' Clark and his people. I am Qui and I speak for all who are enslaved."

The air in the room went dead still. Aelan looked distressed. She extended a hand and started to speak just as two people began to applaud. More joined. Others mumbled support. Almost every head nodded approval. Kelley glanced from face to face. They were ready for a war.

Whether Aelan liked it or not, the meeting was over. Dark man turned and left. Everyone else stood as though there was nothing else to say. Kelley went to Aelan and put his arm around her shoulders. He felt a strange mix of apprehension and excitement, almost a thrill—fighting the bad guys, possibly killing or being killed. She didn't seem to appreciate the adventure.

Kelley held her for a long time until she grew quiet and sighed with resignation, "Damn it, I'm trying to run things as intelligently and peacefully as I can. Why won't they listen?"

He shushed her and pressed her head against him. Someone cleared his throat. Both Kelley and Aelan turned to see Bennie

Sepatski still sitting at the conference table. He spoke in an offhand way. "This meeting must have been difficult for the lady. Let's give her a minute to breathe shall we? How about you walk me to my car, Mister Price?"

Kelley thought that an odd request but Aelan pulled away and indicated with a brush of her hand for him to go.

Bennie led him to a service elevator in the back of the Pacific Voyager offices. Once the door closed he folded his hands before him, rocked on his heels and looked at the ceiling. "Mister Price…"

"Kelley."

Bennie ignored him. "Mister Price, do you know what I do here?"

"Well, Mister Sepatski…"

"Bennie."

"Well Mister Sepatski, I think you are an investigator for Excelsior or Haida or whatever."

"Partly true, but only partly. My real job is to take care of my little girl, Aelan. Patrick asked me to do that before he went—and Mister Price, I take that duty very seriously. You may think you are here just because of Patrick's generosity or strong family ties. That may play a small part but the real reason you are here is to draw fire away from Aelan and the rest of us. Patrick knew of your CIA connection and thought you would be a fine adversary for Clark and his gang. So, you go on with your search for gold and enjoy your inherited wealth. Enjoy them, but take my advice." He gave Kelley a cold stare. "Watch your own ass. I'm here to protect Aelan, not you."

Kelley was shaken. "What do you know about the CIA?"

"It is my job to know things, to find things out. In Bulgaria, you worked for a pharmaceutical company but the paychecks deposited to your account came from a U.S. government source often used by the CIA. You had a classified discrete satellite setup at your 'clinic' and you received a lot of visitors who weren't patients. This stuff is easy to find so don't play innocent. So Mister Price, now, you see, it really is just another shitty day in paradise. I suggest you use your CIA training to protect yourself. I'll take care of Aelan."

The elevator door chimed and Bennie walked out into a parking garage without looking back. Kelley called after him. "Are you going to tell Aelan?"

Bennie kept walking but shook his head "no."

Kelley paced in the elevator and ran a hand through his hair. *How could Bennie know? How could anybody know?* He had to come up with a plan. He had to get control of things.

NOVEMBER 11, 1988

"It seems so strange to be here in a beachfront Waikiki bar after the past sixteen years. Things are going to hell over there. The Thais invaded Laos while the Burmese are busy having a revolution. The Vietnamese are pulling out of Cambodia and reinforcing the Laotian border. All my people are on the run. I had no place to go but here. So here I am, home...sort of."

"It's good to see you, Eli."

"Really? Why's that?"

Patrick Tooney was taken aback. "Eli, we've always been a team. Even though you've been missing–in-action bloody forever, I tried to look out for your best interests. I think I've taken pretty good care of Gina and Aelan while you were off playing G.I. Joe. Anyway, I always thought of us as friends."

Eli Lee grimaced and looked out at the ocean sunset. "Yeh, you're right. You've been a very decent man to my family, certainly better than I have."

There was an awkward silence before Patrick spoke again. "The movie 'Apocalypse Now' made me think of you out there, so far from civilization. So, can you tell me why you went back to the jungle for half a lifetime? It's not that I'm criticizing. I just want to understand."

Eli stared hard at the fading glow as though it might help him find the words. Then he began in a quiet, halting voice. "I went back in early 1972 right after Aelan was born. I went to take Gina's mother back to Laos. That was no easy trick with the war in full swing but she demanded and Gina always did what her mother wanted. The old woman was never happy about coming to America in the first place. When I finally got her back to Laos she wanted me to stay and train her people to fight. I thought it would be a short-term thing."

His tone softened. "The truth is, I felt good about doing it. I felt like I was doing something of real value. For the first time in my life, I was really needed."

He grimaced and sipped a drink. "There was something else. Something that compelled me to help those people." He took a deep breath and spoke in a deadpan voice. "Back before you came to the gunship squadron I had a flight, one particular flight, that changed me, changed my whole being. I had always been a hell raiser, hard drinker, wild man...whatever. I thought the war was a sporting event. We all did. But on this one night during the dry season, I was working on the night observation device hunting trucks."

He was getting into the story and his voice took on an intense, almost urgent tone. "Down near Delta 45, I saw a convoy, ten trucks on a narrow mountainside road. The B-52s had bombed that place so heavily there wasn't a blade of grass left. The trucks were completely exposed. I called out 'I'm tracking movers, large convoy.' The pilot rolled into attack position and I selected the lead truck, held him steady in my crosshairs and settled in. Two bursts from the twenty millimeter Gatling guns and his gas tank blew."

Eli gazed off into another dimension. "I quickly switched to the last truck in the column and called 'tracking.' The pilot fired again and this one exploded like a giant bonfire. It was the tanker truck carrying fuel for the others. It was also higher up the hill so its load of burning fuel ran down the mountain road igniting one truck after another until all ten were blazing.

We cheered, home team touchdown cheering. I remember shouting 'Die, Commie bastards.' Anti-aircraft guns on the ground opened up on us like the grand finale of a fireworks show. We stayed in orbit until the fires burned down and then flew on feeling victorious."

Now Eli sagged back. The emotion of reliving his combat adventure seemed to drain away. Patrick waited, allowing him time. When he spoke again, his voice was different. "The next night we showed up for our pre-flight intelligence briefing and they showed us the reconnaissance photos. The ten trucks were all burnt hulks but, in each, you could clearly see the mangled bodies. Limbs were twisted and frozen in odd poses. Everything was burned black like those cardboard boxes of chicken wings. We all cheered and applauded the death of so many enemy soldiers. Score one for the good guys."

Eli looked right into Patrick's eyes, right into his soul. "The intelligence briefer stopped that cheering cold. He said an Army road watch team had inspected the site. The bodies weren't North Vietnamese soldiers. They were Laotian slaves chained inside the trucks." He took a breath. "Patrick, I burned two hundred innocent people to death. They were helpless inside those trucks. I still carry that guilt like a cactus in my gut."

Patrick saw the pain in Eli's eyes and tried to find some words of comfort but what could he say?

Eli exhaled long and hard. "In some illogical way, fighting for Gina's people made me feel like I was atoning for the crime. I know it makes no sense, but that's how I felt. So I stayed. Truth is, Gina didn't really want me back. She had what she wanted from me. I brought her to America, gave her a child and then took care of her mother. She thought I would be a bad influence on my daughter and she was probably right. It made me really angry. I even changed the birth certificate so Eileen Lee, my daughter, became Aelan Comer. If Gina didn't want me, her daughter wouldn't carry my name. Man, she was furious about that."

Patrick had always wondered about the name change and Gina would never speak of it. "Are you going to see Aelan?"

Eli sidestepped the question and continued his story. "A man from Air America found me in a bar, heard my story and made me an offer. They had some guys in Vientiane coordinating with the tribes but they didn't really know the country or the people. I signed on with no idea what I was getting into. I didn't intend to stay long. In a month, I went from low level Air America employee to warlord of southern Laos. I was learning the language. I had credibility with the people. I was king of the mountain."

"What exactly do you mean, warlord?"

"I mean no-shit-warlord. The Ankha and other hill tribes wanted to fight but they needed a leader. Their culture was polite. It did not prepare them for decisive decision making but they were superb fighters. I filled that leadership void. I took a rag tag bunch of mountain boys with machetes and turned them into a guerilla force that terrorized the NVA. We raided their supply convoys, murdered their officers and blew up everything they built. The CIA gave us weapons and intelligence information and we became a small clandestine army. I kept thinking I'd get them organized, develop leaders among them and then bow out. But it didn't happen. I stayed, absolutely intoxicated with power."

He grinned. "Can you imagine, a misfit drunk like me commanding hundreds of jungle fighters? That movie you talked about, 'Apocalypse Now,' I think it was based partly on me and my small army." He stared back to the sunset. "I loved that time."

Patrick said, "What about Gina? Why didn't you stay in better touch with her?"

"Well, I did, sort of." Eli didn't sound so confident. "She was doing fine without me. All her needs were being met. She had you. She had Sepatski." He hesitated for just a breath and his brows pinched. "We wrote. Well mainly, she wrote to her mother."

Eli looked straight into Patrick's eyes. "You know she and her mother were addicted to heroin. They smoked it, or something like it, all the time back in their village. I knew they were bringing it in with the illegal immigrants. When your gold started running low, you and she were just getting the human smuggling operation going. She said there wasn't enough cash to support it. The heroin trade more than made up for the dwindling gold."

Patrick tensed and turned to look away. "I didn't know for a long time. She kept the books. I still have a great deal of guilt about becoming a drug runner."

Eli scoffed. "You have guilt? *You*...you have guilt? Do you have any idea how many people I've killed? I've burned farms, temples, whole villages. I let myself get seduced by it all. I thought my little private war was more important than my family, my future, even my life. I got so caught up in the violence I lost all sense of right and wrong. I even went back to the burial ground and took gold to finance my operation."

There was bitterness in his voice. "Even after Gina's mother died, I kept fighting." Anger gave way to a despondent whisper. "I can never repent for everything I've done. I don't belong out here in society. I don't even want the gold anymore. I'm constantly afraid I'll just crack and lash out at some innocent person."

Eli Lee was breathing deep. Even in the dimming light Patrick saw his eyes water. "I need some sort of redemption. I need to do something of value but I don't know where to look. I've even gone to church...but it felt as artificial as the Ankha spirit houses. I'm lost, Patrick. I've lost my marriage, my kid, my country, even my soul. I don't know..." Eli let his head fall. He was shaking slightly.

Patrick reached across the table to place an awkward hand on the bigger man's shoulder but Eli lurched away. "I'm sorry. I didn't mean to dump on you." He sucked a deep breath. "I got to go. Thank you for everything you've done for Gina and Aelan. I don't know how I can ever repay you."

As Eli stood, Patrick sat back. His voice turned cool, with no trace of emotion. "There is one thing you can do." Eli stood completely still except for a few blinks of his eyes. Patrick continued. "I think I know where Dewey hid most of his gold. I'm pretty sure it's still there. He's too miserly to spend it."

Eli was a statue.

"Dewey bought a sightseeing tour boat to live on. He keeps it at the Civic Marina." Patrick leaned forward and almost whispered, "I think the ballast in that boat is gold not lead. If we steal the boat and take the gold, we can get out of this damned heroin business and regain our self-respect."

Eli Lee turned and stood against the sunset with his back to Patrick. Slowly his fists relaxed, his breathing returned to normal and an angry scowl eased. When he finally spoke, it was businesslike

"Steal a boat? Sure, I can steal a boat for you."

NOVEMBER 12, 1988

Dewey Block knew that time had not been kind to his body. Almost sixty, he bore the effects of a lifetime of drinking. His belly had fallen below his beltline and now seemed to move independent of his frame. His hands trembled constantly and he had become as bitchy as an old washer woman.

He entered the Pearl City Dragon Lady bar and waved away a waitress. Gina saw him and came out from behind the bar wiping her hands on a towel. "Hello, bad news, what's your story?"

"Gina, is it true? Is Eli here? What's he want? Is he looking for me?"

"Slow down, big boy. Yes, Eli comes home. Says war is over, now it is time to be a normal man." She wiped more vigorously than her hands ever needed. "I don't know what to do. I don't really want him to be around Aelan. He has plans, big ideas." She shot a plaintive look at Dewey. "Everything is going good for us. I don't think we need big plans."

She threw the towel over her shoulder. Gina looked much younger than forty with long, silky black hair that fell onto a matching Mandarin collar black silk dress. Only her voice had aged. It gained the timbre and authority of a wise but stern woman.

"Eli's not going to hurt you. He doesn't want to hurt anybody. He wants war to be over. He forgives you for stealing his share."

Dewey sputtered. "But I didn't steal…and besides, we have enough money. We're doing okay aren't we?"

Gina was patient. "We, the corporation, are doing okay, but only because of the powder. Patrick hates the powder traffic. He has always hated it. He wants out. He and Eli have some sort of big plan."

Dewey put a hand on his bald scalp. "Wants out? How could he want out? That's our money maker." His shaking grew worse. "What will we do? What…?" His voice was almost a scream.

"Dewey, calm down. Come. Come back into the office. We can talk there." She took his puffy hand and he allowed himself to be led, mumbling and cursing, past the bar, past the rest rooms and into a small, paneled office. There she pushed him back into a wheeled office chair.

"Now, big guy, I calm you right down."

From under her desk, she produced a small metal box, extracted a syringe and bottle, smiled indulgently and filled the needle. "Now, we make you relax. Take a deep breath and you will see more clearly."

Dewey panicked and leaped at her. "What are you doing? You bitch, you're trying to kill me aren't you. The three of you have always wanted me dead. I knew it all along. You and Patrick and Eli—maybe even Sepatski—you want me dead."

He was screaming in her face. Gina reached out to touch him but Dewey grabbed her wrist with one hand and took a handful of her hair in the other. Then, in the most athletic move he had made in years, he spun and smashed her against the desk. Her cry of protest was quickly silenced. She slid onto the floor sending the old chair spinning on its ball bearing post.

Dewey stood open-mouthed. He rubbed both hands on his shirt front and whimpered. "I'm sorry. I'm sorry, but you can't take my treasure. It's mine." He was breathing too hard. "Got to do something. Got to fix this."

Gina moaned. Dewey placed a hand over her mouth. "Sh-hh. It's okay. Dewey just lost his temper. It's okay, girl. Stay calm." He saw the needle on the floor and grabbed it and the bottle. He wasn't sure how to give an injection. "Where does it go?" He lifted her slit skirt and ran his hands over the exposed skin of her leg hoping he would discover a good spot. Her skin was warm, smooth, the skin of a beautiful woman, a woman he had always desired.

Dewey Block bit his lip and looked her body up and down.

Patrick handled the big boat with confidence pulling up to a makeshift pier on the Big Island. Eli Lee jumped onto the pier and Patrick tossed him a rope as thick and heavy as a circus tent mooring. Once secure, they surveyed the area.

Patrick shielded his eyes. "I bought this place, almost a hundred acres of rocky land with protected access to the ocean. I mean to build a transition community here." He spread his arms and embraced the view with obvious pride.

Eli was less enthusiastic. "It looks like the surface of the moon. Nothing will grow here but sea grass."

Patrick just grinned. "I'm not trying to make farmers, just citizens. This place will work just fine. Come with me and I'll show you the vault I had built."

Eli squinted and scanned. "I don't see anything but black rock, black sand beach and water. Where's your vault?"

They hiked for less than fifty feet and stopped under the shade of a monolithic black rock that jutted out of the landscape. Patrick pointed behind the rock to marks left by construction equipment. He reached under a smaller boulder and released a catch. The much larger boulder turned out to be a thin shell covering a steel door. It took both of them to open that door and reveal a concrete ramp leading back into the hill.

Patrick beamed. "Here is where we'll keep the gold. It's a fortress with two-foot thick concrete walls and vault doors. We'll load the gold today. Later, I'll build my community buildings on top of it. We'll have easy access without arousing suspicion. Pretty slick, huh?"

Eli only shook his head. But after a moment, he laughed too. "Yeh, Pat. It's pretty slick."

Inside the vault was a small forklift. They drove it back to the boat and began unloading ballast bars. It was tough work. Just getting into the bilge area was an athletic event. The hatch was barely as wide as a man's shoulders and, once in the boat's belly, there just enough room to crawl. Patrick was smaller so he squeezed his way into the under-deck space and began wrestling ballast bars out.

The small man's hands repeatedly appeared and slapped the ten-pound metal bars up through the hatch onto the metal grid floor. Eli collected them. When he had all he could carry, Eli wound his way past the fuel tanks, through the engine room, up the stairs and onto the deck. He estimated each armful to be eighty pounds. To add to his labor, only about half the ballast bars turned out to be gold. The others were just lead but all were painted black. He needed the sunlight to be able to tell which were which and that committed him to carrying, not two tons of gold, but four or more tons of mixed gold and lead.

All afternoon they worked stopping only to down occasional bottles of water. By sunset there were two waist-high pyramids of metal bars on the deck. They were less than half done but the lack of daylight and overwhelming exhaustion brought a faltering, groaning end to their Herculean effort. They slept on the hard board deck of the boat. Without food or pillows or protection from the elements, they slept with the intensity of death.

At first light, both awoke, starving and stiff. Patrick made coffee and found some stale pop-tarts. Then it was back to the task. By early afternoon, the ballast bars were all topside and the gold ones loaded into Patrick's vault. The lead bars remained on deck. They would hire someone to put them back in the bilge.

They found two beers and were starting a sweaty celebration when the ship's radio-phone rang. Patrick roused and limped like an elderly cripple. His muscles protested every step. He answered the phone with irritation in his voice but, in an instant, his manner changed. All pain forgotten, he straightened and nodded. "Yes, I'll be there as soon as I can. No, don't do anything until I get there."

He hung up and sagged with both hands on the console. Then, he collected and walked out onto the deck where Eli sat with a questioning look.

"Dewey's dead. They just found his body. I don't know what this means. Can you get the boat back by yourself?"

"Yes, I think so. But how are you getting back to Oahu?"

"I'll radio for a helicopter from Hilo." Then Patrick looked pained. "Eli, I want you to know that I've always kept our shares honest. Everything is divided into four. One each for Gina, Dewey, me and you. Even while you were gone, I kept your money separate. I know Dewey is, or was, a thief but I want to keep his money for his heirs. I think it's the right thing to do. Are you all right with that?"

Eli hesitated for a minute and shrugged. "Of course. You've always been the responsible one. I trust your decisions. After all, you had no reason to protect my share over all these years. Sure, do what you think best."

WEDNESDAY

Captain Bjorn Olafson stood on the bridge of the great white cruise ship Pacific Voyager Mahalo and surveyed the scene. Inside his air conditioned wheelhouse, he was insulated from the swelter and chaos of the Haiphong dock. But down below, he could clearly see throngs of laborers fighting to get their goods through a bottleneck to the cargo loading ramp. They came with push carts, three-wheeled cargo motor bikes and small trucks. He imagined the sounds of shrill shouting, puttering engines and whining music. All he heard in his high-tech womb atop the ship was the soft blow of the air conditioning system and ever-present background music, Brahms, he thought.

But on the dock, skinny, shirtless men dripped sweat and shook angry fists as they barked insults and fought their way through the melee. Over the enormous ship's ramp hung a faded red banner with a Vietnamese gold star. Beneath it, teams of uniformed men with clipboards processed individual pieces of cargo with the dispassionate calm of bored bureaucrats. The inspectors appeared immune to the heat or the pandemonium around them.

Captain Olafson knew that, after being meticulously checked in and inspected, the drivers and cart pushers would descend into the darkness of a cavernous ship's hold. There, men clad only in shorts and sandals and slick with sweat, would direct traffic in a labyrinth of choking exhaust fumes, oven-like heat and dimly lit cargo bins. Somehow, despite the chaos, it all worked. That always amazed him.

The captain's staff assembled for their pre-departure reports. As he waited for them to settle in, he looked far out beyond the wharf. He stood on the highest object within sight. His ship, a virtual high-rise building, loomed over dockside cranes and Colonial French red-roofed buildings. Even nearby hills seemed puny beside his floating mountain of metal.

He was well aware of the power and influence of his position. A burly man with a jovial disposition, he was also a careful, demanding manager. As his people seated themselves, he asked, "So, how are progressing? Shall we make our scheduled departure time?" He looked first at the maintenance chief.

Engineer Gupta nodded enthusiastically. "Yes, we are doing very good. This time, the fuel is all delivered quite properly. Repairs to the passenger deck number two air conditioning duct are running behind but, no matter. We can depart whether it is finished or not. I see no difficulty to delay our time slot for the Harbor Pilot."

Olafson nodded approval. He turned to a chunky Asian woman. She wore a man's uniform and a butch haircut. "All right Chan, how about cargo?"

She stiffened and took a breath. "There is a holdup. Customs is being bitchy, as they always are. We slipped the inspectors almost two thousand Euros but they're still pecking away, taking their sweet time. They have found at least two opium shipments mixed with the loose general cargo but nothing in the bags of coffee or rice. That's where they usually focus. We'll make it on time if nothing else goes wrong." She sat back as though waiting for criticism. None came.

Without being asked, a man in a chef's coat embroidered with the name 'Caprelli' spoke. "For once, food deliveries are complete on time. We were unable to get sufficient puff pastry or beef but the seafood is all of good quality. With some changes to the menu we will manage.

The captain nodded and asked, "Passengers?"

A dark, thin man with a Semitic profile and British accent snapped his reply. "Yes Captain, all's quite on time. The tourists are wrapping up shore visits and will be delivered back to us at fourteen hundred hours Haiphong time. We'll have head count and baggage check complete no later than fifteen hundred. Everything ship-shape I should say." He sat back with a smirk. "Quite a different story than the Donnybrook at Manila."

Captain Olafson looked pleased. "Thank you Prentice. Thank you all. Well, all right then, let's get this rust bucket ready for cast off at zero six thirty Greenwich Mean Time." He slapped a meaty hand on the table with a laugh to signal the meeting was over.

As the group filed out onto the bridge he tapped Chan's rather manly arm. The captain leaned close. "Everything *else* going well?"

She nodded while looking left and right, and spoke cautiously. "Yes, Captain. We have a total of six forty-kilo packages sewn into life raft casings. They are all slung on the ship's utility boat. From that position, they can be immediately jettisoned. If we have as little as thirty seconds notice of a raid, they will go right to the ocean floor. They definitely won't float. But, if all goes well, we will offload them along with the illegal immigrants when the tour boat meets us near Kauai. Our contact in Hawaii says the buyer is ready... with half a million Euros."

The big man slapped her shoulder playfully. "Good, very good work. So tell me Chan, what will you do with your share?"

The Chinese woman smiled slowly. "I shall buy an American motorcycle and go to Hollister, California."

"What? What is in Holly Steer California?"

She twisted the throttle on an invisible motorcycle and made a varoom sound. "It is the biggest motorcycle rally in the world. There, I will be a... biker chick." She grinned as though she had just been chosen prom queen.

With so much confusion and shouting down on the dock, no one at the check-in paid much attention to the gaggle of eighty or more ship's crewmembers as they pushed their way past the mob waving little yellow shore passes. The placid-faced officials simply motioned them on. The crew stayed together in tight groups to hide children behind them.

The captain watched as his cabin crew with immigrants mixed among boarded undisturbed. Then, he was interrupted by an apologetic steward who scrambled up the outside stair and almost shouted, "The Hanoi buses are arriving early." The steward was still panting from exertion as the captain pushed by him and grabbed a microphone.

He held the mic to his lips and boomed with the authority of a General Patton. "All stations, all decks, prepare for immediate reception of passengers. Clear the gangways and position greeters. All baggage handlers move immediately to your assigned stations." Then he turned and thrust the mic against the steward almost bowling the man over. The steward fumbled and managed a screech over the Public Address system before making an awkward, fumbling translation into Vietnamese.

Like the cast of a theatrical production preparing for the curtain to go up, people swarmed in good order to their positions, adjusted their outfits and put on phony but convincing smiles. Almost everyone was ready as the motorcade of buses plowed through the crowd on the dock. Vietnamese soldiers wearing white belts and matching helmets cleared the way, blowing whistles, shouting and poking slow movers with their white batons. Suddenly, the chaotic dock grew still.

The buses came to a halt with a great whoosh of air brakes. Doors flew open and a seemingly endless stream of elderly tourists groped and stumbled down the steps. There, they were met by a line of slender, attractive women in colorful Ao Dai outfits, filmy silk pants under matching slit side tunics. The women bowed, smiled and draped strings of flowers over the arthritic necks of the tourists.

A grumpy man with bowed legs and a beer belly wore wrap-around sunglasses and black socks with his Bermuda shorts. His Aloha shirt bunched under a wide camera bag strap and his straw hat was ringed with sweat. Upon receiving his flower necklace, he tried to hug one of the Vietnamese girls. She backed away with an apologetic smile and bowed repeatedly. The man's wife, in a cotton print dress that clung to her sweaty haunches, lumbered down the bus steps to swat the laughing reprobate. Captain Olafson watched them and smirked. He sent an aide to invite the couple to dine at the captain's table that evening. They might be interesting.

After the frantic reaction to the early bus reception, things settled into an orderly flow and the big boat launched precisely on schedule. The proud captain, now in his dress whites, ordered a long blast of the ship's horn as it pulled away from the dock. Crowds along the shore waved enthusiastically at the tourists who left so many dollars behind. Tugboats turned the big ship into the Cam River channel and then shadowed alongside, ready to protect it from any obstacle until it cleared the last small sand island. There, the Harbor Pilot boat sounded a farewell blast of his horn and Pacific Voyager Mahalo headed out into the open water of the South China Sea just as sunset turned the sky into blazing, molten gold.

Captain Olafson finished his checklist, reviewed the navigation data and weather strips. Comfortable that everything was under control, he went to the upper dining room and joined his guests. An older Philippine steward wearing a white jacket with gold sleeve stripes began to make introductions. The geezer from the dock didn't wait. He half-stood and thrust out his hand.

"Bertie Ellison. This is my wife, Maude. Pretty slick little operation you got here, Captain."

"Thank you, Mister Ellison. I hope you're enjoying your cruise." They all sat and the captain continued. "You know, you and your fellow passengers are a unique group. Not everyone, after all, is interested in a thirty-day cruise. Almost all our clients are retired, comfortable with themselves and able to survive a month without television or cellphones." He scanned the room and continued. "We have a few writers seeking time without distraction. There are divorcees and other refugees from stressful life situations trying to get away and regroup. There are some who just hate to fly and are willing to take the time for an extended cruise. And then, there are always those who are just seeking the seclusion of the open sea. So tell me, why are you here?"

Bertie Ellison leaned back with a grin. "Me and the old lady decided we were tired of being full-time baby sitters for our grandkids. We was going out to see the world. You know, all the faraway places with strange sounding names, but Maudie's one of them that just won't fly. Me, I wanted to see North Viet Nam." He made it rhyme with ham. "But tell me something, Captain, how do you guys make any money with so few passengers?"

Captain Olafson indulged. "Actually, only the top two of eight decks are for passengers. You are a bonus for us. This ship and its sister vessel, Pacific Voyager Aloha, operate primarily as cargo carriers for shippers with less than container-sized loads. The container ships offer lower prices but they have very high rates of damage, often leave containers exposed to the elements and suffer up to ten percent loss in transit."

He picked up a piece of tableware. "Consider this fork. Craftsmen make these pieces individually, works of art. On our ship, such things are protected in a climate controlled locker and treated with care. We are the preferred shipper for many artisans and importers willing to pay a premium."

Bertie didn't seem all that interested but the captain continued.

"We maintain the upper two decks as luxury suites for cruise passengers. I think you will agree your accommodations are first class, yes? In addition, we are the only cruise ships operating trans-Pacific, the very last passenger ships operating from Hawaii to Asia. And," he sounded proud, "on top of that, we are the only U.S. based carrier to serve Vietnam."

Bertie Ellison perked up. "Yeh, I was particularly wanting to see North Viet Nam. See, I was a B-52 tail gunner during the war. On our bus tour, we got to see a wrecked B-52 tail sticking up out of a pond. They showed us the Hanoi Hilton. They even had a picture of that bitch Jane Fonda on a North Vietnamese anti-aircraft gun." Bertie shook his head in disgust. "We bombed the living hell out of them gooks and now we're paying them to give us tours."

"Gooks?" the captain repeated, losing some of his charm.

"Yeh, that's what we called 'em all—gooks, slope heads, chinks. You remember, that's what all us Americans called 'em."

The captain sat for a moment sucking an invisible lemon. Then, he abruptly stood and straightened his jacket. "Please forgive me. I have just remembered something that demands my attention immediately." He paused. "By the way sir, I am Norwegian, not American. There is no North Vietnam anymore. They won the war so now it's just Vietnam. And, for your information, my wife is Vietnamese. I hope you enjoy your meal. Good evening."

Mrs. Ellison looked shocked. "Well, I never..."

Bertie waved a dismissive hand. "Don't get your panties in a knot, Maudie. He's a foreigner married to one of *them*. You'd expect him to be a weirdo. No reason to fret about it. Just be careful of the food. These people eat anything."

As the captain passed, the steward whispered, "I did not know you were married, sir."

The captain made a casual shrug. "Oh, I'm not."

FRIDAY

In the two days since Aelan's meeting, Qui had quietly organized his own rescue plan. It was very different from the one Aelan thought was being carried out. Bobby, a crane operator on the dock night shift, was a key player. He identified the two Clark containers by serial number and stacked them behind others making it awkward for inspectors and almost guaranteeing they would be overlooked.

In the wee hours of that morning, Qui and seven men dressed in mechanic's jump suits rode a maintenance truck into the customs holding yard using the fake ID badges Bobby supplied. They found the two containers, broke metal band seals and swung the huge doors open to release an eye-stinging odor of urine and rotting garbage.

Eight people who had endured an ocean voyage locked in these portable prisons looked out with owl-like expressions. The adults seemed small and frail as they clutched a few belongings and clung to each other. Four very frightened children still huddled deep in dark corners of the stinking metal boxes. Qui reassured them, speaking broken Chinese. There was always someone in any immigrant group who spoke a little Chinese.

The refugees were packed into the overcrowded maintenance truck and driven out. The adults were given matching worker's jumpsuits. Qui knew this was the most dangerous part of the operation. Vehicle exit searches were common and it was almost impossible to keep the now excited, chattering immigrants quiet. They wanted to look out at their new home. They wanted to cheer. They wanted to sing and rejoice. They were done with hiding and cowering.

But, on this night, the truck passed out of the chain link fenced dock yard with just a wave from a weary guard. Qui and three other men stayed behind. They replaced the immigrants inside the containers, two men in each. Bobby closed the huge metal doors behind them and replaced the soft metal band seals. The men inside settled onto filthy mattresses and waited. Just about sunrise a crane hooked onto the containers and dumped them onto a flatbed trailer one stacked on top of the other. Inside, Qui and his men were tossed and banged around in a chaos of dark, disorienting motion. Portable toilets spilled. Stinking mattresses flew into the air and slapped down along with a rain of dirty clothes and food scraps. Qui tried to protect himself and stay upright. He swore revenge for the atrocities committed against the brave pilgrims who had been forced to endure such hardship.

For an hour, the truck with its container load slugged through stop and go traffic. The containers were heat traps. Qui could only guess the temperature—one hundred, one ten—it could be higher. He should have brought water. Finally, the truck stopped. There was no movement for what seemed like eternity. Qui checked the GPS on his phone, surprised that it still worked inside the big metal box. They were on a back road high in the hills near pineapple fields. He called his location to his backup crew but that was unnecessary. The backup had followed them using a device Bobbie planted.

Then, in a blinding flash of sunlight, the door of Qui's container cracked open. It made a painful, creaking noise. A gruff voice yelled, "Everybody okay in there?" No one answered.

Another voice asked from a distance, "They alive?"

"Don't know. I'll check."

Qui squinted as his eyes adjusted to the brilliant light. He could just make out the form of a big man lumbering up a ladder to the top container door. The man turned on a flashlight. Qui and his companion pressed themselves behind an upturned mattress. They were keenly alert, aware of every sound, every movement. Qui could hear the big man's labored breathing after climbing the ladder.

Somewhere outside, the other man was shouting something. The big man in Qui's container was still huffing as he swept the beam of his light and called repeatedly. "Hello, anybody here? Damn it, is anybody here?" Big man grumbled and picked his way through the stench and wreckage inside the container kicking pots and bottles out of his way, swearing under his breath. When he was close enough to touch, Qui raised his pineapple machete and poked the man.

"Be quiet or I cut you." Qui realized his voice sounded shrill but maybe that was okay. Maybe it would be scary to hear one of the people they mistreated threatening back. The big man stumbled, gasped and fell on his butt.

He sputtered, "What the hell? Jesus Christ, where did you get that? Get away from me." He rolled and struggled to get to his feet, almost whimpering in fear. Qui's companion blocked escape with arms spread, his own machete held high. Big man's panic increased. He pulled something from under his shirt. In the dark it looked like a pistol. Qui's stomach tightened. He took one step forward and, with no hesitation, slashed down hard. The big man made terrible noises and began to flop around like a fish in the bottom of a boat.

Qui and his companion stepped out into the sunlight and saw another Anglo below them. This one had skinny, tattooed arms raised hold-up style. They climbed down the ladder and joined the other two rescuers confronting the tattooed man. Now, four very Asian-looking men with knives and machetes surrounded the skinny white man. He looked terrified, gulped a breath, stammered something and then, in a split second, turned and broke into a gut-wrenching sprint to the forest edge.

The four men watched him go with no effort to chase. Qui raised his phone to his ear. "This is liberation calling. Tell the lady she can send her fake ICE agents home. The rescue is already done. The passengers have been released and are ready to continue their voyage to freedom. They should already be delivered to your designated location. Wish them a big Aloha."

He forced a grin and slapped another man on the back. The four laughed and congratulated each other in varying degrees of accented English. Qui's smile faded. He felt none of the enthusiasm they showed. He left the group and climbed back into the container to stare quietly at the big man's body. He had never killed a man before. Even over all the lingering smells of urine, sweat and rot, there was a butcher shop odor of fresh cut meat and wet blood. There was no pistol beside the body, only a hand-held radio. Qui wasn't sure how to react. He told himself that he had no regrets for killing the man, but wasn't sure it was true.

The backup crew arrived to drive Qui and the others home in an oversized van. It was a celebration road trip with singing and good spirits. Somewhere along the way, Qui used a throw-away phone to call 9-1-1 and report the location of the smuggler's containers and the dead body of the big man. Then he sat back and took a breath.

Through an open window, he felt wind cooled by roadside vegetation. He felt strangely emotionless, almost empty. Qui watched the colorful forest of Hawaii passing by his window and stared into the dark tangle of broad green leaves, vines, flowers and mysterious shadows. In this tapestry of living things, he imagined he saw figures, shapes, eyes. He imagined his ancestors were there watching. They were always there, always watching. Would they be proud? He wasn't sure but he hoped so.

Nelson Clark was shaking with rage. He could barely keep the phone to his ear.

"Dead? Big Louie is dead and the cargo is gone? How? How could this happen? Who the hell stole my cargo? Somebody's gotta pay. Someone is going to pay, by God."

After a hesitant knock, a small blonde woman cracked the office door and put her head halfway in. She almost whispered. "There's a man to see you. Says his name is Kelley Price. Should I send him away?"

Clark stopped in his tracks and let the phone arm fall to his side. Then he snarled, "What? No, send the bastard in."

Kelley breezed by the blonde and chimed, "Thank you Miss Roberts and, may I say, you are the prettiest thing in this whole dismal industrial park. Like a rose in a desert, you brighten the day." Turning, he focused his good humor on mirthless Nelson Clark.

"Morning partner, I've come to collect. I am told your containers went untouched through Customs. I don't know how many people you had in them so I'm not sure how much you owe…"

Nelson Clark was almost purple. He spit as he screamed. "Bastard. You got some balls strolling in here like you own the place. I ought to kill you right on the spot. I ought…"

Kelley held up his hands. "Whoa, whoa, big fellow, what are you talking about? I did exactly what I promised. We paid off the port people and your containers were out of there like greased lightning. What are you upset about?"

"They were hijacked. Someone broke into the containers and hijacked my people. They killed one of my men doing it."

The blonde poked in again. "Sir, I have Eddie Fitzwater on the phone. He's very agitated and won't speak to anybody but you."

Clark punched his phone. "What the hell do you want?" He listened and grimaced. "What? The little bastards had what? Impossible, they are all checked before loading. There's no way they could have been armed." He looked confused. "Well, where did they go after that?"

Nelson clicked off his phone, stared for a minute before slumping into his chair. His voice was quiet now, controlled but still seething. "I know you're involved. I don't know just how, but you are involved. Mister Price, I keep my word but I'm telling you that if I find out for sure you cheated me, there'll be no place for you to hide." Then he stared at the wall and shouted. "Linda, cut this asshole a check for $27,000 for… *consulting services.*"

Kelley grinned and extended his hand. Nelson Clark ignored it and continued a bitter stare at the wall. Kelley shrugged and walked out to get his check from Linda Roberts, the blonde assistant. She looked nervous as she processed the check, constantly glancing through the glass door as Nelson paced, talking to himself and making exaggerated, angry gestures into the air.

Kelley leaned toward her and whispered, "He's not having a really good day."

Nearby, the rescued immigrants were taken to a small apartment building overlooking the Honolulu Zoo. Here, they were given food and clothes and rooms to shower and change. They comprised two families who had never met, even though they travelled for weeks in side-by-side containers. They chatted, drank tea and laughed. The children, all under the age of twelve, ran and laughed and played, as children do.

They were in America. Their journey was almost over and their new lives almost begun.

A few blocks away, in a downstairs room of the Pacific Voyager building, Qui sat quietly enduring the rage of his Dragon Lady. Aelan shook her fists and screamed. He seemed unrepentant. He had, it was true, saved the people who now frolicked near where he sat. Nothing she said could make him apologize. She reminded him that he killed the Clark employee—killed a human being.

Qui bowed his head. "For that I am truly sorry. That man probably didn't understand the terrible thing he was doing. But it was an accident and accidents happen."

Kelley walked in as Aelan was winding down. She clutched her arm and tucked her head in an almost fetal position, or as close as you could come to a standing fetal position. She turned away and seemed on the edge of tears.

He tried to lighten the mood. "I got the check, twenty seven thousand dollars from Clark Containers Incorporated." She didn't acknowledge.

"Come on, you have to admit this has worked out well. The immigrants are safe. We got paid for faking their delivery. All's well..."

Aelan exploded out of her shell. "All's well? Nothing has been 'well' since you arrived on the island. Patrick is dead. I'm left to deal with this mess. Clark is after me. ICE is after me. A man has just been killed by people who claim to support me. A man has been killed in my name. Do you understand? I am a partner in murder."

She was shaking now and her voice was nearly a scream. Kelley grimaced and moved to put his arm around her but she shrugged it off. After a long, tense silence she almost whispered.

"They think you're in charge. All right, you be in charge. I'm going to the Big Island, to the Haida compound. I'll be gone several days. In that time, please try—really try—not to get anyone else killed. I'll call you when we have arrangements for the new immigrants. In the meantime, they can stay here. Qui and his people will take care of them. If you need to contact me, go through Mrs. Adachi."

And with that, she stormed out the door and disappeared into the crowd of visitors headed for the nearby zoo.

Linda, the administrator, kept everyone away from Nelson Clark's office as he ranted. All morning, he paced and shouted, growing louder and angrier. Sometimes she could understand his words.

"Bastard, it's no wonder they killed you. You bullied everyone. Everyone hated you. You bullied me. Damn it, I was your son. You were supposed to protect me, not beat me up. It's no wonder my mother drank herself to death. You made her life miserable. You made everybody miserable." Nelson was near tears. "You always said I was weak." He finally took a breath and stared into the desk chair where his father once ruled, the chair he inherited.

Clenching both fists, he spit the words. "I am not weak. I am going to outdo you in every way. I am going to take this operation big time. I am going to rule the slave trade—rule it. First, I'll take over Excelsior, then the federal inspectors and then the government. Anyone who stands in my way will get blown away. I...will...dominate the trade. I will be the Godfather of Hawaii."

Nelson Clark Junior was shaking, soaked with sweat and looking, not like a Mafia boss, but more like a small, wounded child.

Tongay took a deep breath and poked his big fuzzy head through the door. "Mister Clark, I'm sorry to bust in like this but that Price guy has disappeared. We can't find him nowhere."

Nelson gave Tongay an evil little grin. "Disappeared, huh? He's scared, running scared." He stopped pacing and took a long swig direct from his bottle, grimacing at the liquor's bite. "He should be scared. You go back and find him, find him and kill him... and the Comer bitch too."

Tongay hesitated, shifting from one foot to the other. "Aw, Mister Clark, you don't wanna go killing nobody. Didn't this Price guy do good by you? Didn't he keep his word? What for we want to hurt him?"

"Just do it. That's what you get paid for, doing what you're told. Now do it. Any way you want, but don't get caught. Use your head and don't get caught." Nelson punched two fingers against his own head for emphasis.

Tongay looked at his shoes and started to plead again but stopped himself. "Boss," he said slowly, "Maybe we should scare them instead. I can go tear up their place—make 'em know that we can take 'em down any time we want. They might wanna help you instead of fighting. You could take over their cruise ships. Just think what you could do with those big boats. Think about the money you could make."

Nelson spun his chair like a kid on a piano stool. Tongay saw the drunk consider. "Huh, okay." He stopped spinning. "Now we'll see just who's the Big Kahuna." He shouted, "Now, we'll see who's King of the Island." He threw his head back and laughed like a maniac.

Tongay stood with a pained look. Nelson leaped up, knocking his chair over as he charged around the desk. "Yes, yes, yes… Tongay, go get your people. Go throw our friends at Pacific Voyager a party." Nelson Clark cackled like an evil old woman.

As Tongay left, he saw Linda peeking through the glass partition with a look of horror as though her boss was going nuts right before her eyes.

Much later, Kelley went home, carefully checking to make sure he wasn't followed and that no one had broken into the condo.

He had one message on the answering machine. A breathy, agitated voice almost shouted, "Kelley Price, what the hell have you gotten me involved with? I made a couple of quick calls about this Eli Lee fellow and I feel as though I just swung at a piñata and hit a hornet's nest. I have been called by agency people I've never heard of before. You, my friend, have stirred up a shit storm and I don't know what will come of it. Just be ready. I'm sure you're going to meet some interesting people real soon and these clowns aren't desk jockeys." The message paused. "Be careful Kelley. You're swimming in the really deep water and the sharks are coming."

Kelley sat back with a confused look as the machine informed him that he had no other new messages. He didn't usually drink during the day and certainly not before noon but today seemed like a good time for an exception. He knew Hawaii's bars were twenty-four hour operations. He would find one.

The elevator door chimed and opened on the condo ground floor but he didn't get out. Just beyond the concierge desk Kelley saw Tongay and two slightly smaller clones. The Micros were coming. Kelley pressed himself back into the elevator and hit the parking lot button.

Someone yelled, "Hold the door," and a preppy-looking looking young man bolted inside and let out a breath as though he had been running. He turned and faced the closing door with a cheery smile. Kelley sank deeper into the corner to avoid being seen.

Tongay approached and reached out to stop the door and the young preppie called out, "Going down?"

Tongay stopped, looked up at the elevator display and shook his head before reaching to press a button. Once the door closed Kelley started breathing again. They had been only two feet apart but Tongay seemed unaware of him. As the elevator began to move, preppie spoke. "How's your day going, Mister Price? What say, we go for a drive."

Kelley returned a blank look. Without another word, the two walked to his Audi. He took the coast road while Preppie spoke in a casual tone. "You can call me John. I am a doctoral candidate over at Hi U."

"High You?"

John, the preppie laughed. "University of Hawaii. The postal abbreviation for Hawaii is HI. It's sort of a joke. Anyway, I am also a researcher working for an organization that employed you once." He produced a laminated badge for Kelley to inspect.

"CIA?"

John smiled. "Now tell me, what is your connection to Eli Lee?"

Kelley thought before answering. "I don't have any connection except through Eli Lee's daughter, Aelan Comer. I was simply trying to help find her father."

Kelley drove faster and John had to shout with the convertible top down. "You and your lawyer flew all the way to California and visited San Quentin just to locate her father who, by the way, did not want to be found. Is that right? Come on Mister Price, that's a pretty thin story."

Kelley bit down. "So, what story would you like to hear?"

"I want to hear—the Agency wants to hear—everything you know about Eli Lee."

Kelley thought as he down shifted and accelerated around a curve. "I know that Lee was involved with two other men who claimed to have found a mountain of gold which now seems to have disappeared. He is the last survivor of the group and I thought he might be helpful in my effort at a treasure hunt. He wasn't."

"How did you find out about the gold?"

"From the lawyer, who doesn't think the gold story is true. I thought it would be fun to follow up, that's all."

"And that's why the three Sumo wrestlers were looking for you when you ducked back into the elevator?"

Kelley took a long time to answer. "No, they're really after Aelan Comer. She is a business competitor and they are small-time hoodlums. They think I'm involved somehow."

"Are you?"

"No."

Preppie John looked late twenties, button down shirt and pressed Bermuda shorts—no Aloha outfit for him. He didn't look convinced. "So, what do you know about Lee's history in Southeast Asia?"

Kelley was getting irritated with the interview. "Okay, let's cut the crap. I made an inquiry about Eli Lee in hope of bringing some consolation to the daughter he abandoned while, at the same time, learning more about this mysterious gold rumor. I know nothing about his history except what I was able to pick up in a few internet searches so, now you tell me, what the hell is this all about?"

"Heh, I'm the messenger. You know how this works. They gave me the questions, not the answers. I will tell you this, he has some association to the Triangle group. All the questions came from them."

"What the hell is the Triangle group?"

"Hey, Mister Price, I'm the messenger, remember."

"But you must know something. They must have briefed you on something."

Preppie John considered his words. "Mostly, they briefed me on you. They are concerned that you might inadvertently open a can of worms. I don't know which can it might be. That's all I can share. Please pull over and let me out."

Kelley looked around. "Here? We're in the middle of nowhere. How will you get back?"

John smiled. "Seriously, did you forget who we work for? There's a car behind us monitoring our conversation and ready to provide backup."

Kelley pulled to a stop. "Backup? They're worried about me being a threat?"

John got out and ran his fingers along the Audi TT's door. "Nice ride for an unemployed statistician. Aloha, Mister Price and have a nice day." With that, he walked off.

Preppie John waited until a gray sedan with tinted windows stopped to pick him up. Two humorless men sat in the front. Alone in the back seat, he spoke into the air. "Did you get all that? It was pretty loud in the convertible." A disembodied voice returned, "Yes, we got every word. So tell me Sigmund, what does our behavioral psychologist think of Kelley Price?"

Preppie spoke louder than seemed necessary. "Well, there wasn't enough exchange for thorough analysis, but I think he's being generally upfront. He has secrets but I can tell you this for sure, he's not a pro. His facial expressions, body language and tone all seem genuine with little effort at subterfuge. He's not playing us. He's not acting. I'm sure of that."

The voice came back with a sigh. "Well, it doesn't really matter. He knows now that we're watching him. We'll just wait for his next move. What do you think that will be?"

Preppie was quick to respond. "He'll seek support from the one he trusts most. That will tell us a lot about his priorities. If he goes to the Comer woman, he's probably confused and looking for comfort. If he goes to Clark, he's after confrontation and dominance. If he goes to Bennie Sepatski, we're in trouble."

The voice said, "What if he doesn't go to anybody?"

"Then, he's an unknown. We will just have to watch him."

There was a half-hearted chuckle. "And watch him, we shall. In the meantime, we meet with Eli Lee tomorrow. I'm anxious to see what reaction we get from our former associate."

SATURDAY

Aelan had abandoned him to go hide in the Big Island compound. Kelley had an apartment building full of illegal aliens under the supervision of Qui and his men. He had no idea how reliable those men might be. Now, in addition to the local ICE agents, he had the CIA watching him. He wasn't sure where to turn, who to trust, so he went to the man who first drew him into this mess.

Clayton Sheppard was tending his Mother-in-Law-Tongue houseplant as Kelley climbed the stairs. He almost dropped the watering can.

"My God, are you okay? Where did you park? Did anyone see you come in?"

Kelley held up his hands. "No, I parked in the alley. I don't think anyone followed me. Do you know what's going on?"

Clayton put down the can and pushed his round-lens glasses back on his nose. "All I know is that Tongay Apu has been ordered to kill you. I have a relationship with Linda, Nelson Clark's administrator. She says Nelson is having a total breakdown. Kelley, you need to go to ground until this works itself out. The beach house is vacant right now. Why don't you go there?"

Kelley shook his head. "No, that's too removed. I'm worried about what could happen here and I want to keep up. Do you know where the new immigrants are being held?"

Clayton shrugged. "No, I don't get involved in that stuff."

"Good, then you can't give me up, even under duress."

"Duress?" Clayton Sheppard didn't like that word.

MONDAY

"Where are you taking me?" Eli Lee, in an orange jump suit, shuffled in handcuffs and leg chains.

One of the guards answered, "You are being transferred to Federal custody. That's all I know. You're leaving San Quentin but I got no idea where you're headed." He made a little shrug. "But most Federal Pens are nicer than here. They're less crowded."

They led him to a bare interview room with only one chair. Two men in suits stood with hands crossed before them. One had a small suitcase by his side. The other began to speak without consulting any paperwork.

"Prisoner Eli Lee, by order of Federal District Four Judge Abraham Parker, you are being remanded to Federal Custody in the Oakland, California facility. We will transport you there. All required documents are on file. I have a change of clothes for you. Guard, please un-cuff Mister Lee."

As the guard fussed with his leg manacles, Eli asked with confusion. "Why? Why is this happening? What is going to happen to me in Oakland?"

One of the suits nodded. "That will all be explained. We are just here to transport you. Please get dressed."

Eli doffed his baggy jumpsuit and stood for a moment as the two suits inspected his tattooed body. He gave them a toothy grin before donning a white shirt, cheap black suit and comfortable new shoes. He had a schoolboy grin as he walked around wiggling his toes.

"They fit. I can't remember the last time I had a pair of shoes that fit. Hey, I bet I look almost human." No one responded.

They led him through the endless passageways and locked doors until he could see daylight coming through the glass of the main door, the door to the world. Eli almost choked on the emotion boiling in his gut. He was about to go outside. *How long had it been since he saw a tree or a horizon?*

The guard buzzed and three men in suits walked out. One of Eli's escorts had a thick manila folder of paperwork but there were no guns, no restraints, nothing to keep him from running. But then, he had nowhere to go.

He climbed into the back seat of a government motor pool car and immediately tried the door handle. It opened and he laughed. Working door handles, what a concept. They drove until San Quentin disappeared in the rear view mirror. Then one of the men turned and put his elbow on the back of the front seat to talk.

"Okay, Eli, here's the deal. You're not going to Oakland. The CIA has taken jurisdiction of you from the California Courts. The governor was happy to get rid of an elderly lifer inmate that cost him big bucks. You are effectively pardoned. No one still alive at the CIA knows exactly what got you into prison and why you were forgotten but we mean to set it straight. What can you tell us?"

Eli was cautious. A quarter century of prison made him a very suspicious man.

"Well, I can tell you I'm not elderly. I can still kick both your butts without breaking a sweat. I'm sure you know that I ran a guerrilla group working against Vietnamese occupation forces. When that war slowed down, I took my guys west to the opium dealers of the Golden Triangle and harassed them." He sighed and looked out the car window. "But when George Herbert Walker Bush became president, he immediately cancelled almost all our off-the-books operations. I came back to Hawaii to be with my wife but I had been gone too long. I was accused of murder. The agency squashed that in exchange for doing a hit for them in San Francisco. I was caught, sent to prison and forgotten. I couldn't get anyone's attention for years. Finally, they got me a lawyer who got my conviction overturned but, by then, I killed a man in self-defense. They left me to rot...and now, here you are. Here I am. What's next?"

"You're about to be a free man. I have a briefcase for you. It contains a driver's license, several credit cards, a cell phone and a plane ticket to Honolulu."

"Thanks, but I don't want to go there. My wife is dead. My daughter doesn't know about me and I want to keep it that way." Eli turned and looked at the passing scenery. "I guess I'm just going to try and live out my life, what's left of it."

"Well, you should be comfortable. The Agency has deposited your back pay for your entire prison time plus a hardship bonus. That's yours but we do want something in return. We want you to do a job in Hawaii. Take your time to adjust, but no more than a week. We'll drop you at a hotel and we'll be in touch. Our number is saved on your cell phone."

Eli shook his head. "Free? I'm free, but I owe you a job. There's just no free lunch is there?"

He watched the new cars passing, smaller and plainer than in his day. Traffic was heavier now and people seemed more impatient. Everyone was talking on cellphones. He knew about cellphones from television but had never used one.

The driver dropped him along with the other agent at a downtown hotel, a nice hotel with marble floors and potted palms. A doorman in a long coat welcomed them without paying obvious attention to the teardrop tattoo under Eli's eye. The other agent left Eli standing alone while he did the check-in. All around, well dressed people hurried. Where were they going? What was so urgent? A fountain gurgled somewhere and faint classical music whispered under the noise and bustle.

The agent came back with folded papers and a key card. Eli looked at him and grinned. "So who do you have to kill to get a room in a joint like this?" The agent didn't smile.

The "Kulia" apartment building was a three story frame structure with a black lava rock veneer on the first floor walls. Matching flower boxes thick with tropical blooms separated the building from sidewalk crowds headed to the zoo just across the street. Kelley buzzed at the front door. It took a while for an accented voice to come over a speaker. "This place for residents only."

He didn't see a talk button so he spoke loudly at the door. "I need to see Qui." There was no response. Kelley was just about to repeat his request when the door clicked open. He walked into a dark room with a white wicker couch and several matching chairs. Like everything else in Hawaii, the walls were covered with oversized pictures of flowers and one huge mirror. He sat and waited.

Eventually, a small dark man appeared and motioned for Kelley to stand and raise his arms. After a cursory pat down, the man said, "Qui not here. Come back later."

"No," Kelley said without emotion. "I am in charge now. I want to make sure our guests are being cared for. I will be staying here for a while." The small man frowned deep. He didn't seem to know what to do.

Then a door opened and another man stepped in. This one was a standard older tourist type with mandatory Aloha shirt and shorts. Kelley recognized him from the PASS meeting but couldn't recall his name. This man forced a smile. "It's all right Mister Jong. I know this man." He turned to Kelley and said. "Come, I'll give you a little tour. I'm Peterson, by the way. I work with the Urban Housing Agency. This building is being rezoned for business but a lawsuit has it tied up for years. In the meantime, we're maintaining and using it."

They entered a darkened room that was apparently just an observation booth behind the waiting room's one-way mirror. Next, they passed through a business office of sorts. All the employees were Asian ladies who flashed genuine looking smiles. Beyond a flight of stairs, a cramped communications room was filled with server racks and a spaghetti tangle of wires. Peterson became a tour guide.

"All right then, this is our Comm center. We have encrypted voice and data satellite capability with variable rerouting capability." He smiled. "It's always good to have some sharp I.T. people on staff and Honolulu, with its huge military presence, has a generous supply. We have similar but smaller operations in Vientiane, Hanoi, Bangkok and Hong Kong. We can even contact our two ships at sea. It makes for a very smooth operation with few surprises."

Kelley looked around and nodded. "This is very impressive but wouldn't it be easier to do all this through Pacific Voyager's system. It seems like duplication to me."

Peterson was a tall, bony man with the beginnings of a stoop. Kelley guessed him to be in his seventies. "This *is* Pacific Voyager's Comm center. Their offices are a shell. All the work of scheduling and executing our trips is handled here. ICE could shut down the main offices and we would never miss a beat. Within this building, we also take care of the food service, housekeeping, entertainment and transportation needs for our clients, our new residents, while conducting some training in these areas."

Peterson looked proud of his empire. "So, now let's go meet some of our newest guests." Kelley bobbed his head in agreement and they trudged up a wide marble staircase that echoed children's laughter from above.

Naked and tattooed, Eli Lee slumped in an overstuffed chair and stared out the hotel window. Below him, San Francisco flowed with endless columns of cars and pedestrians, all frantically moving from one place to another. It was as though the city was a living creature with people and cars flowing in its veins.

He sipped from a miniature of Bourbon and winced. It had been so long since he tasted whiskey he had forgotten how it could sting. He was a free man but he didn't feel free. He should be elated but he didn't feel happy. In fact, he didn't feel anything. He wanted to call someone and tell them his good news but he couldn't think of anyone. Gina was dead. Patrick was dead.

Dewey was dead. He pondered for a while. There was still one. There was one person left.

He picked up his cellphone and fumbled with buttons around the edge until the screen lit. He squinted and tried to focus old eyes on the tiny icons. There was an image that looked like a telephone receiver so he touched it. 'Voila,' a dialing page appeared. He punched zero. The phone buzzed a few times and an automated voice came on listing a menu of options he didn't understand. Eli tossed the cell phone and picked up the hotel house phone. This time 'zero' brought a cheerful voice.

"Yes, Mister Lee, how can I help you?"

"I'm trying to get directory assistance for Honolulu."

"Certainly, sir. You must first dial nine for an outside line, wait for a dial tone and then dial four one one. A small charge will be added to your bill. Is there anything else you need?"

It worked. A human voice came on the line and asked, "Directory assistance for what city?" He sat back with a feeling of accomplishment. "Yes operator, Honolulu, Hawaii, a mister Benjamin Sepatski."

Bennie Sepatski checked the caller ID. It was an out-of-state call. Somehow, he had a bad feeling.

"Hullo."

"Bennie, this is Eli Lee. I'm out. I'm released, free in San Francisco."

There was a long tense silence before Bennie spoke. He could feel adrenalin pulsing. Eli Lee was the one man on the planet he truly feared. He knew what the man was capable of.

"Hello Eli. Are we good?"

"If you mean, am I coming to kill you? Naw, we're good. I've had decades to deal with things and I've made peace with the past. Everybody's dead, Gina, Dewey, Patrick—all dead. Aelan's independent and doing well. The past is past. I'm ready to let it die and forgive the people who lived it."

"And that includes me?"

"Yeh, Bennie, most of all you. I understand things now. Gina's world was different. To her, sex was just like food, water or air. When you're hungry, you need to eat. When you're suffocating, you need to breathe. When she was horny, she found a man...she found you."

Bennie tried not to sound whiny. "Eli, she was always a wife to you. She always said Aelan was your daughter. The biology wasn't that important. You were her man and you were her child's father. She really believed it."

"Yeh, I suppose. But I gotta tell you, it drove me crazy when I found out she was sleeping with you and every other swinging dick in town."

"Eli, it wasn't that bad. She wasn't from our culture. Sex was a friendly act for her. It didn't mean she didn't care about you. She didn't understand our American exclusive partner attitude. She used to say, 'Man not own me. I am not slave.' But she was a good wife to you otherwise."

Bennie paused and his voice softened. "You know she was the strongest, sharpest woman I ever met. She was a real force of nature. I'm sorry old friend, but I was drawn to her like iron to a magnet. For me, it was serious. For her, it was just friendly sex. She broke my heart Eli, because it was you she cared about. Even when I found out that Aelan was my biological child, it meant nothing to Gina. You were Aelan's father."

Eli spoke with resignation. "Boy was she pissed when I got drunk and changed the birth certificate."

Bennie's tone lightened. "Oh, my God, I thought she was going to kill you. It's a good thing I didn't understand the language. Her words might have scarred me for life."

Eli too, seemed to unwind a bit. "So, tell me something, Bennie...did you kill Dewey?"

The phone was quiet for an eternity before Bennie Sepatski answered. His words were cold and hard. "It had to be done. He killed Gina. I'm sure of it, although I don't know just how. He was after you, you know. He was crazy mad, said you were trying to steal his boat before he could make a getaway. I shot him right there on the dock. His body fell into the drink and the tide took it out. He had already called the Coast Guard to report the boat stolen. That's why they stopped you. When they checked the registration, Dewey's name matched the report of the body on Waikiki Beach. I'm really sorry to have caused you that hassle."

"You know I wasn't really stealing the boat. Patrick told me it was urgent that I get it moved somewhere Dewey couldn't get his hands on it. None of us knew that Gina had just died."

"I knew," said Bennie in a thin voice. "I knew because Dewey told me he had just killed her. He called her terrible names. Said her kid, our kid, was a bastard. I couldn't stand it. I plugged him right there, one shot to the chest."

"All these years and I still don't get it. Why would he do it? Why did he kill her?"

Bennie chewed on his lip before answering. "My guess, and it's only a guess, is that he was angry that he was the only one she wouldn't have sex with and he was tired of being the outcast of the group. She did treat him pretty bad." After a breather Bennie continued. "You know, he never did own up to taking the major portion of gold. We all knew he did it. If it wasn't for Patrick, I would have killed him years before."

Eli Lee sighed. "Yeh, Patrick. You all treated me as the leader but it was Patrick who was the brains of the operation."

"Actually," said Bennie, "if we were honest, we'd have to admit that it was Gina who was the brains."

"Yes, you're right. God, I miss that woman."

"So, how long you been out?"

"Couple of hours. I'm like a little kid just figuring the world out. It was a deal they worked without consulting me. In exchange for my freedom, I have to do a job. I'm coming to Hawaii...but I might have my own plans when I get there. I thought you might be willing to give me a hand."

Bennie's answer was flat, without conviction. "Sure Eli. Sure, I'll do anything I can."

FOURTH TUESDAY

Bennie Sepatski waited patiently at the baggage claim area. He wasn't even sure he would recognize Eli Lee after so much time. Passengers streamed by, most laughing tourists excited about starting their vacations. One of the last to deplane was a rangy man in a white long sleeve shirt. He had Marine Corps short hair and a teardrop tattoo under his eye.

Bennie knew the teardrop was the prison mark of a killer. It was definitely Eli and time seemed not to have softened his appearance. If anything, age made him more intimidating.

They were the same height and met eyeball to eyeball. Bennie held out a hand. Eli looked and considered before shaking. Neither man smiled.

"Everything go okay? I know flying is a lot less enjoyable than back in your day."

Eli made an exaggerated shrug. "Well, you would know. You've been out here in the world living the good life." Then Eli lightened a bit. "Everything is so God damned complicated and there aren't any people to talk to. You get your ticket from the computer. You check in on a little machine. You check baggage at a scale where they barely even look at you. Everybody acts like they're doing you a favor just to take your money. And what about the stewardesses? They used to be pretty young things. Now they look and act like cops."

Bennie heard the buzzer warning that the baggage conveyer was about to start. "What's your bag look like, Eli?"

"I have two. They're both black cloth with little pull out handles. Kind of clever, those handles and rollers on suitcases." Bennie looked for the newest and cleanest luggage. He found them on just their third trip around the conveyer. Outside, in the parking lot, Eli stopped and squinted up at the sun. He smiled through yellow teeth. His voice was soft. "This really brings back the memories. We were going to rule the world. We were rich beyond belief and we could do anything, have anything, be anything. How did it all go so wrong?"

Bennie loaded the bags in his trunk. "I have a room for you at the Reef Hotel. It has internet and easy access to downtown. There is a rental car reserved. You can pick up the keys at the hotel desk."

Bennie paused and sounded flustered. "Eli, what are you doing here? What do you want?"

Eli Lee leered. "I have to be somewhere, why not here?"

"What about the job you said you were here to do? What do you need from me?"

"I don't know yet. I'll get in touch when I'm ready."

"I'll give you my number."

"Don't bother. I have everything I need. But I want you to tell me about this kid nephew of Patrick's. His name is Price, Kelley Price. I need to know about him."

Kelley took it all in, actually enjoying his tour of the Kulia House. The top floor held "guests," the recent arrivals taken from

Clark's containers. The scene in that room looked like a happy elementary school class. It made him smile.

The children, dressed in fresh new American clothes, chattered and watched television as an older lady spoke in their language and explained what was going on. The kids all seemed to be between six and twelve years old. Kelley wasn't a good judge of age. They giggled and pointed with unrestrained joy. The four parents sat at a round table as a patient woman talked them through a picture book about American cars and traffic. There was a smell of French fries.

Professor John Peterson was still talking and Kelley refocused to hear what the old man was saying.

"We don't normally bring clients here. Education usually begins at the Haida compound but we had instructors available so why waste the days. We're very proud of our curriculum. In thirty days, we have most of them, at least the ones under fifty, able to speak enough broken English to get around town. By sixty days, they are driving and shopping. At that point they are sent to live with sponsor families."

"How long do they stay with their sponsors?"

"That's kind of open-ended. Some develop strong bonds and stay for years. Others want independence and wean themselves in just a few months. The children, of course, learn faster. Some of the older folks never achieve full independence. But it is a tight community and they look after each other. We have started several businesses to offer employment but we insist that only English be spoken."

"What kind of businesses?"

"Well..." Peterson seemed to be enjoying the chance to brag. "On the Big Island, we have a distillery up and running to produce a unique Hawaiian rum made from local sugar cane. It's been very successful and we're branching into wine and liqueur. Tourists buy it by the case."

Kelley was intrigued. "What else?"

"Of course we interview the clients to find marketable skills. Artisans and garment makers are in demand. We have a group of stone masons who do superb work creating water features and gardens for wealthy clients. Every worker is given a social security number, contractor's license and necessary permits, all created by our staff at Haida. Social security is obviously the biggest challenge."

Peterson hesitated as though unsure just how much detail to share. "We use numbers from many sources. We even solicit the relatives of recently deceased Asians not to file for death benefits so we can recycle their number and name. We have a dedicated and very capable contact in the Social Security Administration. She's great with computers."

This was exciting. A complex interactive system with secrets, this was exactly what Kelley Price was good at doing. He was anxious to get deeper into the details. Peterson seemed equally eager to explain all he knew. The older man spoke faster, words seeming to tumble out. His hands were in constant motion pointing and gesturing.

"Our two Pacific Voyagers are older cruise ships leased along with basic crews. Excelsior augments those crews with our own people. They blend in completely, working side by side with the professionals to allow our people to develop skills. The long voyage back to Hawaii offers an excellent way to ease the clients into a western cultural environment."

"Yes, I can imagine that. Tell me though, how do you find your clients? Aelan made that sound like a great mystery." Kelley was getting more enthusiastic.

"Oh, it's certainly no mystery. The four overseas stations are manned by only two people each to limit exposure of our methods and contacts. All of the operators are former clients or relatives of clients. It's a tight inner-circle that doesn't let information leak... ever. Our security has never been broken. They receive travel requests for potential immigrants only through an established system of former immigrants' relatives. Before accepting anyone, we investigate to ensure their identity and to assess whether they will be successful in a new culture. The process also serves to weed out con men, crooks and other undesirables. We only serve people who truly want a better life and are prepared to sacrifice for it."

Kelley felt comfortable with that. "Also, they must have a significant amount of cash, right?"

Peterson looked offended. "No immigrant pays the $20,000 fee out of pocket. The money is always provided by a source known only as "The Bank."

Kelley probed. "Is it an actual bank?"

Peterson shrugged. "Money is transferred into one of our overseas Pacific Voyager accounts and it is always from the Bank of China. Whether that is just an intermediary I don't know. I do know this. The two Voyager ships operate at break-even rates. All profit comes from the clients and our paying cruise passengers. It is all processed as passenger revenue for the IRS. Our paperwork is audit-ready and looks completely legitimate."

"How many passengers per trip?"

"Usually twenty to sixty clients and about two hundred regular paying passengers."

"Okay, you have two ships taking thirty day cruises. That doesn't seem like enough to sustain such a big operation. Where does the rest of the money come from?"

"You should really ask Aelan. She keeps the books and she's very good at it. You must remember that the clients are our core business, our *raison d'etre,* but we have many side businesses like the distillery. We also have sizeable interests in pineapple and mango plantations, jewelry and shirt factories and a new construction venture. These provide cash flow as well as employment for clients." Peterson stood a little straighter. "And unlike so many other businesses, we pay our taxes right here in America."

They were interrupted by a dark, strikingly beautiful woman in a business suit. She had a cover-girl smooth mocha complexion, sparkling obsidian black eyes and hair to match. The super model took Kelley by surprise and he forced himself to close his mouth.

"Mister Price?" Her voice was as polished as her appearance. "I'm Sandra, Sandra Collins. I will be your assistant here at the Kulia House. I'm sorry to interrupt but we have a situation."

Peterson stepped back and deferred to the beauty.

"Mister Clark's associates are attempting to enter the offices of Pacific Voyager. Mrs. Adachi has initiated a lock down and wants to know if she should call the police. What should I tell her?"

Kelley felt no stress. For the first time in recent memory, he felt confident, in control. "Do we have camera feeds from the office?"

Peterson chimed, "Yes, of course. Right this way."

As they passed, Kelley shot a glance at Sandra, "My assistant, huh? I'm looking forward to having you under me. Wait, that didn't sound right."

She made an indulgent face as though used to inappropriate comments by men.

He was immediately embarrassed. "No, I meant under me in whatever capacity you perform."

Her next look wasn't so charitable.

He sucked air through his teeth. *Just shut up, Kelley. You're acting like a junior high school kid.* "Miss Collins, are you a volunteer here?"

She raised eyebrows. "I certainly hope not. I have a mortgage to pay." Now, Kelley did shut up.

Peterson led them to the server room, turned on a bank of monitors and opened a speaker connection. Kelley regained composure and shouted.

"Mrs. Adachi, where are they?"

"They're in the outer office," she responded in a calm voice. Peterson pointed to one screen that showed Tongay and several other men vandalizing the reception area.

"Is the staff all secure?"

Adachi's voice was businesslike. "We're in the back room. If you think it best, we can use the fire stairs to the floor below."

"How much damage can they do to the outer office?"

Peterson answered. "It's a false front, purely cosmetic. Everything entered on the receptionist computer is ported here. Even the files are phony."

Kelley took a deep breath. "Okay, Mrs. Adachi, let them have their little party. You and the other ladies hunker down and be quiet until they have blown off some steam."

A sharp voice came back over the speaker. "Hunker, Mister Price? I'm afraid I don't know how to 'hunker.' We shall be quiet and watch the melee but I would very much appreciate it, Mister Price, if you would bring an end to this vandalism and intimidation."

Kelley turned and grinned. "Mister Peterson…"

"It's Doctor Peterson."

"Sorry, Doctor Peterson, can you make an untraceable call from here?"

"Of course."

"Great. Please call the fire department and report smoke coming from the top floor of the Pacific Voyager building." Without taking a breath, Kelley continued. "Miss Collins…"

From the back of a crowd gathering around him a sharp voice responded, "It's Mrs. Collins."

"Sorry, please get Bennie Sepatski on the line."

Almost before the words were out of his mouth, a series of dial tones came over the speaker followed by a bored Sepatski. "He-l-low, who's this?"

"It's Kelley, Kelley Price. Clark is in the process of trashing the office at Pacific Voyager. He strikes me as a man with the mentality of a baboon. I don't think he should be allowed to intimidate us without retribution. I want you to make him think twice about messing with us?"

"Us? Just who are you talking about Mister New Jersey? I told you before, I watch Aelan's back, not yours." The line went dead and there was a long moment of silence as Kelley bit his lip. Then a quiet voice from the crowd, "I can do it. I would like to do it."

All faces turned to Qui who stood expressionless. Kelley thought it over. "What can you do?"

"A baboon steals your bananas until he gets his fingers whacked. I will whack this monkey for you."

"I don't want anybody whacked. No one gets hurt, understand?" But Qui was already gone. Kelley turned to Peterson, "Is he violent?"

Peterson shrugged and shook his head. "I really don't know the man well. He's quiet, kind of brooding. I know that he's very dedicated. His family was almost wiped out in some sort of government crackdown back in Laos. He has been relentless in trying to get more people evacuated from the hills there."

Kelley felt his first wave of doubt. Maybe his first decision in calling for a payback against Clark had been too aggressive. This man Qui was an unknown to him. And why were all these people—well, except for Sepatski—deferring to him without question or hesitation? What had Aelan told them? Why had Peterson shared information about the overseas recruiting with him that Aelan claimed not to know? Was he the new Master and Commander, or was he the new fall guy?

On the screen above Kelley's head, the image of a diminutive Mrs. Adachi moved to open a desk drawer and take out an automatic pistol that looked far too heavy for her. She seemed quite comfortable with the gun as she chambered a round and sat, staring patiently at the hidden door to her outer office. There was a loud clatter as file cabinets in the outer office fell and computers smashed. Something hit the oversized picture of a cruise ship that served as a secret door to the back offices causing it to crack open a few inches.

A big meaty hand appeared and eased the door open just enough for Tongay to poke his head through. Alarm showed in his eyes and he glanced first at Mrs. Adachi and then back into the outer room. He put a finger to his lips indicating silence and then withdrew. The door eased back closed and the destruction continued until overtaken by the sounds of heavy boots and shouting firemen in the outer hall.

On the big screen Kelley saw Mrs. Adachi smirk as she whispered to the others. "All right ladies, it's time for us to leave now." She slid the big pistol back into its hiding place, stood and straightened her outfit.

THURSDAY

Eli Lee wore a bright red flower Aloha shirt with the top three buttons undone to reveal the tattoo of a Chinese dragon on his chest. Elaborately scrolling vines mixed with skulls, daggers, horned devils and naked women on his exposed arms and, of course, there was the teardrop under his eye. He did not look like an insurance salesman.

Linda, Mister Clark's assistant, stood up as Eli marched in. She clasped a stack of papers to her chest and took a step back from him.

"I'm here to see Nelson Clark Junior," Eli rasped. Her voice quivered. "Do you have an appointment?"

Eli grinned through crooked, yellow teeth. "Yeh, I got an appointment. Tell him Mister Moneybags is here and I'm going to change his pathetic life. And tell him not to be cute. I don't have much time." Eli enjoyed intimidating people and he had a natural bully's flair.

Linda stepped back and went to Nelson's office door still clutching her papers as she looked back over her shoulder. Eli followed so close he knew she could sense him there. She knocked once and bit her lip. Eli brushed by and opened the door himself.

Nelson Clark jumped out of his chair with an open-mouth look of alarm. He clawed at his desk drawer. Eli plopped in a wooden chair. "Don't waste your time pulling a gun. I'm not here to hurt you. I'm here to deal." He looked around at the damaged office. "What the hell happened here?"

Clark let go of the drawer handle and stood straight. "Container mover accident, nobody got hurt. So, who are you and what kind of 'deal' do you have in mind?"

Eli sat back with a broad, ugly grin. "This place looks like a tribe of monkeys tore it up." He turned serious and leaned forward to stare. "Nelson, you're really small time but you have something we need. You have an established smuggling operation. I see by your clothes and what's left of your furnishings you aren't a man who is concerned with fashion trends but there is one current trend that can make you wealthy, fabulously wealthy. The American public has rediscovered an old reliable friend…heroin. My clients have an abundant supply and need to get it into the U.S. of A. You have a buddy named Diggins who used to take care of you. We're in the process of rehabilitating Agent Diggins so he can help again."

Nelson showed confusion. "Who the hell are you and why are you telling me this? There are dozens of other freight forwarders on the dock."

Eli answered with a drawn out "Yeh-h-h, but most of them have scruples. You, on the other hand, don't seem to be above anything. So, here's the deal. We need two containers a day. The cargo will be bags of coffee grown in Thailand's hill country. It's completely legitimate product to be processed by the Kona Coffee people. We're just going to add a couple of dozen kilos of Number Four heroin to each container load. We'll take care of all handling. You can claim complete ignorance if anything goes wrong.'

Nelson regained some of his composure. "And just why would I be inclined to do that?"

"For about a million dollars a month. Our lawyer will create a public stock offering and magical investors will pour money into your little company. You'll be rich. Your bank account will be full and you will have no liability."

Nelson squirmed but could not hide his delight. Without any further questions he blurted, "All right, let's do it." He stood and extended a stiff arm handshake.

Eli didn't move. "We don't need to shake on it. We trust you. We know you won't let us down. Because, if you do"—the awful grin—"we'll kill you...and your family and everyone you've ever known. So basically, you just schedule our shipments and stay out of our way."

Nelson ignored the threat, retracted his extended hand and grinned like a schoolboy. "Okay, I'm ready. What should I do first?"

Eli bobbed his head left and right as though debating. "Well, stop the human trafficking crap. It's high risk, low reward. It gives you too many possible leaks and, if you're discovered, you could bring down our operation. Ditch that and let's get serious about the coffee trade." Eli looked around. "And get some more professional looking office space. This place is a dump."

He abruptly stood and turned, words trailing after him. "We'll be in touch." As he left, Eli heard Linda say, "Who on earth was that?" Nelson sounded befuddled. "I'm not sure. I guess I should have asked more questions."

Eli smiled and kept walking. *You sure should have, like who is going to be running Clark Containers after you're gone, you moron.*

Ricky Pho was a man of contradictions. He was thin, six feet two and athletic, but with a pumpkin round face. His heritage was disputed. Some said Vietnamese, others Cambodian. He never spoke of his history but he remembered clearly that, as a child, his ethnic Chinese family fled Burma and bought passage to Hawaii from traffickers. His father had been a doctor and his mother a teacher who wanted to escape the upheaval of Burma's "killing fields." In Hawaii, they were sold as field laborers.

At thirteen, he escaped and took to the streets where he found the drug trade. He wasn't a user. He was an entrepreneur, buying cheap and selling high. Intelligent and a born hustler, he rose quickly in the business. Once he had money, he tried to rescue his parents but it was too late. His father died in despair. His mother was an empty shell after so many beatings and rapes. He put her in a nursing home where she just sat and stared. His sister had disappeared, probably sold.

He set out to find her and his search brought him into the underworld of sex slavery. A world he saw as evil but enormously profitable. He started recruiting young girls and soon his noble brotherly search was forgotten. Ricky Pho was getting rich. He made contacts throughout Asia and developed a reputation for reliability in a world of unrelenting sleaze.

Though he could still be found on the nighttime streets of Honolulu, he spent most of his time in the Chinatown office where he handled his main businesses. Eli Lee came unannounced to Ricky's unassuming two-room walkup. There, he saw a businessman sitting before an array of monitors. It looked more like a stock broker's digs than those of a drug dealing pimp.

If Eli's ex-con appearance intimidated Ricky Pho, he didn't let it show. "Hi, can I help you?" Ricky sounded as casual as a Wal-Mart greeter.

Eli immediately liked the young businessman. "Yes, I'm here to make your life much easier. You have no reason to trust me but all I ask is that you listen. Don't say anything until you hear me and have time to check me out. Does that sound fair?"

Ricky sat back in his chair, cautious but curious.

Eli went on. "You are an exporter of a high-value product that brings in a fair income. I don't care about that." Now Ricky tightened up. "The girls have nothing to do with your main importing business. That's what I'm here to talk about. You deal with Pacific Voyager for moderate volume shipments of my employer's product. He isn't satisfied with the arrangement. He's worried about Pacific Voyager's security."

Ricky spoke with the precision of a trial lawyer. "I don't know what you're talking about but, if I did, what are you proposing?"

Now Eli Lee grinned and got serious. "Okay, we need to increase the flow of shipments and guarantee security. I have made an arrangement with Clark Containers. You already work with them in your flesh trade. We want to start shipping coffee from Thailand to Hawaii and we want you to manage operations here in Honolulu. We don't trust Clark to do the details but you've already shown your skill there."

Ricky was scowling now. "I still don't know..."

"We intend to greatly increase the shipments. The sacks of coffee *will* clear Customs and Ag. We need you to arrange pick up and distribution. You will be paid the same percentage you get now but on a greatly increased business." He paused for a long, silent minute of dead air between them before continuing. "Don't say anything now. Here is a business card you will recognize. Call your contacts and verify my offer. We're all going to make money on this deal."

Eli produced a small plastic zip-lock and dumped out a card covered with Chinese characters. There would be no fingerprints or traceable marks on the business card. Ricky picked it up and sighed. "So, if I wanted, how would I contact you?"

Eli was already walking out. "You don't. I'll contact you. Check me out first. You'll be ready to talk when I come back."

FRIDAY

The ultra-modern glass and steel office building rose among many similar structures that formed Hong Kong's distinctive skyline. These man-made monoliths were vaguely reminiscent of the karst towers of Laos. Mid-level in the tall edifice, a full floor was devoted to the Chi Rho Trading Company, an exporter of agricultural products. Its owner and CEO was Nguyen Chi.

Silver haired and immaculately manicured, he was an astute businessman with an eye to the future world's needs, particularly its most profitable needs. His assistant was a stern Chinese lady with eyes that never seemed to blink, a mind that stored more information than Google and an animal-like sense of underlying agendas. Nothing and no one got to Mr. Chi without Mrs. Ling's approval. That included a phone call from Hawaii.

She approached the white haired man behind his desk of polished stone and spoke in a crisp voice. "Sir, there is a man on the phone who calls himself E. Li Lee. I do not know of him but I recommend you accept the call.

Nguyen Chi looked at her and his normally reserved face broke into a grin. That seemed to unsettle Mrs. Ling.

"Actually Ling, we both know of Mr. Lee, only we call him 'Attila.' Please be so kind as to connect me and, of course, to record the conversation." Nguyen Chi sat back in his wine leather chair and picked up the phone.

"So this is the famous Eli Lee. It's been a long time since I've heard the voice. Indulge my suspicious nature, if you would. Where did we first meet?"

The voice on the phone was rough, made scratchy by a lifetime of abuse. "Nguyen, you must be getting senile in your old age. We met at the Erewhon hotel in Udon Thani. You charged me 250 Baht a day to take me sightseeing and, in return, I brought you to America."

Chi laughed hard and a strand of white hair fell across his forehead. "It is you Eli, you old dog. I see you aren't calling from a prison phone. What's up old friend?"

"I'm free, Nguyen. They let me go, but I'm broke. I need some cash flow so I've set up an arrangement that will benefit us both. It will reduce your risk and I will get a taste of the money on this end. A man named Ricky Pho will be contacting you shortly. He is reliable."

There was a pause as Nguyen Chi processed the information. He spoke carefully. "Does this mean you want me to stop dealing with your daughter, Aelan?"

"Yes, Nguyen. I want her to retire. I do not want her exposed to any more danger."

"All right, Eli. If you say so, I will work with Mr. Pho. I already have some dealings with the man." There was a moment of awkward silence before Nguyen spoke again, this time in a much more serious tone.

"Eli, I know quite a bit about what you did for the hill people. I know what you must have endured. My words are insignificant in comparison, but I speak for generations of free men and women when I say, very humbly, thank you."

For a second both men could hear themselves breathe into the phone before Eli said, "I appreciate that," and hung up.

Nguyen the businessman, drug dealer, former taxi driver and now wealthy family man gazed out over the Hong Kong harbor bustling with commerce and wondered how much of the wealth it represented was the result of the slavery Eli Lee fought to stop.

Mrs. Ling saw him standing at the window and spoke softly. "Sir, your eyes are sad. You must not feel guilt. You have been, and remain, an honorable man. I do not know much about this Lee but he has upset you. Please, do not lose courage because of anything he has said."

He acknowledged her with a slight nod and continued to stare far off. "You should have known this man in his prime. He was like a god. Fearless, he stood against enemies many times more powerful and, for years, made them flee before him. What have I done? I ship a few people to America. I bribe a few politicians. All this I do with money from illegal operations. How shall I be proud of this?"

Mrs. Ling always knew what to say. "You would find your answer in the eyes of children born to parents who were once slaves and now have hope and opportunity. They are your legacy, not the heroin that funds your operation."

He turned to her with a soft look. "I wish I could believe that as much as you. Tell me, again Mrs. Ling, why is it that I did not marry you?"

"Because sir, as you often remind me, I am something of a bitch." They shared a smile.

SATURDAY

Mr. Hajita knocked softly and Aelan immediately opened the door of her room at the Haida Compound. "Good morning, Miss Comer. Are you ready?"

"Dressed, packed and ready to go at six o'clock just as planned." There was a childlike air of excitement in her voice. She had always been the accountant, the office-bound business manager, never the front line operator. Now, she was actually taking the boat to rendezvous with a cruise ship in mid-ocean. It seemed like a real adventure.

The eastern horizon was just turning dull gray but things were already bustling around the boat dock. Aelan had a quick coffee and pastry at the imitation Starbucks while she and Hajita watched out the window. People dressed as tourists with cameras and tote bags were queued up to load. There was even a banner written in both English and Kanji welcoming the "Kansai Touring Company." It all looked very believable even if the sign and the name of the company were Japanese and the players in this little drama were not.

Hajita walked her to the ramp. They shook hands and he left without speaking. The crew and passengers were all Asian, all fairly recent immigrants, all excited. They treated Aelan as a celebrity, bowing and smiling and offering help with her bags, with her coat, with everything. It both pleased and embarrassed her.

They cast off and she took a position on the ship's bow. Once beyond the sheltered cove, the boat gained speed slapping against waves. Sunrise came with an almost violent brilliance that forced her to shield her eyes. As the boat continued to accelerate, wind whipped her hair and collar. She gripped the rail and leaned forward, swaying against the boat's motion, taking in the feel and smell of the ocean spray. It reminded her of the movie Titanic. She wished she had worn a scarf. *Wouldn't it have been wonderful to let a long scarf trail as they cut through the wind and waves?*

For an hour she stood straight and tall like a sailing ship's figurehead as they plowed through long miles of ocean swells. Small islands passed and sea birds chased her along, diving and squawking. The sun and salt spray made her cheeks redden and sting. She laughed like a child, loved every second, every sensation, and promised herself she would keep this memory forever.

The waves increased and, reluctantly, she abandoned her perch to wobble her way back toward the passenger compartment. The boat began to pitch like a funhouse ride. Loose items rattled as the prow rose and then slapped back down with enough force to shower the deck and make knees buckle. She groped to find a seat. *So that's what the term sea legs meant.*

Someone brought her an iced tea. Someone else offered a seat cushion. Everyone wanted to talk to her. They were excited, hopeful. They were on their way to rescue new arrivals. This was a day of celebration.

The trip was long and tiring. By early afternoon, Diamond Head, the iconic extinct crater of Oahu, came into view. They docked at the private estate pier owned by a member of the PASS group. Most of the passengers went to guest quarters for the night but Aelan took a loaner car and headed for downtown Honolulu.

She left the car in the Zoo parking lot, made her way to Kulia House and used her key to the back door.

Someone shouted her name and the staff rushed to welcome her. Well, all but Sandra Collins who stood back with a petulant look. Aelan was getting used to her celebrity status. She chatted for a while before turning to Sandra. "So, how is he doing?"

Sandra chose her words. "He is decisive but not impulsive. He has much to learn but seems to accept help and even instruction. I think he'll do fine."

"You mean better than I would?" Aelan's voice was matter-of-fact but her head toss seemed combative.

"I didn't say that. I think he has a lot to learn but he seems competent." Sandra's eyes were steady on Aelan.

"Well, we'll just have to see, won't we? Is he in?"

Sandra's shoulders squared and her chin rose. "Just left, actually. If we had known you were coming..."

"No matter. Is everything arranged for the transfer?"

Before Sandra could answer, John Peterson walked in. He gushed when he saw her. "Aelan, my dear. I am so, so happy to see you." His smile seemed heartfelt. "We have everything under control. The ship is informed of rendezvous location and time. Weather is forecast to be perfect. I see no difficulties. Can you stay for a bit? I'd love to talk."

She softened her stance and smiled at her old friend. "I wish I could but time is very short. Do you know how I can contact Kelley?"

"Yes-s-s but he's going to be tied up for a bit. He's gone to meet Nelson Clark. It seems our container friend has a proposition for Mister Price. I can only speculate what it might be. Perhaps you would like a cup of tea. It's my special blend from Singapore."

"Thank you, John. Maybe later. Do you know where they are to meet?"

"Yes, certainly. They will be at the Halona Blowhole in…" He checked his watch…"fifteen minutes."

Kelley left his car in the public parking area and walked to the fenced overlook. He had selected the public place, a tourist attraction, thinking the crowds would provide safety. The concrete viewing area perched on a promontory well above heavy waves that crashed with a steady rhythm. Every seventh wave caused the blowhole to erupt.

Halfway down the rocky cliff, a five-foot-high white column marked the blowhole, an old lava tube connected to the ocean. When the biggest waves broke against the rocky shore, they compressed air into the water-filled tube to spew a geyser thirty feet in the air. It was Hawaii's answer to Old Faithful in Yellowstone.

But where were the crowds? Only a handful of tourists gathered at the fence to watch. Kelley scanned the area. There was no sign of Clark. He checked his watch with a nervous glance. He should have brought some backup, but who? None of the people he had met in Excelsior seemed like fighters, except perhaps Qui and maybe Sepatski. He should have postponed the meeting or even refused to come. But Clark sounded so earnest. Maybe even panicky. Kelley hated to pass up an opportunity to negotiate. It's always easier to get concessions when your opponent is stressed.

Then Kelley saw the convoy and his chest deflated. Two, then three big SUVs pulled into the lot. Tongay was the first to step out joined by five other Micros almost as large. This wasn't looking good. Nelson Clark and three Anglos who looked like motorcycle gang alumni followed. Ten to one, these were not good odds.

Kelley took a really deep breath. He wasn't sure he had enough bravado to cow this crowd, but what else could he do now? With an overly confident wave he shouted over the sound of surf.

"Mister Clark...Nelson, over here."

Nelson Clark seemed to have developed a tic that made his head jerk every few seconds. He looked angry as he arrayed his small army, positioning a few Micros to the left, others to the right and the bikers behind him. Forces in place, he chugged toward Kelley, arms pumping, lips tight like a playground bully going into battle. The few tourists watched the unfolding drama with concerned looks. A mother hurried her two pre-teens away, shushing their protests.

Nelson had to shout over waves and a wind that made his comb-over flap. "Okay Price, here's the deal." His tone was hostile but his voice a little too high-pitched to be taken seriously. "I'm getting out of the people moving business—completely. Too much grief. I'm going to give all my contracts to you. Do you understand? I'm *giving* you my business. You can move the people on your boats." He paused and moved close to drill Kelley with his stare. "We have about twenty passengers currently en route. After that, I have contracts for just under a hundred more. They're all yours. All I want in return is a position on your board and a payment of five grand per head for all the names I provide. That's pretty damned fair, don't you think?"

Kelley was thinking, thinking as fast as he could. There had to be more to it. Nelson Clark was not a generous man. Kelley tried to stall. He didn't like being pressured like this. "I don't know. I'll have to bring this proposal to the board and have it voted..."

"No." Nelson shook his head and the tic made his jaw flinch. "This ain't no proposal. I'm telling you how it will be. Either you play with my rules or I trade you for somebody else who wants the money. I'm tired of your smart ass New Jersey mouth so I'm telling you...you either step up or get stepped on. Got it?"

You either step up or get stepped on. Got it?

In Bulgaria, with no American TV, Kelley had watched the Sopranos DVDs over and over. They reminded him of his New Jersey youth. He remembered an episode where he'd heard this exact bit of dialog before. That realization made him relax, fueled his ego. For a moment, he forgot the nine other tough guys watching from the parking lot. He straightened to his full height, a good four inches taller than Nelson, put on a swagger and reached out as if to grab the smaller man's collar. He was about to act out the rest of the Soprano episode scene when he heard Aelan yelling, "Duck, you idiot, duck."

Her voice was like a splash of cold water in his face. He realized he had Nelson by the neck. *Okay, maybe it wasn't the smartest move to grab this middle-aged psychopath in front of his personal army.* Kelley froze, unsure of his next move as the reality of his situation set in. Courage flowed out his body as though someone has just opened a spigot. He made a weak smile and stepped back. Two guns fired, he wasn't sure from where.

Nelson waved his arms and screamed. "Stop it, you morons. You'll hit me." The would-be gunfighters looked at each other without acknowledging who fired the shots. Nelson shook his head. "Dumb shits, all I can hire are dumb shits." Then he reached under his shirt and pulled his own gun. "And you, you really are the king of the dumb shits. Now, turn your ass around and start walking. What the hell were you thinking? You going to take on me and all my guys? You're even dumber than I thought."

Kelley had to agree. Grabbing Nelson was a pretty dumb stunt, but what about Aelan? He was sure he heard her voice, pretty sure anyway. He looked all around. She wasn't anywhere he could see.

Nelson Clark poked him with the pistol barrel. "You total dumb shit. I was trying to help you and look how you treat me. Now you're getting nothing. You understand, nothing? I'll just get rid of you and your girlfriend and then I'll run your little cruise line myself. How's that sound, dumb shit?" Nelson was spitting his words.

Kelley didn't quite have a plan. "Now, Nelson...can I call you Nelson?"

"Jump," Aelan yelled from somewhere.

Jump? To where? There was only one possibility. As Nelson Clark looked away toward the voice, Kelley vaulted the spectator fence. He half ran, half slid down the steep lava slope propelled by gravity and adrenaline. He passed the blowhole marker and leaped toward the water, hoping to catch the surf at a high point.

For a long second he hung in the air, legs and arms bicycling. Bad luck, he was well short of the water and slammed hard onto the rock ledge. He rolled, lucky not to have broken anything. Catching his breath, he scrunched his back against the rock. Maybe they wouldn't come after him. *Yeh, right. They'll just pack up and go home, forget the whole thing...or maybe they'll go after Aelan.* He couldn't let that happen. He had to help her.

Kelley peeked up over the wall of rock that shielded him and was met by the barrel of a large gun. One of the biker boys had followed over the fence and now held a western six-shooter pointed right between Kelley's eyes. He fought panic. "Whoa now, cowboy. Let's talk this over."

A plan of sorts was forming, a bad plan but what else did he have going? Kelley shuffled along the lava rock wall to his right with his hands held over his head. A small wave exploded on the rocks below drenching his pants and shoes. "Just let me get up over to the ledge so we can talk, okay?" He watched the blowhole out of the corner of his eye and listened to the breakers, counting for the one he knew was coming. He moved slowly, waiting for the crash, timing his movements. Then, when it seemed right, he broke, clamoring back up the slope with every bit of remaining energy.

The biker yelled something and followed, but cautious of his footing on wet lava stone. Kelley bolted up the steep hill to grab the marker pole. Then he stopped and grinned. Biker boy, just two steps behind, paused as well, huffing from exertion and looking confused. He wasn't confused for long.

A hollow gurgling sound made the biker look down between his feet just as the blowhole exploded. It hurled him high into the air. He spun and screamed. The water's force was suddenly spent and he fell back to earth, arms and legs flailing. The blowhole made a loud sucking noise as it drained back into the sea. Biker boy bounced once but Kelley didn't stay around to see it. He was already gone, running with all his heart, his soaked pants and shoes squishing with every step.

Nelson Clark stood at the parking lot fence and fired once, twice. "Dumb shits, I'm surrounded by dumb shits." He turned to his entourage with an exasperated open hand. "I try to help this clown out and look what the dumb shit does. Okay, go ahead, kill him."

The whole contingent lined up shoulder-to-shoulder and began firing. That is, all but the crumpled biker boy who still lay sprawled and moaning on a shelf of flat black rock. Gunshots crackled like a shooting gallery but, despite all the sound and fury, none of them were marksmen. Kelley's dash took him to cover behind a small stand of gnarled, wind-twisted trees. He found a path and raced down into a shallow ravine where sunbathers lay scattered on towels. They seemed not to have heard the shots over the surf's noise.

Across the small beach, another path led back up to a different part of the parking lot where Aelan waited with crossed arms and a look of absolute disgust. "Get in you idiot. Hurry. What were you thinking?"

He had no answer as he slipped into the passenger seat and slumped in docile silence. Nelson and his goons were just reaching the beach below. She drove fast and hard. There weren't many options for evasion on the coast road and she knew Nelson Clark's army would soon be hot on the chase.

"Want to tell me what that was all about?"

Eli Lee walked the streets of Honolulu. He was having trouble dealing with so much freedom. After twenty years in a jail where every minute of your life was controlled left him a little overwhelmed. There were so many tiny decisions. He had to decide what to do, where to go, how to go. He could handle the big things. It was the little day-to-day, minute-to-minute details that stressed him. *Should he have coffee? Should he walk the beach? Should he kill Nelson Clark?*

That could all wait. He was going to meet his daughter. Eli Lee, code name Attila, the terror of the Laotian jungle, was afraid. He knew of her life from Patrick's constant updates. Patrick loved the girl. Bennie Sepatski loved the girl. Gina, his dead wife, loved little Aelan with the ferocity of a mother lion. To Eli, she was like a religious icon. He worshipped her but she was almost a mythical being to him.

It had taken some doing to find out where she lived. Even Clayton Sheppard, the lawyer, claimed not to know. He paused outside the Pacific Voyager building, then took the elevator to the sixth floor. Six was a lucky number for the Ankha people. Her condo door was unmarked but security cameras stared down at him. *Good girl, being careful.* He knocked. No answer. He knocked again. Nothing.

His cell phone buzzed and he fumbled. *Why did these things have to be so damned complicated?* He answered, talking loud as though the electronics needed amplification. "Hello. Hello. Is this thing working?"

"Eli, this is Sepatski, something's going very wrong. The people at Excelsior are in a panic. They want me to rush over. Aelan's on Route 72, the coast road, and she's running from something or someone. She was shot at and the shooters are in pursuit. Can you meet me at the zoo?"

Eli switched to his action mode. "The zoo? If she's on the road, why would I go to the zoo?"

"That's where she is almost certainly headed."

"Almost? That isn't good enough. I'm headed out to intercept her. Keep me advised of what's going on." He tried to hang up but couldn't remember how. *Do you swipe or punch. Screw it. The stupid phone would go off on its own…probably.*

Eli cut through traffic, risking a ticket but he wanted to get out of the town's congestion as fast as possible. Once on the coast road he could floor it. But what kind of car did she drive? How would he even know which was hers? He wasn't even sure how to get to Route 72. That question was answered in just minutes as police cars with sirens blaring raced by him. He fell in line following them, keeping pace until he saw a non-descript Toyota Corolla roaring at him, weaving and passing lines of cars.

The police, probably intent on reaching the shooting scene, ignored the reckless driver. Eli did not. As the Toyota passed, he saw the woman driver and her passenger. It was Kelley Price, the man who had come to San Quentin looking for information on the gold.

Even though his driving skills had deteriorated after twenty years in prison, Eli Lee slammed on the brakes and did a smoking skid turn across the median that would have made a stunt driver proud. Then he floored it and hoped his little four cylinder rental could keep up.

Quick glances in his mirror showed nothing unusual for a while but, just as they approached the heavier city traffic, a big, black SUV appeared behind him. *Hello. Who are you and why are you threatening my little girl?*

He slowed until the SUV was just about to pass him and then hit the brakes to slide into a tire-smoking sideways skid-stop that effectively blocked both lanes of the road. The hard-braking SUV fishtailed leaving black skid marks as it jolted into Eli's rear fender.

Two huge Polynesian looking men jumped out. They pounded on his fender and shouted. Eli got out with an apologetic shrug. One of the Micros reached to grab him but Eli grabbed faster, twisting the man's arm backward and driving him to his knees.

The accomplice hesitated and then charged. Eli released the first Micro and jumped to kick the charger up high, right in the jaw.

He didn't go down but he did stagger and shake his head. The first Micro was trying to get up but he was a huge man and it took a lot to get all that flesh mobilized. Eli ended that effort with another kick, this one to the temple. Micro number one collapsed. Micro number two, somewhat recovered, drew back a fist. Eli popped a punch that broke the big man's nose. Then a kick to the knee that toppled him and another to the forehead that turned off the lights.

With both men down and their SUV now blocking the road, Eli removed their keys, got back in his slightly bent car and drove off, careful to obey all speed limits. He tried to call Bennie Sepatski but the demands of the tiny cell phone screen and driving a car after a twenty-year break were too much. He tossed the phone and pressed on.

Kelley was still trying to explain his "plan" to Aelan as she drove. Spoken aloud, it sounded foolish, even to him. He had hoped to meet Nelson Clark at the blowhole and negotiate a deal to end their childish conflict. No more smashing each other's offices. No more tough-guy confrontations, just live-and-let-live business. He really didn't have much leverage, certainly not compared to the threat of Nelson's gangster wanna-be associates.

Kelley had allowed his ego to get out of control. It happened many times before and it always led to disaster. This time, however, he was determined not to give up and sink into depression and self-doubt. *Damn it, he could run this operation—if Aelan would let him.*

She was talking, chiding, telling him where he went wrong. Then she stopped in mid-sentence. "There's a car following us. It's a sedan with a bent rear fender, not one of Nelson Clark's." Kelley turned to look. He thought he recognized the driver. "It can't be. Eli Lee is in prison." Aelan looked confused.

Kelley was suddenly back in his boss mode. "Make the next right and then three more rights to see if he follows. She did and the bent car hung on their tail. As Aelan stopped at a red light, Kelley jumped out yelling to her, "Get back to Kulia. I'll catch up."

He stood in front of Eli's rental car and spread his arms. Eli Lee tried to go around but Kelley played football blocker moving side to side. Eli rolled down the window and growled. "Get in the car, asshole, and quit aggravating me." Kelley hesitated and considered his options. It was a short list. He got in the car and Eli drove off staring straight ahead. "Okay, asshole, where is she going? I want to meet her."

"Did you escape?"

"Naw, pardoned, part of a court ordered reduction in California prison population. I came back here to do my bucket list and that includes meeting my daughter."

"So, you're not a fugitive or anything?"

"Naw, just a law abiding citizen living out my golden years. Now, where is she going, asshole?"

Once again, Kelley didn't really have a plan. "To the zoo, follow signs to Ninth Street, then Kalakawa." They drove in silence while Kelley studied the face of this man the CIA called Attila. Who was he really? What was he really? After a short internal debate, Kelley called Aelan's cell. She answered breathless.

"The man who was following you is not associated with Clark. He wants to meet. How about the Kona Coffee shop? Park in the alley so you can make a quick getaway if the goons show up." He held the phone away from his ear as she came back with an angry stream of abuse.

Eli Lee grinned. "She sounds like a real pistol, my little girl."

Kelley walked in the front door and the coffee shop crowd went silent. Behind him was the big tattooed man with scars and scary eyes. Aelan sat at a back table holding a paper cup before her face. Her eyes flicked all around. Kelley stopped before her and took a deep breath. "Aelan Comer…I would like you to meet… Eli Lee."

The whole world froze. There wasn't a sound for a long, long time. Aelan's face twisted with emotion. Kelley thought he would have to take the initiative.

"May we sit?" Her mouth tried to form a word but Kelley didn't wait. He pulled out a chair and motioned for Eli to do the same. "Eli is free."

She found her voice and it was sharp. "Is he? How nice that he wanted to see how I turned out after growing up without a father. How nice that he came to see me now that my mother is dead, my stand-in father Patrick is dead and my life is in turmoil. Has he come to wish me well and…?"

Eli looked down and spoke with his low, rough voice. "No, I have come back to apologize and offer whatever help I can."

She jerked her head to look away and her voice grew thin. "Oh, why now?"

He still stared at the table. "Because now I can. I have had a long, long time to sort out my priorities. I am sad that I missed out on so much but I thought I was doing the best thing. Your mother didn't want me to be in your life. She thought I was a bad influence."

Aelan was about to snap back when Kelley's phone chimed. He listened and then became a drill sergeant giving orders into the phone. "Get out of there right now. Take all the ladies. Use the freight elevator and go to the garage. Split up and make your way to Kulia House. I don't think they know about it."

He turned to Aelan. "Nelson Clark has his gang attacking your offices again. This time they aren't vandalizing. They came with guns drawn. I told Mrs. Adachi to evacuate."

Eli Lee sat back and nodded as though acknowledging the obvious. "I would say, Mr. Price, we need to get over there and protect Ms. Comer's assets. I think it's time you used some of that CIA training."

Kelley's face dropped. "How do you know...?"

Aelan gaped. "You're CIA?"

Kelley looked like a schoolboy caught cheating. "Well, so is he." His voice sounded whiny, adolescent.

"What?" She almost screamed. "What the hell is going on?"

"Time enough for that later. Let's go end this foolishness." Eli Lee was standing now, towering, really. He had the natural ability to command and it was hard to resist. Kelley stood without argument as Aelan looked from face to face. She slammed down her coffee and stood. "Oh shit, I'm coming too."

Eli started to protest but Kelley shook his head. "Don't waste your time. It runs in the family." Eli Lee found himself following as Kelley and Aelan marched out the door. He took a breath of resignation and said, "We'll take my car."

He opened the battered rental car's door and yanked a side panel loose to probe inside. He pulled out three handguns and distributed them. "I don't have any extra ammunition so be careful and don't waste any."

It was all business now. No one was angry. No one was ruminating. No one was thinking of anything except saving Pacific Voyager. The three unlikely commandos drove off without a plan or even a real objective, except to stop Nelson Clark.

In the underground parking lot, Mrs. Adachi waved from a delivery van where she and four others hid. As he approached, she looked hard at Eli Lee but kept her usual sarcasm in check. "There are at least six Micros, maybe more. They are going from door to door checking everything on the entire floor. They have guns drawn like you see on cop shows."

"Okay," now it was Aelan taking charge. "We'll take the freight elevator and stop one floor below. Then we'll go up the fire stair. There is a connecting hall that will get us close to the receptionist desk. We'll see what's going on from there." There was no argument.

They waited in front of the freight elevator. No one spoke but Aelan shot quick sideways glances at the other two. The elevator chimed and the door began to open to reveal three surprised Micros inside. Kelley raised his gun. Eli and Aelan did the same. The Micros froze.

Eli growled, as he did so well, "Outside, hands on your head, fingers clasped." They complied and he ordered them to their knees.

Mrs. Adachi joined the group. Her eyes were just about the same level as Eli Lee's belt buckle but her voice had a matronly authority. "I'll take care of these three. You go on."

Eli gave her an approving look. "Okay, but first we take their weapons. We could use some additional firepower." Mrs. Adachi made an agreeable nod and held up the oversized semi-automatic Kelley had seen her take from her desk once before.

In the stairwell on Pacific Voyager's floor, Kelley used his pocket screwdriver to remove the door handle, just as he had done before. He cracked the door to peek. There was no one in the hall. He motioned and the others followed silently. They slid along, backs against the wall, guns held high. There was no sound but their own breathing.

At the empty receptionist's desk, Eli Lee took a deep breath and burst into the center of the hallway, dropping to one knee and pointing his pistol. The other two snapped into firing position behind him. There was no one there. The hidden door behind the big picture was ajar. Aelan went forward to stand flat, back against the wall. She shot a quick glance into the door opening and pulled back. She held up a hand with all fingers extended and then bent each one in succession to indicate there were five people inside. She pointed to her left and held up three fingers and then pointed right with two fingers.

Eli Lee grinned. Kelley thought he must be proud of his daughter. She held her gun high and nodded. The two men nodded back. Then, in a violent move, she turned and charged into the room. Her two companions were a split-second behind. They all fell onto one knee in firing position.

"Everybody freeze." Eli Lee was a hard man to ignore when he gave an order. Three Micros and two bikers were just standing around as though waiting. They looked stunned and all raised their hands obediently. Aelan found twist-ties in the storage closet and they bound the five men, hand and foot.

Eli collected a plastic bag full of guns and then began an interrogation. He was in good form as he bent close to Tongay, the biggest of the group. "Where is Nelson? What is he up to?"

Tongay Apu shook his head. "I don't know, man. He's acting real crazy. He's telling everybody he's going to be rich. Hell, the man's already rich. He wants to take over this whole cruise ship thing. He told us to wait here for Miss Comer and Mr. Price and kill them. But I wasn't going to let that happen. I wasn't going to kill nobody."

Eli moved over to a biker and grinned wide. "Nice tats, where'd you get them?"

The biker wore a denim vest with lots of patches and elaborate stitching of a skull and crossbones. He turned his head away. "Little shop near Kaneohe."

Eli grinned and displayed his bare arm. "Know where I got mine, brother?" He sounded absolutely evil. "Laying in a bunk in San Quentin while I served life for murder...actually several murders. Now, why don't you help a brother out here? Where's my buddy Nelson?"

The biker whined, "I don't know, man. He said he was gonna get the guy we shot at back at the blowhole. That's all I know. Like the big guy said, we was just waiting here."

"Where? Where was he going to get Mr. Price?"

Tongay spoke from across the room. "I'm not sure, but he knows where Mr. Tooney used to live. Mr. Price lives there now. I know because that's where Price caught me by surprise and knocked me out. Mr. Clark might be headed there."

Eli stood and looked at his companions. "Who is going to stay with these fine citizens while I go chat with Nelson?"

"I'm not going to miss that," Kelley piped. "Me either," Aelan added. "Tell you what, we'll have Mrs. Adachi babysit them all."

They parked in the underground garage and took the elevator to the fourteenth floor. There was no thirteen. Eli led the other two musketeers back down a fire stair to Kelley's condo level. Aelan muttered, "Mother always said twelve was an unlucky number. She was unhappy that Patrick lived here."

Kelley tried to make small talk. "Where did you and your mother live when you were together?"

Aelan thought for a moment before answering. "We had an apartment building near the bar. We used it to house new arrivals in the early days."

They were getting close. Kelley pulled his pistol but kept up the chatter. "So, you knew all about the smuggling operation even as a kid?"

"I was never a kid. I was born into the business and lived in the midst of strife. My father chose to go fight for mother's tribe. They both seemed more concerned with helping those people than raising me. I have been a war orphan my whole life." Aelan was whispering but the bitterness showed through. Then, after a breath, she asked, "When were you going to tell me about the CIA?"

Eli cut them both short. "There will be time. Who has the key?"

Kelley and Aelan answered in in unison. "I do."

"Swell, you're sleeping with my daughter." Eli spoke through his teeth.

Aelan shot back. "It's not like you have the right to claim any parental rights, Mr. CIA jailbird." Immediately, she looked as though she regretted the childish outburst.

Eli ignored her and pointed with his gun. "Price, you unlock the door and, on my call, push it open and stand out of the way. I'm going to dive in and…"

But they were caught by surprise when the condo door they were discussing suddenly opened. One of the bikers Kelley had seen at the blowhole froze with the doorknob in his hand. He gasped, stepped back and slammed it back shut with a click of the lock.

"Shit," Eli almost sprayed the word. "Any other entrance?"

"Just the balcony." They answered together

Eli shook his head. "Okay, I'll go in from the adjoining balcony. Price, can you pick the neighbor's lock?"

"Oh, don't be silly," Aelan said as she went to the neighbor's door and knocked. No answer. She yelled against the door. "Mrs. Delany, it's Aelan Comer. I'm locked out."

After a moment, an elderly lady in a faded muumuu, answered. "Of course, dear. Come in and use my phone to…" Eli and Kelley barged right by her.

As they passed, Kelley held out his hand. "We haven't met yet…" The old lady recoiled and put her fingertips to her lips.

Eli Lee went to the kitchen and retrieved a butcher knife. He surveyed the wall and set to carving out a large piece of wallboard. The old lady was horrified as he damaged her wall. Aelan took her by the arm, reassuring her that everything would be all right and led her back into a bedroom. Eli ripped out insulation to reach the drywall sheet on Kelley's condo wall. He carefully poked and twisted the knife until he had a pinhole, just large enough to peek through. He pressed his face between studs and broken plaster and swiveled his head to see the whole room.

Pulling back, he whispered to Kelley. "Just two men and they're preoccupied talking." He added with a disgusted tone,

"Amateurs. They should be spread out in defensive positions. Okay, I'm going out to the balcony. You go to the front door. Use your key to unlock it and step aside. Count to ten and swing it open. They'll be watching the door. I'll come in behind them from the balcony." He slapped Kelley on the shoulder and went to the balcony glass door.

Kelley knew it was at least a six foot jump between his balcony and the neighbors. That's a long way down from the twelfth story. But that was Eli's problem. He went to the hall to wait. Seconds later a gunshot echoed and he heard a commotion inside. Kelley fumbled with the key as two more shots sounded. Panic made him clumsy. He threw open the door and leveled his pistol to the backs of Nelson and two bikers…two not just one. Eli had missed one in his survey of the room. They were all three gathered, looking out the balcony door with guns drawn. They must have surprised Eli.

Kelley took a breath and tried to imitate Eli's gruff voice. "Drop 'em. Hands up and stand still." All heads turned to him. They ignored his macho demand and started firing. Kelley shot once before falling back into the hallway. He pressed himself flat, took a ragged breath and collected. The door was still wide open. He popped his head out for just a second to peek and was rewarded by another pair of gunshots. One shattered a hallway light fixture.

Heads began to appear from doorways all along the hall. Kelley motioned with his gun for the residents to go back inside. He squatted and tried a low peek. All he could see was the back of the couch. He thought for a second. *If I can't see them, they can't see me.* He made his move. One quick scramble, low along the floor. Once behind the couch, he drew his legs up tight to make the smallest target.

Clark was talking. He and his men obviously hadn't seen Kelley's move. "You two, one on either side of the door. I'll cover the balcony. If the asshole tries to jump again, I'll be ready. If he comes in the door, waste him. Got it?"

Okay, two men were about to move to the door. Kelley would be exposed. *Two men and he had only one gun. No, wait, he took another gun from one of the Micros in the elevator.* Kelley pulled it from his belt and made sure the safety was off. Sweat dripped in his eyes. He wiped his brow with one of his gun hands and forced himself to breath. He was pressed hard against the couch. *Careful, don't make the damned thing move.*

His peripheral vision told him one man just came alongside on the left. Kelley held both arms extended crucifix style, only with guns instead of nails in his hands. Left man's focus was ahead on the door. He didn't notice the figure crouched at knee level. The other man crept into view on the right. That one did see Kelley and blurted something.

Kelley fired twice from each gun. He didn't aim, didn't even look. In fact, he squinted, almost closing his eyes at the blast and recoil. *How could you miss at two feet?* Both men yelled. One got off a wild shot before falling. That man continued to moan and writhe on the ground. Kelley, still scrunched into a ball, kicked the pistol from the moaner's hand. *Now for Nelson.*

Kelley took a chest full of air and leaped to his feet, both guns extended forward. Nelson was waiting, already aiming. They stood for a long second, gun against gun, no more than five feet apart. Nelson's jaw flinched. He was shaking slightly as he demanded, "Any last words, dumbshit?"

Kelley said nothing. He just fired both pistols. Nelson convulsed and his mouth fell open. The stricken man looked down at his now bloody chest and let out a long breath before the gun pivoted off his finger and he collapsed in a pile.

Kelley Price was shaking hard. He started to wipe his face but hit his nose with the gun he had forgotten he held. It smelled of gunpowder. He backed toward the door and his voice came small and weak. *I just killed three men.* He walked unsteadily to the neighbor's door where Aelan met him.

Her eyes showed that she understood the threat was gone. "Come. Help me with Eli."

Kelley was almost sleep walking as he shouldered Eli Lee's arm and helped the wounded man hop to the freight elevator. Luckily, there were no other occupants as they descended. Eli was drooping, becoming dead weight. The parking garage was empty of people. They loaded him into the back seat of the rental and drove out just as the first police cars arrived with sirens screaming, lights flashing, amplified radio transmissions booming off the garage walls.

Aelan drove. Kelley sat beside with a blank stare and asked, "Where are we going?"

She forced something like a smile. "To Clayton Sheppard."

Eli gurgled from the back seat, "Call Sepatski. Have him meet us. Then, call this number." He rattled off a phone number with an area code Aelan didn't recognize. Kelley dutifully left a voice mail for Bennie Sepatski and then dialed the number Eli gave.

A recording answered saying. "Please enter your access number." Eli's bloody wet shirt heaved as he dictated a string of numbers to be typed and then held out his hand for the phone. Eli waited and then spoke as though for a recording. "Attila is down. Clark is down. Pho is onboard and so is Chi. Recommend you implement Operation Roundup at this time. Your local contact will be Z-Pat. Attila is going dark." His voice faded and he handed the phone back. He wheezed, "I don't know how to hang up."

He needed a doctor. Aelan knew that. They all knew that. They also knew that he would not accept the risk of going to a civilian doctor. Eli leaned back in the seat, breathing deep as if on a ventilator. It was a bad time but Aelan had a question and needed an answer. Eli appeared to be dying. She tried to sound calm.

"Please tell me the truth. Was Patrick Tooney my real father?"

Eli's voice was wet and breathy with hesitations and gurgles. "Patrick thought of himself as your father but he was injured in the war and could not have children. The truth…the truth is that Patrick, Sepatski and I all thought of you as our child. Biology didn't seem that important. Gina didn't want any of us to get too close to you. She didn't think we were…worthy."

"Sepatski?" Aelan sounded confused but Eli had slumped. There would be no more questions. She pulled into the alley behind Clayton's law office. The lawyer was there waiting and so was Bennie Sepatski. They hefted Eli into the storage room of "Mister Chang's Very Good Chinese Restaurant" and laid him on a stainless steel table.

Clayton Sheppard seemed to take it all in stride. "The doctor will be here in a few minutes. I assume you will all want to disappear. Here's my proposal. Aelan and Kelley helicopter to Haida and wait while we create new identities for you. Eli Lee will join you as soon as he is able. Sepatski will coordinate with the DEA to complete the operation. I know that Eli intended for Ricky Poh to take over from both Clark and Pacific Voyager in the drug business. I can facilitate that transaction."

Aelan seemed perplexed. "You knew about all this? You knew about my father, the drug smuggling, everything?"

Clayton, no longer acting the silly wimp lawyer, was all business. "Yes, and there's something else I know. Patrick Tooney is not dead. He is in Laos and he would like you all to join him… if that's acceptable to you."

"Not dead? Who's in the box? Who did we bury in the woods?" Aelan asked but Clayton just shrugged. She was in shock. Kelley was confused.

Eli Lee was coughing blood and wheezing as he lay on the table. He took a deep, wet breath and said, "Aelan, my daughter, do it. I have never asked anything of you before but I want you to do this. Go to Patrick. Go and see what he wants. Take New Jersey with you." His voice trailed and his arms went limp at his sides.

Aelan pursed her lips as though ready to argue. Bennie Sepatski looked at Eli Lee laid out like a side of beef and reached out to touch the man's shoulder. "Will he live?"

Clayton bit his lower lip and answered. "I don't know. The doctor is on his way. We can only hope…"

Bennie Sepatski clenched his fist and looked down on Eli's face as the big man drifted from consciousness. "So, Sepatski will coordinate with the DEA. Sepatski will be the errand boy. I hope you do die, you overgrown bastard. You cheated me. You all cheated me. You wouldn't have been so damned rich if it weren't for me. I made it all possible back when I ran the Air Force Aerial Port. You never..."

Bennie sulked for a moment before he looked up as though explaining himself to the others. "Eli, Patrick, Gina, even that fool Dewey, they split the money four ways. I got fifty grand, a crummy fifty grand. They're worth hundreds of millions. I deserved more."

Aelan moved to him. "Bennie, I never knew. Why didn't you ever mention it?"

"Mention it? I begged Patrick. I begged Gina. She gave me a little and told me to invest it. I did, and now my oil well ventures are paying off, but that's not the point. I was one of them and they cut me out, ignored me. They treated me like an outsider. They never..." He took a breath and faced away from them. "I only stayed here because of you, Aelan. I only stayed to look after you."

She sounded earnest. "And you did, Bennie. I am so grateful for everything you've done. Please don't let anger keep you from helping my father. He may be dying."

"Your father, Eli Lee, the man you call your father..." Bennie turned to the wall and crossed his arms tight but said no more.

Aelan became business-like. "We can discuss this later. We have other matters to deal with." She paced and gestured. "Clayton, don't bother with a helicopter. Kelley and I will take the Excelsior boat out to our scheduled rendezvous with the cruise ship and then return to Haida. That should be safe. Mrs. Adachi can run the front end of Pacific Voyager. Sandra Collins can manage operations at Kulia. Hajita handles the Haida compound and Bennie, you're the only one who can coordinate everything. I will go to Laos to meet Patrick and find out what's needed to manage the Asian operations. Any questions?"

No one responded. After a long silence she continued. "Clayton, can you manage everything with the doctor?" He nodded with confidence. "Bennie, are you okay with everything I've said?" He still faced the wall but his head bobbed in agreement. "All right. Kelley and I need to get going. We'll take Eli's rental car and dump it from the dock."

She went to Eli and bent over his body, hesitated and then placed a small awkward kiss on his forehead. His skin was cool and salty from sweat. She stood and found her voice. It was small and weak. "Come on Kelley. We have to hurry." Regaining composure, she announced, "Everyone, keep me informed."

Kelley drove. Aelan sat staring straight ahead. Neither spoke. There was just too much to deal with, too much to sort out. Better to let it settle down first.

The estate where the boat docked was a sprawling tropical garden. A red brick driveway curved under exotic trees heavy with blossoms. Birds chattered and flew with little regard for human activity. The main house was an imposing castle of lava stone and wood in the craftsman style.

Their wrecked rental car looked out of place entering such a grand setting. They were about to park when a gray Ford sedan screeched in behind them, blocking the drive. Kelley hit the gas to escape but immediately another gray car skidded to a stop in front of them. He yanked the steering wheel and pulled onto soft grass where his front wheel drive car dug in, spinning tires and spewing dirt. He was going nowhere.

Two men approached but showed no guns. Kelley kept his ready but out of sight. The first guy made a circular motion with his finger and Kelley lowered the window a little. That's when he noticed the man's coiled wire earpiece.

"Mister Price?" Kelley nodded. "Mister Cowling needs to speak with you. He'll be here in a second. In the meantime, please don't do anything foolish. Would you and Miss Comer step out of the car? We just need to talk to you."

Aelan leaned across Kelley to put her face near the half-open window. "Who are you and why should we do what you ask?"

Earpiece guy shrugged. "Fair question. I'm John Bolt. James Cowling is my boss and head of the Honolulu office for the Drug Enforcement Agency. We just received an urgent call to detain you but file no charges. Your rental car has a tracker so we picked up your signal and followed you here. That's all I know." He put a finger to his earpiece. "Ah, Mister Cowling is just pulling in. Why don't we all go sit on the patio?"

James Cowling appeared, fleshy and flustered, bustling like a bureaucrat late to a meeting. He was talking on his phone and nearly tripped on a concrete patio step as he gestured with his free hand. He plopped into a wicker chair and leaned back looking exasperated. John Bolt held out a hand in their direction and said, "Mister Kelley Price and Miss Aelan Comer."

James Cowling nodded in a perfunctory way. "Yeah, I know. Okay first, it is my sad duty to report that your father, Eli Lee, has just expired. Please accept my sympathy and that of the agency, Miss Comer. Although I did not know the man, did not even know of the man, I am told he was a courageous agent who worked more than fifteen years for us. His actions as an undercover agent inside prison resulted in hundreds of arrests and severely hampered the illegal drug trade in California."

"What?" Aelan looked unpinned. "Eli's dead?" She paled noticeably and her voice trembled slightly. "You say he worked for the DEA in jail? What about the CIA?"

Cowling, having caught his breath, said, "I know nothing of any CIA involvement but, frankly, this whole operation bypassed us. Now, we are going to need statements from both of you. Apparently, there have been three deaths in a home recently titled in your name, Mr. Price. We'll need you to come down to the office."

Kelley had been thinking, sorting, and gaming the situation. "Are we under arrest?"

Cowling looked surprised. "No, I just need your help in understanding what happened. We'll take your statements, pass them to headquarters and see what happens, that's all."

Aelan started to speak but Kelley took her by the arm, squeezing harder than necessary. "I need to speak to Miss Comer for a moment." He pulled her aside ignoring her confused protests.

She whispered but with the intensity of a hiss. "What's the matter? He said we aren't under arrest."

"Aelan, I killed three men back at the condo. Now, I could probably escape conviction of murder charges by claiming self-defense but once they got us in custody, think of the other problems. ICE will get involved, the local police, the FBI. We could be in court for years and eventually one of those charges will stick. We have to get out of here."

Cowling shouted, "What's going on? We need to get down to the office. Come on, you two."

Aelan's phone rang and she answered almost by reflex. "This is Aelan Comer, who are you? What? No, why? We're being held by a Mr. James Cowling of the DEA. Yes, I'll put him on the line." She stepped close and handed the phone to a suspicious Cowling who answered in a gruff voice.

"This is Cowling, who's this? Yeh, I know that. Hell no, I'm not letting them go. I don't work for you." He listened and his face reddened. Everyone seemed intent on the conversation which was now becoming a shouting match.

Kelley leaned close and whispered to Aelan. "Start working your way back behind the bush. We're going to make a dash for the car behind us." They inched back, step at a time. Cowling held the phone away from his ear and a voice raged so loud they could hear it twenty feet away. They could only decipher the last few words which were "Don't fuck this up any more…"

Kelley glanced down into the DEA car's window. "Good boy, you left the keys." He eased open the door and Aelan did the same on her side. Once inside, he started the car and began a slow quiet roll backwards. Incredibly, they were almost out of sight before the first shout."

"Hey, stop where you are."

Kelley gunned the car backwards down the driveway and out into a stream of traffic. Horns honked, tires squealed and drivers swerved to avoid them. Kelley spun and tore off, weaving in and out of lanes. Aelan was breathing hard. "Okay, now we're officially fugitives—and car thieves to boot. So what's our plan?"

He tried to sound confident. "Well, we're going to go back where they least expect us, right where we just were. As close as we were to the dock, they gave no indication they knew about the boat. It's supposed to leave in half an hour, right? Well, let's see if we can be on it."

He turned into a shopping center and parked behind a supermarket. "Come on, I see a bus stop. Let's take a little ride back to the dock."

Honolulu's bus service was reliable and cheap. It was a great way for tourists to get around, and it worked just as well for people on the run from the DEA. The two fugitives boarded and sat without words but neither looked composed. Flashing cop car lights sped past. The police were chasing ghosts.

When they got off the bus, the flurry of activity at the mansion had died down and the boat dock, hidden behind dense foliage a quarter mile south, was quiet. They walked confidently, boarded without hesitation and made departure right on time. As the boat motors churned in reverse, they watched DEA agents on shore still standing around the house, apparently unaware of the boat casting off just five hundred yards away.

The first few hours aboard were tense but as the islands disappeared behind them and they forged out into open water, the sense of impending danger eased. Kelley joined Aelan who stood at the bow. She held her head high into the wind.

"I love the feel of this. I should have done it long ago." She took a deep breath of sea air and seemed to bathe in the moment. Then, spell broken, she turned to him.

"What should we do? Do you really think we should go to Laos?"

He leaned on the rail holding a drink in both hands. "I think we have to. How else will we ever find out what is really going on?" He sipped. "We need to know. We can't spend our life on the run and, and very obviously, Patrick Tooney is the key to everything."

She nodded and continued making love to the wind. "Do you really think he's alive? And, if he is, how in the world do we find him?"

Kelley smiled at her. "I think I know the answer to the second question. Patrick left me a coded message on a fake stock certificate. Do you remember, you were surprised he left the stocks? Well, I went to see Eli Lee in prison and he told me it gave the location of their gold hoard in Laos. How we get there, I have no idea."

She thought for a time. "Do you believe Eli is really dead?"

"I don't know. I don't believe you can count on anything with these Golden Boys."

She almost laughed. "What a family I was born into. You know, I thought I hated him but I may have just misunderstood Eli Lee. I wish I had the chance to know him."

Kelley sipped again. "Better you than I. The man scared the shit out of me."

They met up with the Pacific Voyager Aloha ship in international waters and came alongside. The sun was just setting. A bright orange utility craft began shuttling passengers from the sightseeing boat to the cruise ship and bringing immigrants on the return. Aelan explained.

"It is a one-for-one swap. Each new immigrant is manifested using a real person's ID. That person boards here and we take the immigrant who used his name back to Haida. That way manifests and head counts always match. If ICE comes to check in

Honolulu, everything looks perfectly legitimate. Every passenger checks out."

When the last passengers boarded, the utility boat crew tossed six emergency life raft bags onto the deck and sped off. Aelan knew, but did not explain, that those were the heroin packages that would be sold to keep Excelsior's cash flow positive.

The trip back to Haida on the big Island was long. All night and most of the next day they navigated a twisting route designed to keep them away from heavily travelled boat routes.

When they entered the small harbor at Haida, a cheering crowd waited at the dock. There was music from drums, cymbals and some stringed instrument. The ramp came down and new arrivals went sheepishly forward to a crowd who alternately bowed and then embraced them. The joy of the moment thrilled Aelan and maybe even Kelley.

She looked over her little empire and wondered what the future held. If she went to Laos would she be able to return? Would everything fall apart? Why did Patrick fake his death? There were so many unknowns. Might as well let them go and enjoy this moment.

An older Asian woman with bent posture and missing teeth came to Aelan, bowing and shy. She held out a hand to touch the shoulder of the woman to whom she owed her new life and spoke unknown words but the message was clear. Aelan bowed back respectfully and the old woman backed away making the "wai" gesture, hands well above her head.

FIFTH TUESDAY

Aelan, now Gwen Stanton, appeared studious in severe black frame glasses and a short haircut. Kelley, now posing as James Stanton, looked younger with his new short blond hair. The passports they presented were well worn, filled with fictitious stamps suggesting many previous European trips. James and Gwen Stanton cleared passport control at Honolulu International Airport with a cheerful smile

As Mr. and Mrs. Stanton, they were about to take a tour of Southeast Asia that included Cambodia, Thailand and Vietnam, or so they said. They rode business class to Hong Kong for a one-day layover.

After checking into a hotel, Aelan left Kelley to sightsee while she visited Chi Rho trading company. Mrs. Ling greeted her warily in the outer office.

"Good day Ms. Comer. We have spoken on the phone and I have seen your picture but I must confess I do not recognize you."

"Yes, that is intentional. I have met with some difficulties in Hawaii and found it necessary to alter my presentation."

Another voice from a nearby office, "Aelan, my dear, you cut your beautiful hair. Oh, your mother would be furious." Nguyen Chi approached and gave her a grandfatherly hug. "Come into my office, dear. Mrs. Ling, please order some tea and then join us." He took Aelan's arm and escorted her into a museum of an office.

It was all glass, marble and polished granite, slightly smaller than a tennis court and filled with statues of lions, dragons and Asian kings.

She took a moment to survey the opulence. "Mr. Chi, can you tell me truly, is Patrick Tooney alive and, if so, how do we contact him?"

He hesitated as the tea arrived and Mrs. Ling sat quietly to the side. Nguyen poured and offered delicate china cups to the two ladies before speaking. Then he sat and rubbed his hands together with a satisfied smile. Aelan was attentive as she sipped.

"First, my dear, some background. Your mother and her mother and your father and I began this enterprise many years ago. It was shortly after your birth. We began importing opium and later, refined heroin to wholesalers in Hawaii who sent it on to California. When Patrick Tooney found out, he was furious."

Nguyen paused as if choosing his words. She showed no emotion and he went on. "We placated him by agreeing to set up an ongoing sting operation. President Reagan's "war on drugs" program was a big thing back then. Eli was working for the CIA and used them to establish contacts. We sold drugs and kept the money. Then we passed the names of the California buyers to the new Drug Enforcement Agency and they arrested the street dealers who, by their nature, aren't very smart. This program has been in play for more than twenty years now and they are still being arrested as fast as they appear."

Her eyebrows knit and he looked away, suddenly distant. "This past summer, someone in the San Francisco mob finally fingered Patrick. They put a hit on him and he was shot, not once but several different times. One head wound has left him somewhat impaired. In any event, he was now a marked man and so, decided to fake his death. You, my dear, have done a commendable job of filling his shoes. Patrick feared for your life so he created a buffer. He left all his declared assets to Kelley Price, a man with loose connections to the CIA. Patrick thought this would effectively remove you as a mob target."

Aelan tried to stay composed. "This whole thing is a ruse? Patrick is alive but he left me without a word and dumped the entire operation on my shoulders? Then he sent a nephew he barely knew to take over?" She inhaled and clasped her hands in a tight knot, waiting until everything calmed, both inside and out. Nguyen and Mrs. Ling waited with legendary Oriental patience.

Finally, Aelan found her voice. "And Eli, how does he fit into this?"

Nguyen worked his lips before answering. "I'm not completely sure. He called me last week but it was a very brief conversation. All I can say with certainty is that he wants you out of the drug business. He wants me to deal exclusively through Ricky Poh."

Aelan leaned forward. "But without the drug money, how will I finance my relocation service?"

Nguyen Chi sat back and steepled his fingers, more relaxed now. "Patrick doesn't think that will be a problem but he is waiting to explain that to you in person. He is in a remote Laotian village near your mother's home. I can have a plane fly you into Vientiane if you like."

Nguyen hesitated, regaining his paternal tone. "Aelan, I know you better than you may imagine. I was there when you were born. I worked for your grandmother as translator and assistant. I knew Gina, your mother, very well…and your father. In fact, I probably know Eli Lee better than any man alive. I am here for you if you need anything… anything. You have only to ask."

She shot back immediately, "Is Eli alive? Can you tell me that?"

"I truly wish I could answer, but I do not know. As you are certainly aware, there has been no official acknowledgement of his shooting. He hasn't been treated at any hospital that reports publicly. That is somewhat hopeful. If he were dead, why would the authorities cover it up? I have called Clayton Sheppard, the lawyer, but he's disappeared as well. I only hope Patrick can answer the question. He has always been the man with the answers."

Aelan was still perplexed. Nguyen glanced at a scrolling monitor on the wall. "And now, my dear, I fear our conversation must close. I have urgent duties. Please be careful and give Patrick Tooney my warmest wishes." Nguyen Chi came from behind the desk to hug Aelan and then stepped back.

Mrs. Ling led her to the outer office to book a flight. As she typed, Mrs. Ling spoke softly. "You know, he idolizes Eli Lee, always has. And you, he has followed your life ever since you were born. He considers himself a part of your family." She stared up at Aelan. "Please do nothing to harm him. He is a good and decent man."

Aelan nodded but did not speak. The meeting had released a flood of emotions, decades of emotions she had always kept in check. Now they threatened to erupt. She had to get out of there to somewhere private...and quickly. She grabbed the paperwork and fled without another word.

Nguyen Chi approached and placed a hand on Mrs. Ling's shoulder. The woman responded softly. "You didn't tell her."

"It was not my place to tell her. She will learn soon enough." He looked down at Mrs. Ling with compassion and almost whispered. "Thank you for everything."

She put her hand on top of his and both stared at the door Aelan Comer had just walked through.

WEDNESDAY

Kelley thought the flight to Vientiane was spectacular but bumpy. Huge thunderstorms climbed into the stratosphere. Their business jet seemed tiny as it winged through canyons of air between the monster clouds. Luckily, Vientiane was clear and their landing uneventful. Nguyen had a Range Rover and driver waiting to take them into the jungle. The driver seemed to know where they were headed without asking.

Kelley sank into a leather seat and became a spectator as an exotic world passed by the windows. All along the way, vendors in straw cone hats squatted roadside to sell fruit or mats or, strangely, scrap metal. Aelan lectured him, as she did so often. "The metal they sell is recovered debris from American bombs. More bombs were dropped on Laos during the so-called 'secret war' of the 1970's than fell on Nazi Germany during World War II. Now, these munitions have become a major source of income for scavengers."

He saw the forlorn look in her eyes, the kind wealthy westerners get when they contemplate the plight of underdeveloped populations and feel momentary pity. She kept the Wikipedia lecture going.

"Laos is one of the poorest countries in the world. It really isn't a cohesive country at all. It's more a coalition of tribes loosely federated under a communist central government but still paying lip-service to a king who has little more than ceremonial power.

The hill people have been conquered and enslaved by one dynasty after another. They have been ruled by China, Vietnam, Burma, Siam and several indigenous factions." She was distracted as they passed a temple of carved stone with giant sitting Buddha statues flanking the steps to a conical building. She continued in a flat voice. "I think that dates to the Siamese occupation."

Kelley cut in. "That's interesting but you're jabbering to avoid talking about what's going to happen here. Do you have any idea what we're walking into?"

Aelan's voice was quiet, almost meek. "No...and I'm frightened. Everything I thought I knew about the important people in my life has turned out to be a distortion if not an outright lie. Everyone has lied to me." She pressed her face to the window as a boy leading a water buffalo passed and waved.

Kelley shot back. "Well, I didn't lie to you."

"No? When were you going to tell me you worked for the CIA?"

Kelley threw up his hands. "Oh, for pity's sake, I was a contractor doing a legitimate cancer study. I just got funding from the CIA to allow them to use the facility as a safe house. That doesn't count as a lie."

They both stared out their respective windows. No one spoke for the next hour as they climbed higher into somber mountains of gray stone and thick jungle. The Range Rover handled muddy roads competently but still, they bounced and skidded enough to throw objects around.

The driver checked his paper map and pointed. He said something that Aelan understood. "It's just ahead," she said with a touch of apprehension. And there it was. A sunny valley opened up before them. It held a recently constructed enterprise of mud roads and bamboo buildings arranged in a circular layout. Smoke rose from several buildings and outdoor pits.

The village or settlement or whatever, was busy. People dressed in shorts and sarong-type wraparounds scurried about, pausing for only brief glances at the car. Several serious looking men in brown military shirts carried rifles but seemed unconcerned. Aelan seemed to come alive as she craned out the window, taking it all in. For the moment, her mood brightened. People greeted her with a smile and she responded.

The driver asked someone directions and then pulled up to a large thatch-roof house bristling with antennas. There, on the porch, stood Patrick Tooney.

He seemed smaller than Kelley remembered. Short and slight with wispy gray hair, sharp features and thin legs under baggy shorts. His right arm trembled—the palsy Aelan spoke of. Patrick came down three porch steps favoring his right leg but still graceful, almost elfin in appearance. All in all, he wasn't an imposing figure.

Aelan shot out of the car and rushed to overwhelm him in a tearful embrace. Kelley stood by the car and waited. He could hear her almost wail, "I buried you. I grieved for you. You abandoned me. I was nobody. I'm not white. I'm not Thai. I'm not Polynesian or Lao or anything. My mother was my only tribe. She and her faraway, strange people. When she died you were my only link back to her." Aelan was shaking with what looked like a mix of anger and despair. "Why didn't you tell me this was all just some sort of scam?"

Patrick took her by the shoulders and pulled her tight. He seemed genuinely pained. Kelley could barely hear his voice. "I'm sorry but I had to leave, and fast. Clayton helped me stage my death. He's good at that kind of thing."

She drew back. "Clayton Sheppard, the silly little lawyer with a bow tie?"

Patrick smiled. Now composed, his voice took on a surprisingly deep timbre for a small man. "Eli recruited him years ago."

"Is Eli alive? You came back from the dead. Did he?"

Kelley leaned to hear. "Yes, he's alive but he's never going to be the same. The bullet clipped his spine. Eli may never walk again. We're trying to get him to a hospital in Bangkok. It's one of the best. I hope we'll all be able to see him before too long. I want him to know that his plan is being implemented."

She wiped her eyes, inhaled deep and her shaking subsided. "His plan? I thought this was all your plan."

Now it was even harder for Kelley to hear. Patrick spoke in a conspirator's near-whisper. "We are about to take down the entire Asia-Hawaii heroin operation. Aelan, you and I…we're out. As we speak, Nguyen Chi is closing his office and going into hiding. Ricky Pho has been arrested along with two dozen west coast dealers. Bennie Sepatski is leading the DEA people around the islands, picking up one dealer after another. ICE has arrested Agent Diggins."

Patrick paused but the excitement made his arm shake more violently. His voice quivered as well. "I am finally free of the drug curse. It took a bullet in my head, but I'm free. We all are."

Kelley felt obliged to speak. "Patrick, Uncle Pat, if you're out of the drug business, are you also out of the human trafficking business?"

Patrick Tooney pursed his lips and glared directly at Kelley. "You know, I never liked you. Even as a kid, you had a snotty, superior attitude. Your mother indulged you too much, spoiled you. I brought you to Hawaii purely as bait, never expecting you to become so involved with Aelan." He sighed.

Kelley almost stammered, "But your letter…the words you said about me and my mother. They were touching…"

Patrick looked away and his scowl softened a bit. "I was just setting you up." After a long, empty pause, he continued. "But, I have to admit, you turned out to be a colorful addition to the plan. I'm frankly glad you killed Nelson Clark Junior. The world is better off without that man. More than that, you were an unpredictable player. It was your intervention that motivated the CIA to get Eli out of jail. He had long ago been handed over to the DEA as an informant, and they didn't ever plan to let him out. You stirred up a real inter-agency cat fight. Better yet, you kept everyone confused about what was going on, and that let Eli get all the moving parts lined up."

Aelan cocked her head. "Eli knew you were alive?"

Patrick looked at her. "Of course, it was his plan all along. He has been a shadow force in everything I did over the past forty years. Eli was a true believer in the Ankha cause. He never gave up on them, and he kept his promise to Gina that he would help her people," He turned back to Kelley with a sour tone. "I guess I'm grateful to you."

Kelley tried not to be offended. "But my question was…what about your human smuggling? Will that go on? And how will you fund it?"

Patrick sniffed and then crooked a finger. "Come. Follow me." He limped but kept a stiff, almost military posture as he walked and talked over his shoulder. "Eli Lee fought in these hills. At first, the CIA gave him arms and support, but that ran out as the U.S. withdrew from Southeast Asia. He kept his guerilla army financed by using the gold from the temple. Do you know about that?"

Kelley shrugged and said, "Lima Golf three three zero, one zero zero. Is that near here?"

Patrick stopped and smiled. "Yes, exactly. Those are the GeoRef coordinates for an ancient temple. We buried the major gold stash in tombs there. Eli used one crypt but left the others untouched. I have now opened them."

He swept his arm. "Look around you. This is our future. We smelt the gold and make jewelry. We will soon employ hundreds of craftsmen and turn out enough to make us a leading supplier of Saudi Arabia, Pakistan and India. There is enough gold to last twenty years. Our refugee program will continue, now funded by the same Vietnamese gold that has driven our lives and our destiny for more than forty years."

Patrick's arm trembled visibly. "These people you see here working the smelters and jeweler's benches are earning their travel. They are the next generation of American citizens and, as long as I live, they shall have their chance for freedom, prosperity and a dignified life in our country. At the same time, they are creating Ankha jewelry preserving the symbols of their culture. Gold is immortal and their heritage will be preserved for mankind."

Patrick Tooney inhaled the damp smell of red earth and thick vegetation and looked defiant. After a long silence, he spoke, but too softly for them to hear clearly. Still, they understood.

"I knew I would die here. I was meant to die here. What better place? Here, I am free. Here, I am absolved of all my crimes. Here I shall fulfill my destiny. Here I shall be buried….near my gold."

Aelan took Kelley's arm. They both saw Patrick Tooney turn his face to the sun and close his eyes. He seemed lost in his thought, lost in his memories.

THREE MONTHS LATER

A chauffer held the car door as a man in an expensive suit climbed out of the Mercedes limousine into a steamy Bangkok afternoon. The man squinted up at the sign written in Thai, Chinese, Arabic and English. He could read three of the languages but they all said the same thing, "Khom Gold Exchange."

He smiled and spoke to himself in English. "You have been very busy, Mr. Price, very busy indeed."

The unassuming storefront building sat among other similar businesses on a bustling commercial street just a few blocks from the financial district. Inside, it was staffed by white shirt workers in cubicles surrounded by walls of scrolling monitors that displayed financial information from world markets. A window air conditioner hummed as it blew little attached ribbons.

A pleasant Thai lady in a silk blouse and plain no-nonsense skirt stood from behind the reception desk. She paused deciding which language to use.

The man helped her by asking in English, "Good day, I should like to speak to Mr. Price, if you would be so kind."

The lady made a tiny head bow and smiled politely. "And who may I say is calling, sir?" Her accent was slightly British.

He returned the bow and said simply, "A friend of Aelan Comer."

The lady extended a hand toward a small visitor's couch and disappeared. Nguyen Chi sat and took in the scene. It was, he decided, just a façade. The monitor screens were just TV sets, all tuned to the TVB Pearl financial networks to give the look of a financial business. From the corner of his eye Nguyen saw a tall American emerge from one of the offices. The man came cautiously, looking suspicious as he extended a hand. Nguyen stood to shake.

The blond, short-haired man grinned and spoke in an overly casual way. "How do ya do? I'm James Stanton, manager of the Exchange. We don't have anyone here named Price. Can I be of service, sir?"

Nguyen grinned. "You may relax, Mr. Price. I know everything about you and it is I who may be of service. You have established yourself very quickly as a reliable supplier of gold products. Very cleverly, I might add. Now, I am a man with many connections and I am anxious to join in the operation and growth of your business. I believe my acumen in government and informal networks of influence will greatly facilitate your transportation and handling needs in a very challenging Asian business atmosphere. In return, I ask only that you allow me to meet with a very old friend."

Kelley scowled, his tone still defensive. "What old friend?"

Nguyen paused for longer than was comfortable. "I want to meet Eli Lee. Please call Aelan and she will verify that I, Nguyen Chi, am a trustworthy friend."

Kelley's face lost all expression. His tone was curt. "Please, step into my office. It's in the back." Nguyen went, with an almost cheerful confidence.

Kelley excused himself to step into the hall and make the call. As he spoke into the phone, he gestured as if in an argument. Finally he hung up and stared for a time before rejoining the businessman. Tea was served. Nguyen thanked the receptionist and spoke to Kelley. "Did she convince you?"

Kelley nodded but it was obvious, he was not really convinced. "So what exactly can you do for me?"

Nguyen held his tea cup in both hands and inspected it as he considered his words. "I have powerful allies in the government as well as the, shall we say, non-governmental agents, who control commerce here. In addition, I have contacts in the Swiss banking world who can handle tricky money transfers from Arab states. The Middle East market is ripe for a new provider of scarce gold. It is the standard of wealth there, and I want in on your enterprise. I am not greedy and I am completely honest. More than that, I want to help Aelan."

Kelley nodded. "She said you were her godfather."

"Oh, that makes me very happy to hear but it's not exactly true. I am her father's friend."

The front desk lady interrupted with a light knock and a peek through the office door. "Sir, he is here. He said you asked him to hurry."

Eli pushed by her and thumped in, relying heavily on an ebony cane with a carved cobra head. Thinner now, he was as frightening a figure as ever. Tall, broad and covered with tattoos and scars, he could have been a character in a horror movie. Eli's grin was at once warm and chilling.

Nguyen leaped up to embrace him and Eli gathered the much smaller man in his arms letting the cane fall. The bear hug lasted until Nguyen finally stepped back and dabbed at his eyes. His voice was breathy.

"Eli Lee, I always prayed I would see you before one of us died. Now my wish is granted."

"Oh, don't get all sappy. I intend to live a long time." Eli pointed to Kelley. "Maybe this Jersey boy will actually marry my little girl and adopt a grandbaby for me."

Nguyen and Eli Lee both looked at Kelley, who stammered. "Well, we're already sort of married...passports and papers say James and Gwen Stanton."

"This is true?" Nguyen looked pleased. "Oh, her mother would be so happy. She wanted a big family. Tell me is Aelan happy? I so want her to have happiness."

Eli and Nguyen both turned to stare at Kelley who took a step back and cleared his throat.

"I think she is. We are now James and Gwen Stanton and we've settled pretty comfortably into Bangkok's expatriate culture. We live together in a large open bungalow surrounded by tropical plants and an electrified security fence. We never officially married, since we never officially existed, but I think we're both comfortable with our new lives. Somehow, she feels as though she belongs here."

Nguyen nodded and looked very much like a pleased grandfather.

"As for me," Kelley seemed to lighten up. He took a deep breath filling his lungs and closing his eyes. "I wake every morning to the smell of blooming orchids, sip strong Thai coffee and watch boats navigating the Klong waterway. For me, this is a chance for a complete do-over from what was previously, a quite unremarkable life."

He made eye contact with Nguyen who nodded agreeably.

Kelley returned the look. "I know I feel happy here. She makes me feel happy. I only hope she feels the same."

Patrick Tooney woke in a sweat. He tried to sit up but the effort exhausted him. Falling back, he raised a shaky arm and beckoned. The Ankha woman attending him brought a cup of water but he waved it away.

"Is he here yet?"

She nodded and placed a gentle hand on his fever-slick forehead. "He is coming. He will be here very soon." Her English was good.

Patrick stared up at the rotating ceiling fan of his newly constructed building. It still smelled of fresh-cut tropical wood, a heavy sweet scent. He started to laugh at his situation but that brought an agonizing wet cough. "Hurry up old friend. I don't know how long…" Before he could finish the thought, Patrick was distracted by a commotion outside. Then he heard the thump and scrape of a cane across the wood floor.

"Is that you, Eli? Is it you?"

"Yeah, yeah, it's me. What's all this about? I thought you were too tough to ever die."

"I wish, Eli. I got a fever and my brain has gone haywire. I keep seeing ghosts, hearing ghosts. I hear Gina talking to me, calling to me." Patrick hesitated to catch his breath. "I'm scared, Eli. I'm not afraid to die. No, I'm ready to die. I just don't want to go to Hell. I've done so many bad things, so many…"

Eli Lee maneuvered his body into a bedside chair with a grimace and a grunt. His right leg extended like a useless log. He shifted and balanced both hands on the head of his cane. "You know I don't believe in any of that magic stuff—Heaven, Hell, angels, demons—whatever. But I gotta tell you this. If there is somebody somewhere keeping score, I think you are way ahead on points. How many people do you think you brought to the States and gave new lives? A thousand? Maybe Two thousand?"

Patrick sagged, his head back, mouth open, trying to suck in air. He felt Eli's hand on his arm as the big man spoke.

"Listen Pat, you took care of my family while I was off playing Jungle Jim. Aelan is a good person, a fine girl, and it's because of you. Gina lived a good life, again because of you. Patrick, you have lived a good life, a saintly life. I am proud to be your friend."

The small man tried to smile. His voice was hollow. "Eli, I want you to take over things up here at the factory. You speak the language. You know the...people. You...care about the..."

Patrick felt phlegm rattle in his chest. He knew what it meant. With great effort, he whispered, "Bury me in the old temple where I can look out on my mountains. Bury me... where the evil spirits fear...to...go."

He hacked one last time, stiffened and let out a long gasp. Then Patrick Tooney lay still and silent. The Ankha woman raised her arms and wailed in anguish. Outside a crowd murmured and then began to sing some strange song.

Eli Lee stood for a second with clenched teeth, fighting to prevent his lower lip from quivering. Then, he took a deep breath and reached down to cross Patrick's arms over his chest before lifting his limp body. The big man was clumsy without his cane but he managed to carry Patrick's body and limp-walk to the door. Emerging into the bright daylight, he stood before the assembled singers, the people of Patrick's new gold rush boom town.

"Come," Eli commanded. "We must go quickly."

In death, Patrick Tooney's expression was contorted, but it almost looked like a smile as the Laotian sun fell on his pale face one last time.

Aelan and Kelley traded stories of the day's events. She said they must have Nguyen for dinner. The man who had been Eli's old driver, translator for Gina's mother, as well as Aelan's old drug dealing partner was fast becoming a part of their new life. She and Kelley laughed and argued and offered each other advice. They had become partners in life and in business, partners who never went to bed angry.

She had forgiven Kelley for his small deception about his CIA history. She had almost completely forgiven Eli for abandoning her and then for almost dying. She was working hard to forgive Patrick for faking his death and then leaving her to deal with the mess. With Nguyen, there was nothing to forgive. He alone had always been honest. She didn't think about Bennie Sepatski very often at all.

Kelley said he had to meet Nguyen and Eli for a late night discussion of how the Lao jewelry factory should be run now that Eli was in charge. Aelan agreed to stay out of that side of the business at Eli's request. So now, it would be a guys-only meeting. That's how deals were done in Bangkok, by well-dressed men, late at night, in dark café booths with plenty of "Running Deer" whiskey, laughter and stories of the old days.

Aelan watched Kelley go out into the noisy, crowded Bangkok night full of "Tuk-Tuk" tricycle cabs, street vendors and multi-national pedestrians. She would have liked to be there with them but she honored Eli's request to distance herself from the gold trade largely run by gangsters.

Her house lady, an Ankha woman of thirty or so, spoke as she turned down the sheets and laid out slippers.

"You have good man, you know."

Aelan wasn't fluent in the language but she managed. "I know. He still needs training but, yes, he is good."

The woman smiled with a gold front tooth. "He has soft hand but strong heart for you. The spirits smile. Your mother is very proud of the man you chose."

Aelan faced away and looked out onto the porch. She thought for a moment and then spoke to the housekeeper, but even more, she spoke to her mother's ghost.

"Did I choose him? I don't remember ever making that decision. I just remember that he needed me…and I guess I needed him."

Aelan listened to the Bangkok night. There were the ever-present insects and night birds. There were street noises in a city that never really wound down. But there was also a sound of gentle wind blowing through her spirit house. Aelan focused on the tiny doll-house-sized pagoda structure on her porch. It was covered with silk ribbons and candles, tributes to her ancestors' spirits who were supposed to dwell within. There was a ribbon for Gina's mother and now one for Patrick. She knelt and touched the ribbon for Gina.

You planned all this, didn't you? So many years ago, you had it all laid out. When you told Eli to go fight for your people, when you told Patrick he had to import drugs, when you made Sepatski set up the first refugee safe houses, you had already planned out our lives and we were just playing out the roles you set. None of us had a choice, did we?

Aelan felt no anger. She lit a small candle in the spirit house. Then, she stood back and admired the flicker of flame. It looked alive. Gwen Stanton, Aelan Comer, Eileen Lee bowed before the spirit house and made a "wai" gesture, praying hands clasped above her head.

The world was in perfect order.